WHITEOUT

BOOKS BY LYNETTE EASON

WOMEN OF JUSTICE

Too Close to Home
Don't Look Back
A Killer Among Us

DEADLY REUNIONS

When the Smoke Clears
When a Heart Stops
When a Secret Kills

HIDDEN IDENTITY

No One to Trust
Nowhere to Turn
No Place to Hide

ELITE GUARDIANS

Always Watching
Without Warning
Moving Target
Chasing Secrets

BLUE JUSTICE

Oath of Honor
Called to Protect
Code of Valor
Vow of Justice
Protecting Tanner Hollow

DANGER NEVER SLEEPS

Collateral Damage
Acceptable Risk
Active Defense
Hostile Intent

EXTREME MEASURES

Life Flight
Crossfire
Critical Threat
Countdown

LAKE CITY HEROES

Double Take
Target Acquired
Serial Burn
Final Approach

BOOKS BY DANI PETTREY

ALASKAN COURAGE

Submerged
Shattered
Stranded
Silenced
Sabotaged

CHESAPEAKE VALOR

Cold Shot
Still Life
Blind Spot
Dead Drift

COASTAL GUARDIANS

The Killing Tide
The Crushing Depths
The Deadly Shallows
The Shifting Current: A COASTAL GUARDIAN *Novella*

JEOPARDY FALLS

One Wrong Move
Two Seconds Too Late

Shadowed: An ALASKAN COURAGE Novella from *Sins of the Past: A Romantic Suspense Novella Collection*

Deadly Isle from *The Cost of Betrayal: Three Romantic Suspense Novellas*

WHITEOUT

TWO ROMANTIC SUSPENSE NOVELLAS

LYNETTE EASON
AND DANI PETTREY

BethanyHouse
a division of Baker Publishing Group
Minneapolis, Minnesota

"Snowbound Secrets" © 2026 by Lynette Eason

"Buried in Shadows" © 2026 by Gracie & Johnny, Inc.

Published by Bethany House Publishers
Minneapolis, Minnesota
BethanyHouse.com

Bethany House Publishers is a division of
Baker Publishing Group, Grand Rapids, Michigan

Printed in the United States of America

All rights reserved. No part of this publication may be reproduced, stored in a retrieval system, or transmitted in any form or by any means—for example, electronic, photocopy, recording—without the prior written permission of the publisher. The only exception is brief quotations in printed reviews.

Library of Congress Cataloging-in-Publication Data

Names: Eason, Lynette author | Pettrey, Dani author | Pettrey, Dani Buried in shadows | Eason, Lynette Snowbound secrets

Title: Whiteout : two romantic suspense novellas / Lynette Eason and Dani Pettrey.

Description: Minneapolis, Minnesota : Bethany House Publishers, a division of Baker Publishing Group, 2026.

Identifiers: LCCN 2025038379 | ISBN 9780764245978 paperback | ISBN 9780764246081 casebound | ISBN 9781493452484 ebook

Subjects: LCGFT: Fiction | Christian fiction | Thrillers (Fiction) | Romance fiction | Novellas

Classification: LCC PS3605.A79 W48 2026

LC record available at https://lccn.loc.gov/2025038379

Scripture quotations in "Snowbound Secrets" are from The Holy Bible, English Standard Version® (ESV®), copyright © 2001 by Crossway, a publishing ministry of Good News Publishers. Used by permission. All rights reserved. ESV Text Edition: 2016

Scripture quotations in "Buried in Shadows" are from the Holy Bible, New International Version®, NIV®. Copyright © 1973, 1978, 1984, 2011 by Biblica, Inc.® Used by permission of Zondervan. All rights reserved worldwide. www.zondervan.com. The "NIV" and "New International Version" are trademarks registered in the United States Patent and Trademark Office by Biblica, Inc.®

This book is a work of fiction. Names, characters, places, and incidents are the product of the author's imagination or are used fictitiously. Any resemblance to actual events, locales, or persons, living or dead, is coincidental.

Cover design by Faceout Studio, Addie Lutzo

Published in association with Books & Such Literary Management, BooksAndSuch .com.

Baker Publishing Group publications use paper produced from sustainable forestry practices and postconsumer waste whenever possible.

26 27 28 29 30 31 32 7 6 5 4 3 2 1

BURIED IN SHADOWS

DANI PETTREY

To Jess

Here's to our first project together!
I had the most fun working on the story with you.

Please Join Us for the Marriage of

Izzy Brunswick & Talbot Wentworth

WEDDING PARTY

Bridesmaids

Cassandra Parker, *friend of the bride*

Mia Beckett, *friend of the bride*

Amy Bishop, *friend of the bride*

Nat Wentworth, *cousin of the groom*

Penelope Wentworth, *cousin of the groom*

Savannah Brunswick, *cousin of the bride*

Kendra Kade, *friend of the bride*

Groomsmen

Joel Brunswick, *brother of the bride*

Jayce Brunswick, *brother of the bride*

Scott Brunswick, *cousin of the bride*

Lyle Wentworth, *cousin of the groom*

Brady Chase, *friend of the groom*

Heath Dalton, *friend of the groom*

Devon Hamilton, *friend of the groom*

PROLOGUE

HER BREATH BURSTING in her lungs, Cassie Parker readied to take a step, her bare foot hovering over the wooden floorboard. *Please, don't creak.*

She placed her foot on the floor, praying for silence.

Creak.

She closed her eyes, cold wafting over her trembling limbs. She held still. So still. Her lungs burned. She released her held breath and took another shallow inhale.

Creak. The sound echoed from the front of the house.

No.

Creak.

Closer this time—heading toward her.

She'd done what he'd said. Broke it off with Joel. Left the love of her life standing at the altar, so why was he back after a year of silence, instead of keeping his end of the bargain to leave her be? What had she done? Not seen Joel. She loved him too much to risk his life at a psycho's hands.

Creak.

She stiffened. Soon she'd feel his breath on the back of her neck, smell his musky cologne.

The moon slipped from the cloud cover, shining down to the courtyard in the center of her home, illuminating him. Faceless, but very, very real—a knife in hand.

Run, you idiot. Run!

Breaking into a sprint, she dashed for the front door.

Creak. Creak. Creak. Footsteps clapped behind her.

Just keep going. Keep going.

Reaching the door, she fumbled with the chain, finally dropping it against the metal door with a clang.

Hands soaked with a cold sweat, she struggled to grasp the dead bolt.

Please. Please. Please.

He was nearly upon her.

She scrambled to get the dead bolt unlocked, then opened the door to find him standing there.

Cassie bolted upright in bed, sweat-drenched and lungs burning. Her gaze flashed to her bedroom door. Still locked with the bar across it.

Windows. She darted a glance at each. All down. The extra locks she'd installed holding.

Struggling for a solid breath, she got to her feet, the floor frigid beneath them.

Reaching in her nightstand, she retrieved her SIG, clasping the gun in her left hand.

You're overreacting. It's been a year. He's not here.

Make sure, a voice whispered on the howling wind.

She grasped the bar and, taking a deep breath, lifted it up and opened the door to darkness. Grabbing the flashlight she'd positioned on her dresser, she clicked it on and stepped into the hallway.

Sweeping the house in fear he'd be hiding around the next corner, she moved in a swift manner, following the pattern she used every night to clear her home before bed. Every night and every time she returned to her home.

It'd be a year without a note. Without any sign of him, but he terrorized her still.

When she reached the kitchen, her rigid muscles eased some, her breath less shallow.

Thank you, Lord.

She leaned back against the kitchen counter, her gaze falling to her open cookbook in its wooden stand on the granite countertop.

She lifted her flashlight, centering on the book.

Horror coursed through her at the sight of the linen envelope.

He was back.

ONE

JANUARY 30

CASSIE APPROACHED the stunning Silver Pines ski village the following day, her insides still tingling from the letter's reminder to stay away from Joel. After a year, she'd hoped she was finally free, though his last letter before disappearing warned of what would happen if she reunited with Sheriff Joel Brunswick, and she'd refused to risk Joel's life—no matter how much it destroyed hers.

Now he was back. Because she was seeing Joel this weekend? They were hours away from her home at the Cedar Loft ski lodge in Silver Pines, Colorado, so how did he know where she was?

Her skin crawled. Had he gone through her things? Seen the invitation to the four-day wedding party weekend for her bestie in the trash? She'd learned not to keep personal information lying around. Her planner stayed on her phone, and her phone stayed on her. But somehow, he knew. But how?

Taking a stiff inhale, the winter chill burning her lungs, she pushed those thoughts away as she passed by the Silver Pines Resort, continued through the quaint ski village all the way to the opposite end, and pulled into Cedar Loft Resort's parking lot. She prayed the four-hour drive to the Colorado destination was enough to leave him behind, but fear whispered otherwise.

She grabbed her gear, checked in at the lodge, then walked

through the upper part of the idyllic ski village to find her cabin. Cedar Loft consisted of the beautiful lodge—only a few years old—and outer cabins only reachable on foot—snow shoes optional.

She rested her mittened hand on the outer doorknob of her cabin. He couldn't be here. She exhaled. Yes. He could, but . . .

Please don't let him be here. No more letters. Let me be free.

At least for the long weekend, culminating in Iz wedding Talbot. She didn't want her horror ruining another Brunswick wedding, and more importantly, ruining the wedding of someone she loved so dearly—*again.*

She opened the door and pulled her gun from her waist holster. Entering, she held her breath. She hated herself for letting him bring her to this level—scared, trepidatious . . . borderline paranoid. But he had. She couldn't shake the sensation of always being watched, of the prickly fear creeping up her neck that he'd been in her place, touched her things . . .

"Stop it! He's not here. You are fine!" Maybe if she repeated it enough, she'd believe it. Doubtful, but worth a shot.

Clearing the main room, she smiled at finding a note from her bestie—thankfully, no envelope with her name scrawled in black across it or she'd have freaked. *His* always came in expensive linen envelopes. How something so beautiful could bring such pain she didn't know.

She cleared the rest of the cabin and came back to read Izzy's note.

> *Welcome to the Silver Pines ski village! Our first excursion begins at one p.m.*
>
> *Meet on Cedar Loft's main lodge's porch at ten till.*
>
> *Dress in snowboarding gear.*
>
> *We're going to have a blast!*
>
> *Izzy & Talbot*

A deep swell of dread swirled through her. Not for seeing her stalker but for seeing Joel. It'd been a year, almost to the day—the perfect day they'd spent before their wedding.

Tears burned her eyes, dropping on the note and smearing the ink.

He'd ruined her life. Taken away the man she had loved—loved *still*.

Even after her move from Jeopardy Falls to Taos, all the precautions and sacrifices, he'd still returned.

Please, Lord, I beg you, let me be free. I don't know what else to do.

Sheriff Gonzales, of the Taos sheriff department, didn't know what else to do. Given it'd been a year without contact from her stalker, he'd set the case on the back burner.

Joel worked the case to the bones in Jeopardy Falls, then he joined forces with Sheriff Gonzales after she moved, but the case still refused to be solved despite their best efforts.

Her fists tightened, the note crumpling inside her left hand, and she forced herself to take a deep breath.

He's not here. He's back there. She exhaled and sank down in the oversized leather chair, resting her head in her hands.

Please help me not ruin Izzy's wedding like I ruined her brother's. And guide me to the right path when I return home.

She'd alerted the sheriff before she left and prayed he was already making progress. Glancing at her watch, she had a half hour until the meet-up.

Changing into her snowboarding gear, she stepped out into the crisp air. Not knowing which cabin Iz was in and not wanting to go knocking on all of them, she set out for the lodge and the coffee shop she'd spotted at the base of the trails. There was always time for coffee.

Snow crunched beneath her boots as she huffed her way to the edge of the small forest separating the cabins from the main lodge.

The snow gave way under the cover of evergreens. Only brown needles and pinecones littered the ground.

Coming out on the other side of the woods, she spotted the exterior ordering window of the Brew Through.

Five minutes in line and another few placing her order later, she studied the gorgeous Cedar Loft lodge, the Silver Pines lodge far in the distance, and the quaint, tranquil ski village surrounding her. A beautiful place to be wed, especially since Iz and her brothers had grown up on this mountain. Their dad's best friend owned the Cedar Loft, and Cassie had heard all kinds of stories about their childhood antics at the original lodge, which apparently remained standing, but she had never been to the ski village herself.

"Your order, love," the lady at the Brew Through shop said, leaning out the sliding window to hand her the hot cup of steaming cocoa with two shots of espresso. The scent of sweet marshmallows, dark chocolate, and rich espresso carried on the blustering wind.

"Sorry. Daydreaming," Cassie said, taking the cup.

"We all do it, darling. Enjoy your drink." She slid the window closed.

Cassie stepped out of the way for the growing line of customers, most with skis on their feet or snowboards tucked under their arms. Fresh snow filled the air, twisting in mini cyclones. She made it around to the front porch, where she found Iz and Talbot waiting—alone.

"There you are," Iz said. "I was about to track you down."

"Am I late?" Cassie glanced at her watch, then gave a sheepish smile. "Sorry. The coffee line must have taken longer than I anticipated."

"It's okay. You made it." She wrapped her arm around Cassie's shoulders, leading her around the corner and down the small slope to two helicopters waiting for the wedding party. A regular day of snowboarding would've been too dull for one of Izzy's adventures.

She looked questioningly at her bestie.

"Heli-skiing." Talbot smiled. "You're in our copter." He pointed to the nearest one as the other lifted off.

Whoosh. Whoosh. Whoosh.

Helicopter blades sliced through the air.

Trepidation shot through her. While she enjoyed heli-skiing, and carving fresh powder was addictive, the ride there skyrocketed her anxiety.

Iz reached over and squeezed her hand. "It'll be okay, I promise. We're just taking it to the west side of the mountain."

"The untouched side." Talbot stepped back and gestured for them to go with a sweep of his hand. "After you, ladies."

Iz climbed in first, and Cassie followed.

Talbot, Izzy, and Brady sat rear facing. Heath, who worked with Cassie and Devon at the ME office, sat near the open bay door, forward facing. Her two coworkers had grown tight with Talbot over the past couple of years at all the group barbeques and outings, and now they were a close part of the gang. She scanned the seats again. Jayce and Mia had their seats, leaving the only empty one next to . . .

Joel.

Had it really been a year since she'd seen him? It seemed like yesterday, or at least her feelings were the same as back then. Despite what Izzy claimed, he couldn't possibly still hold feelings for her.

His gaze met hers, and he nodded. "Cassandra." His gaze pierced to her marrow.

Cassandra? He hadn't called her that in years. Not since they'd first met when Iz brought her home to hang out in junior high. Cassie. For one wonderful and frightening year, she'd been *his* Cassie. But not anymore.

She settled in her seat, and before she had her headset in place, the copter lifted off, rising in the air. She longed to reach for Joel's hand as she had so many times before. Instead, she balled her hands in her lap.

Joel's gaze bounced over them, then he directed his attention forward. She could practically feel the warmth of his body, his thigh inadvertently brushing hers as they hit turbulence, but he kept his focus on the windshield.

She, on the other hand, couldn't keep herself from staring. It'd been a year since she'd seen his strong shoulders, his chiseled arms visible under his pushed-up sleeves, the hunter green Henley shirt bringing out the green undertones in his blue eyes. His jacket lay across his lap.

His gaze flashed to her. She glanced down but not fast enough. He'd caught her staring. Heat rushed to her cheeks. She braved a glance back up, meeting his gaze head on.

Deep emotion filled his eyes.

But which emotion?

TWO

"ALL RIGHT, FOLKS. Here you go," the pilot said, hovering just over the snow.

Joel leaned forward, taking in the pristine powder beyond Heath's shoulders. "Where's the other copter?" he asked.

"We do two separate areas," the pilot said, "but don't worry, they're just on a parallel run on the other side of that thin tree line. You'll all end up at the same place, or they can cross over."

The excitement of untouched slopes raced adrenaline through Joel's limbs—new slopes he'd never been on. He bounced his knee, raring to go, but everyone had climbed up to the door before him, save Cassie.

His chest squeezed. *Cassie*. He swallowed, aching for a distraction.

Any distraction, Lord.

"Have a blast," the pilot hollered over the thwacking blades. "Be at our pickup point by four, or you'll be tempting the blizzard blowing in tonight."

"Roger that," Heath, the first jumper, said, followed by Iz, Talbot, and Talbot's extreme sports buddy, Brady, then Jayce and Mia, leaving Cassie and Joel alone.

"After you," he gestured for her to go. He'd bring up the rear.

"Thanks." A soft smile graced her lips. One that sliced right through him. How could he still love her after she'd left him with zero compassion?

She jumped, and shoving the consternation from his thoughts, he followed, hitting the powder, then rocking his snowboard and digging in sideways to a stop beside Cassie, who'd done the same based on her position.

"You okay?" he asked.

"Yeah. No. I just wanted to say how sorry I am."

He arched a brow. "For?" He knew darn well what for, but he wanted to hear it. Wanted to know why. The question had plagued him for three hundred sixty-seven days.

She dropped her gaze, then met his. "For leaving you at the altar with no word."

"Why'd you do it?"

"I can't explain."

"Can't or won't?"

She bit her lip—pink lips he used to kiss. Lips he'd thought he'd kiss forever.

"Won't, but there's a reason why."

"And that is?"

She shook her head.

"Gotcha. I'm not worth an explanation." He pushed off without looking back, praying the brisk wind would slap his steadfast feelings for Cassie out of his mind as he gained ground on the first group, now less than a hundred yards ahead.

Heat seared my limbs, and I fought the urge to move. They'd talked. The two of them *alone*. What had she said to Joel? Told him why she'd left him? Told him she still loved him?

Biting my lip—clearly too hard as blood slipped across my tongue. I spit it out. Just as I'd spit them out.

Them. There was no *them*. Didn't they understand that by now?

Gripping the binoculars, I tracked them down the slopes.

They needed to understand they'd *never* be together.

Messages hadn't worked.

It was time for decisive action.

THREE

SNOW FLEW in Cassie's wake as she blazed a fresh trail, joy alight in her. This was freedom. If only she could find it in her own life. But she pushed that aside and soaked up the peace being in nature always brought. Spending it with the man she still loved brimmed her happiness over. But she was simply fooling herself. Iz claimed he still loved her, too, but how could he after what she'd done? Even if she'd done it for the right reasons. Regardless, after a year of not seeing him, just having him near warmed her immeasurably more than the physical exertion heating her limbs.

Until the realization smacked her hard that even if he somehow managed to forgive her and, against all odds, still loved her, she couldn't be with him. *He* would see to that. And she loved Joel too much to endanger his life.

Anger pulsed heat through her limbs. A stark contrast to the frigid air engulfing her. She had to find a way to end this. End *his* control over her.

A deep and guttural roar rent the air, shaking the ground with violent energy.

Turning, she froze in fear. A volcano of white exploded, and a giant wall of white rushed at her.

"Cassie," Joel said, his mouth wide in a holler, but the sound dropped to a whisper before it reached her under the mountain's furious snarl. "Avalanche. Brace for impact."

His words hit a flash of a second before a wave of white and debris lashed over her, tumbling her in its ferocity.

Breathe. Take a deep breath and hold it.

She tried, but snow surrounded her, pummeling her along its jagged path.

Managing to get her arm crossed over her mouth, she fought everything trying to rip it away. *"Like you're going to sneeze. Keep it there."* Joel's words during their avalanche training before they started heli-skiing a few years ago raced through her dizzied mind.

Beacon. She prayed her beacon was on because she was under the fury—an inconceivable force rolling over her, ripping at her limbs, and tossing her like a rag doll.

White enveloped her. Flashes of light followed by deep, entrenched darkness.

Please, Lord. Let me survive. Please don't leave me.

Not in the vacuum of white.

Roaring beat against her eardrums.

Thud.

Pain ricocheted through her body as she collided into something hard and unrelenting. A tremendous weight rushed over her, consuming her. She fought to suck in a gulp of air, but it was too late. She was encased in its icy grip.

Pressure squeezed all the air from her lungs, suffocating her in darkness as the avalanche roared overhead—the sound almost deafening.

I'm going to die.

Hot tears mixed with the cold surrounding her.

I never got to tell him. I don't want to die without telling him. Please.

Trust me, Cassie, the Lord's voice whispered over the turmoil.

Snow pressed at her lips, trying to force its way in. She clamped her jaw, hoping the pressure would stop.

Be still.

That was the last thing she wanted to do. She wanted to fight, but as she embraced it, her flustered mind began to clear from the encroaching panic.

Backpack.

She pulled the string to inflate it, praying it would pop her to the surface, or at the very least, create a bigger air pocket around her. But nada. No balloon. No popping pocket of air. *Nothing.*

She tugged harder.

Nothing again.

Panic swelled, her body shaking from the deepest fear she'd ever experienced as cold seeped through her, the pressure unrelenting to the point of snapping her like a twig.

I'm going to die.

Buried in white.

Never found.

FOUR

JOEL CLUTCHED the thick tree trunk for sweet mercy, his head pressed against the rough, scaling bark. A cascade of white roared down the mountain—its force lifting his legs up behind him like they didn't weight a thing. Locking his arms tighter around the tree, he held on hard—fearing they'd break under the amassing pressure.

Please help me to hang on.

His life literally depended on his slipping grasp. His legs flung like a rag doll behind him.

Give me the strength I don't possess. I need Your strength.

"God is our refuge and strength, an ever-present help in trouble."

The words from Psalms broke through his panicked brain but didn't douse his frenzied concern for Cassie. She'd been right in the avalanche's path—nowhere near the tree line. While he hadn't physically seen her go under, he dreaded the worst. Being trapped in the undertow, pushed and dragged in its furious path, scraping the bottom of the earth. So much like a fierce ocean wave stealing your breath. *Breath.* He hoped if Cassie was dragged under that she'd gotten one strong breath before the snow closed in around her.

Please, Lord, let her be alive. Please don't tear her away from me again.

The roaring freight train of snow whooshed over him at lightning speed—the noise and pressure deafening.

Would it ever end?

What seemed an eternity later, it finally settled. The thick wave of rushing snow stilled, the mountain eerily silent. No sound of birds or voices or wind. Just desperate silence.

Cassie.

He moved, or attempted to move, but the packed snow—so high it nearly covered his head—held him fast to the tree. He wriggled, trying to yank his arms free, but no movement. He needed to be shoveled out.

Unable to shift his head more than an inch, he glanced out of his peripheral vision, taking in the devastation—rocks, debris, and mountains of snow.

The wind smacked his cheeks. Cyclones of snow swirled along the surface—the sky a furious charcoal.

Don't let the blizzard loose. That's all they'd need.

Please. Not until everyone is safe.

His prayer wasn't answered as fresh piles of snow broke from the clouds, mixed with pelting ice.

"Joel! Joel!" Izzy's called, her voice high-pitched, frantic.

Thank you, Lord. His sister was alive. There was one relief. He ached for more.

"Here!" he called, blinking his snow-caked lashes. His sunglasses must have torn off in the avalanche's wake.

He spotted Iz and Talbot in his peripheral vision.

They climbed up through the thigh-high snow, plowing for him.

"Oh, thank goodness," Iz said, reaching him and resting a hand on the tip-top of his shoulder—barely an inch above the packed snow line. Talbot approached seconds later.

"You okay, man?" he asked.

"I could use a shovel out." And fast.

"Of course, dude." Talbot pulled his avalanche shovel from his pack, unfolded the handle, and locked it in place. Iz did the same.

Soon he was free, but his arms and hands were numb. He shook them out, and they flopped about, unfeeling.

"How is everybody? How is Cassie?" *Please say she made it out of the furious path of destruction.*

Iz bit her bottom lip.

He narrowed his eyes. "What?" he asked, but he already knew the answer.

She sniffed. "Everyone is fine, thankfully, except—"

"Cassie," he breathed.

Iz nodded, tears welling in her eyes.

"We'll find her," Talbot said, his voice calm and firm with conviction.

Would he be so level if it were Iz in Cassie's place? But calm was good in at least one of them. Talbot would think clearly, and that's what they needed. But Joel was far from that level. Panic rushed hot adrenaline through his frozen hands, bringing them back to life with excruciating pain as blood once again began to flow.

Not wasting a second, he broke into a run for the weathered-looking group gathered in a circle. "Did any of you see Cassie go under the avalanche?" Negative answers sounded. He turned back toward the slope, scanning the snow and debris-strewn earth, anxiety pricking at his soul as he shouted her name again, waiting, pleading with God for her to answer.

"But she was about a hundred yards from me when it hit," Devon said.

"Me too," Mia said. "Maybe less."

It was something. "And where were you two in relation to her? It might help pin her location."

"Almost a hundred yards downhill," Devon said.

"I was a bit lower," Mia said. "I turned and saw Cassie flying off the outcropping, and then it started."

"Okay," Joel said, moving before he finished his question. "So about seventy yards up the slope from here?" He'd only been fifty yards away from her, but the tree he'd clung to blocked his view of everything but brown bark and a wall of snow.

"Yep," Devon said, and Mia confirmed the distance.

Joel broke into a flat-out run uphill, tumbling forward with his flailing momentum. He landed on his knees, cold creeping into his bones. Righting himself, he continued the climb—his legs still struggling to wake up—to work right. Could anything be more infuriating? Time was of the essence and his body was taking its sweet time coming back to life.

"Cassie," he bellowed, progressing through high snow drifts—his steps deliberate, his legs shaking.

Other voices chimed in, calling Cassie's name—the crew spreading out and upward.

"We have a starting point," Izzy hollered.

He halted and turned to face her. "We do?" Hope lanced his soul.

"Yes, but we have to keep in mind how far the avalanche may have carried her," Iz said.

"I know." The thudding of his racing heart whooshed through his ears, making everyone's voices sound distant and echoed.

Please let me find her alive.

He couldn't imagine a world without Cassie, even if she was never to be his.

The thought of losing Cassie to the avalanche reverberated through his distressed mind.

"Joel." Iz tugged his elbow.

"What?" he snapped. "Sorry."

She shook it off. "Jayce made up a search grid by sections."

He swept his gaze over the crew systematically forming into a grid formation, all beginning to search their sector for Cassie with their lancing probes.

"What about her beacon?" What was wrong with him? He should have thought of that first. "Her balloon?" Why hadn't she pulled it? Was she unconscious?

Please, Lord, let her be awake.

He hated the thought of her awake and terrified under the snow, but she'd have an air hole if she was conscious.

"I'm getting no signal from her," Talbot said.

Had the weight of the avalanche crushed it? Was her balloon malfunctioning? It didn't matter why both weren't working. Just that they weren't.

He grabbed his lancing probe from his pack. "Where's my grid?"

Talbot walked it out for him.

He swallowed, his throat raw. Snow drove sideways lashing Joel in the face, the encroaching blizzard picking up speed. Only a short window existed to locate Cassie before she'd suffocated under the snow. An air pocket only lasted so long, and with fresh snow piling on . . .

He tightened his jaw, unwilling to go there. They'd find her. He wouldn't stop until they did.

Twenty minutes later, he moved to the next unsearched grid, his arms heated and trembling, his steps staggering, his legs listless.

Please, Father, let this grid be the one. "Please," he breathed. The ferocious blizzard growled in the oncoming night, swallowing the light.

A thousand different scenarios raced through his mind. He worked from the bottom left edge of the grid. Across the delineated space, his heart sinking with each empty quadrant. Their chance of finding Cassie—of her surviving until they found her . . . Time was swallowed in an endless void.

FIVE

DARKNESS OOZED OVERHEAD, slipping through the white snow.

Stay calm. They'll find you. He'll find you.

Joel wouldn't stop until he did, but would it be too late? Her hope of being found alive dwindled as time slipped by—both too fast and too slow. Her heart raced.

How long had she been under? Long enough she couldn't feel her feet. *Frostbite.* She swallowed. *Please, let them find me—whole.*

Her foggy mind slipped in and out of consciousness. She dozed off, then startled awake, her eyes thick—weighted.

Her arm protecting her tiny bubble of air throbbed in the awkward position. Sooner or later, it would drop in exhaustion, and she'd suffocate. Snow crept closer and closer to her mouth. The roaring over, now was the avalanche aftermath—the snow settling, slinking into crevices of air, sealing the earth and everything under it in its icy casket. Tears pricked her eyes—the only warmth she'd experienced since being swallowed whole.

She'd heard the gory and heartbreaking details of avalanche victims—snow found down their throats, through their sinuses. It would slip through her crevices just as it was the earth's.

She'd die. Die without ever telling Joel the truth.

Unwieldy grogginess and fierce cold battled to take her, and her grit to hold out was slipping away.

Please, Lord, if You're going to take me home . . . just let me fall asleep without pain and wake up in Your arms.

Slipping toward sleep, she fought to keep her eyes open, but the heaviness was too much.

Slipping.

Slipping . . .

What was that? She struggled to listen. *Please don't say I'm hearing things. That I'm that far gone.* She listened again. *Please.*

Sound reverberated above. Something slicing through the ice. Again and again.

Oh, thank You, Lord. Had someone found her? She tried to yell, but her voice was a hoarse sound that didn't even qualify as a whisper. Tears should be flooding her eyes, but all moisture was gone.

Something poked her arm, the pressure deepening.

"I found her!" Joel's voice radiated through the snow.

Oh, thank You, Lord. Thank You. Thank You.

He'd found her. If anyone could have, it was Joel.

He hadn't given up on her, and she wouldn't give up on him. On them.

She'd tell him the truth and, *if* he still loved her as Izzy claimed, they'd hunt down her stalker together. Either way, Joel deserved the truth.

If being so near to death taught her anything, it was not to leave anything on the table. And when she got out of here, she'd not die with regrets. Not like she nearly had.

Anxiety and relief churned in the pit of Joel's stomach. He'd found her, but was he in time? He hollered her name without reply.

Scrambling to shovel her out without hurting her, he worked fast but with deftness.

Iz and Talbot joined him, then Scott and Heath, all working to shovel Cassie out. Snow flew in the air each time a shovel tossed back.

He swallowed the acrid taste in his mouth, his stomach churning.

Was she still conscious? Breathing?

Adrenaline coursed through his veins.

Wait. He slowed. What was that?

He narrowed his eyes.

A glimmer of color flashed before them, then vanished.

He knelt, digging with his hands until a patch of blue appeared. Cassie's snowsuit.

"She's here!" He squeezed his eyes shut for a breath of a moment. *Thank You.* Hot tears sizzled down his frozen cheeks.

He dropped onto his stomach, everyone following suit, each straining as far as they could reach to shovel the remaining snow surrounding Cassie out with their hands rather than risk hurting her with shovels. Painstakingly, they uncovered Cassie inch by inch until she was visible six feet down.

Frigid air seared Joel's lungs.

Shadows covered the sky in the dawn of night.

Faster. They needed to work faster, then find shelter. Get Cassie and everyone warm somehow before they all froze to death.

Clicking on the flashlight from his pack, he swept it over Cassie's face, praying the light would reveal her alert and conscious. She inched her arm up to shield her eyes or attempted to, but it barely budged—as if frozen stiff. But her beautiful green eyes blinked—her lashes caked with snow, no doubt the avalanche had tripped her sunglasses from her face as well.

Ice crystals clung to her hair peeking out of the flower-patterned stocking cap.

"We've got you," he said. "We've got you." His chest tight, he raked his gaze over her—thankfulness and concern churning in his gut.

Blue lips. Shivering. Pale face with white spots.

"She's in hypothermia! We need to get her someplace warm and fast."

"Joel." Izzy rested a hand on his shoulder.

"What?"

"Her leg." His sister gestured down.

His gaze tracked to Cassie's right leg crooked sideways at the knee. No bones protruding, thank goodness. Perhaps a badly twisted knee, a torn tendon. So many things it could be. But examining her leg needed to wait. The priority was hefting her up out of the hole before snow collapsed in around her.

"We found her," Iz yelled in the background of his focus, her flashlight sweeping back and forth.

Talbot's joined hers.

Joel studied Cassie's face pinched in sorrow, or was it relief? On the brink of crying, but no tears fell. "We need water. She's dehydrated." His words cast white clouds in the beam of Izzy's flashlight.

Izzy grabbed the pack off her back. "I've got some." Reaching into her bag, she fished out a bottle of water and tossed it to him.

Catching it, he jumped down to Cassie's side and brought the bottle to her blue lips.

"Here, sweetheart," he said, not even pausing to consider why that had slipped from his lips. Joy at finding her alive was what mattered, that and getting her shelter and warmth. The rest of the crew appeared at his side one by one until the full party encircled the hole.

"What do we do?" Devon asked. "Is she all right?"

"She will be." He'd make sure of that. Whatever she needed to heal, he'd give.

"What do we need to do?" Devon asked again.

"I need a coat," Joel said, taking off his without hesitation.

"Joel," Izzy said, concern lacing her voice. "*You* already have hypothermia. I see all the signs. Get someone else's."

"I'll be fine. Plus, I'd wager nearly all of us are experiencing some level of hypothermia." They'd been out in the elements too long, and with a blizzard howling around them, it was only going to get worse.

Devon and Talbot's cousin Lyle handed him their coats.

"Thanks. We need to build a makeshift gurney and get her out of here."

"What do you need?" Brady asked.

"We need to widen the hole so two of us can fit down here to lift her out. I also need two long sticks—thick as you can get."

"That shouldn't be a problem with all the debris," Devon said.

He nodded, and Brady and Devon bolted for the tree line while his cousin Scott and Heath helped widen the hole—giving him room to work.

Joel draped his coat across Cassie, her teeth chattering. "Hey, Cassie," he said, trying to get her to focus her gaze on him. It took a moment, but she did. "I'm going to get you out of here, okay?"

She gave a nod, the movement stiff.

"You trust me, right?"

She dipped her chin an inch.

"Good."

The guys returned with sticks more reminiscent of poles.

"Perfect."

They handed them to him in turn, then taking their coats, he fashioned the gurney parallel to Cassie on the snow.

Stabbing bolts of ice streamed down with the falling snow.

"Okay," he said, his voice full of emotion, full of love. Even if she didn't love him back, he still loved her. "You ready?"

She gave a slight nod.

"Okay. I need you to be the fierce woman I know you to be. We need to lift you onto the gurney, then up out of this hole." Six feet under the snowline. So very close to death. He shook the cobwebs of thoughts from his brain and refocused his attention on getting Cassie out of the hole. "Moving you is going to hurt, but I know you can handle it. You're my tough girl."

She nodded once.

"All right." He took a deep breath and blew it out. "Be as still as you can." He turned his attention to the guys. "Okay, Jayce and

I will lift her onto the gurney, then we'll each take a corner," he said, addressing Brady and Devon, "and lift her up and you two help pull her out of the hole."

"Roger that," Brady said as he and Devon perched themselves at the edge of the hole, ready to pull the gurney up and out.

Jayce dropped in the hole beside his brother.

"All right." Joel rested his hands on Cassie's shoulders for a moment. "You've got this," he assured her before turning his attention back to Jayce. "Grab her ankles, and I'll get her upper body. We move on three."

Jayce nodded.

"I'm going to slip my hands under your arms, okay?"

A murmur escaped her lips, his heart warming at the first sound she'd made since they'd found her. It was a good sign, even if she couldn't form words yet. He shifted, slipping his hands under her armpits, then looked up at Jayce. "Nice and smooth. One, two, three."

They lifted.

A cry tore from Cassie's blue lips.

"I'm sorry, honey." He and Jayce lowered her onto the gurney.

Her pained face softened as Jayce released his hold on her ankles.

"All right. One more time, sweetheart," Joel whispered. "It shouldn't be as painful, but we have to lift the gurney up and out of here. Remember, deep breaths in and out of your mouth."

She nodded, her neck moving with more ease.

Jayce hiked his end up as Joel stabilized Cassie by bracing one hand on her shoulder. Devon and Brady hauled her out, resting the gurney on the snow.

"Good to see you," Devon said. "I can't tell you how glad I am that you didn't become a crime scene for me to work."

"You and me both," she chuckled at her coworker, but it came out as more of a cough. Her gaze pinned on Joel. "Good to see you all."

"Let's all take a corner," Joel instructed. "And we'll rotate turns with Heath, Talbot, Scott, and Lyle."

The group of four men nodded.

"What about ski patrol?" Heath asked. "They'll be coming soon, won't they? I mean, we're not stuck out here, are we?" Panic embedded his faltering tone.

"They can't cross the avalanche," Talbot said. "Just like we can't."

"Helicopters?" Heath asked, the anxious pitch of his voice rising.

"Not in this blizzard. They'll be grounded," Joel said. "We're on our own, I'm afraid."

SIX

"WE NEED SHELTER FAST," Jayce hollered against the rising wind. "A cave? We could build a fire, get out of the snow."

"Let me get my bearings," Joel yelled back. He needed to think despite the numbness spreading through him—blood being siphoned from his extremities in an effort to protect the heart.

A cave wasn't a bad idea, but there was something else on the cusp of his brain—a whisper not defined but insistent. He shook out his free hand, trying to wake it up, get the blood flowing before hypothermia shifted to frostbite. *Help us, Lord. Direct us. We cannot see, but You can see as bright as day.*

He exhaled, his breath a white vapor among the white surrounding them. There was no way to make it back to the main lodge, the avalanche had seen to that, cutting out any pass to it. Except, perhaps, the top rim, but with the risk of falling, that was suicide. They'd have to wait to be rescued before they could make it back to the lodge. The same low whisper resonated in his ears. This time clear as a bell. *Lodge.* "That's it!" *Thank You, Jesus.*

"What's it?" Jayce asked, despondence edging his tone.

"The old lodge."

"Didn't they tear it down?" Iz asked, huddling against Talbot, his arm draped around her shoulders.

"Not yet. I talked to Stan recently." His dad's best friend and fourth-generation-owner of Cedar Loft.

"Okay." Jayce coughed, raw and deep.

"He said he didn't have the heart to tear the old lodge down." His great-grandfather built it, and Stan wanted to fix it up someday. But they didn't need to hear all that. Only the news of refuge. Ice pellets bounced off his back. "If I have my bearings right . . ." *Come on, Boy Scouts, don't fail me now.* "It should be due west."

"And how far?" Iz asked, her voice quivering, her teeth chattering.

He swallowed. He'd hoped to keep that part to himself.

"Bro?" Iz said, more insistent.

"Let's just say due west." He held her gaze, well, the outline of her body in the bluster of the fierce storm.

Wind howled, the only sound surrounding their party in the burgeoning whiteout. "Let the group know where we're headed and to pull in ranks. Losing someone's far too easy in these conditions."

"I'll let them know," Talbot said, hitching his step. "I'll be right back." He kissed Iz's cheek, or so it looked through a world drenched in white.

Five minutes later, Talbot back at Iz's side, Heath led the way with his flashlight swathing across the shower of snow. The light faded within feet, succumbing to the darkness. Every so often, Heath turned, swiping the flashlight across their party to make sure everyone was still with them. Mia hung at the back, Amy trying to yank her forward, pushing to her to keep going.

Heath shifted, and the light bounced off Cassie's ghost-white face. *Frostbite.* Increasing his strides, Joel hurried the pace, adrenaline burning his thighs.

"Slow down!" Amy yelled. "Mia's struggling."

"We can't slow down." He'd leave it at that. Elaborating on the alternative would only cause panic.

"I'll help her," Scott said, falling back.

Brady shifted his hand on his corner of the gurney, repositioning his hold. "Seriously, how far to this lodge?"

Joel glanced over his shoulder at the group stumbling through the snow behind him, snow too thick to make out faces beyond arm's length. "A quarter of a mile."

Brady's shoulders drooped.

"We can make it," Joel hollered, hoping his voice would carry on the rushing wind. "Keep moving!"

He shifted his thoughts off their situation and on to the lodge of his childhood summers and holidays—the best memories warming him. He'd always wanted to bring Cassie to the old lodge but never under these circumstances.

She shivered beneath the coats draped over her, her heading bobbing to one side.

Faster. Move faster. Battling the painful numbness threatening to consume him, he strove to raise his legs higher with each step, plowing through the snow, now crusting with a layer of ice.

Everything in him ached to lie down and rest his eyes.

He shook his head. *Keep moving. Keep moving.*

Maybe if he repeated it enough, his exhausted body would heed his direction. His leg hovering above the snow, he teetered—the gurney wobbling in his hand.

"Whoa!" Jayce said.

"Sorry." He stabilized. "I've got it." *No. You. Don't.* He swallowed, his throat raw and closing in. *Father, I can't do this without You. They are all looking to me. Please equip me to lead them to safety. Lead the way.*

They *had* to keep moving. Otherwise, they'd fall asleep and never wake up—at least not on this side of heaven.

"He is my refuge and my fortress, my God, in whom I trust."

Joel tightened his grip on the gurney, his fortitude strengthened.

Cries sounded on the howling, blustering wind.

Mia.

Had she fallen? Surely Scott would get her through. His cousin, having spent holidays with them at the lodge, was familiar with the distance left. He could spur Mia on, if she wasn't too far gone.

It wasn't the same lively lodge they remembered—the one

bustling with people. It'd been abandoned for years. Who knew what condition they'd find it in? Or what supplies might be there. But the old lodge was their *only* option.

"H-how . . . ?" Iz stuttered. "M-much . . . longer?"

"Not much," he hollered back, hoping his voice would carry on the wind.

They plowed rather than stepped through the snow—striving against its full, wet weight, exhaustion and frostbite threatening to grip hold.

Please, Father.

Desperation clawed at him.

You can't make it. You'll fail them all. The taunts slipped in his ears in a haunting whisper.

He shook his head and ignored the lies . . . or perhaps the truth.

Shapes took form ahead. Were those . . . ?

"The tree line," he yelled, gratitude welling in his chest.

"What tree line?" Lyle yelled.

"*That* tree line." Joel pointed his hand, unable to get his fingers to respond. "The lodge sits on the other side and down the slope."

"Finally," Heath grunted.

Everyone's steps were invigorated with the news. Cutting a swath through the wooded trail, they moved swiftly through the narrow forest, the snow thin on the pine needle–covered ground. Relief filled him. *Nearly there.*

Something shifted to his right. A dark shadow in the white world surrounding them.

Joel halted, his body tensing. *What was that?* Were his eyes playing tricks on him? He prayed so, but his gut shouted otherwise.

"What's up?" Brady asked, tugging the gurney forward.

Joel pulled back.

Movement fluttered to his three o'clock—fast and fleet. He stiffened, his frozen limbs hardening. Was it a mountain lion?

The rest of their party continued to move.

"Still!" he hollered, and they all fumbled to a halt after gathering around.

Talbot and Iz hitched up beside him.

The shadow slunk through the woods.

Not the way a lion moved, more like a . . . *wolf*.

"What is it?" Nat asked, huffing. Bending at the waist, she braced her hands on her knees.

"Wolves." Heath's voice heightened a pitch.

"It's *one* wolf," Jayce said. "Don't scare everyone."

"One can still do a lot of damage. If he pins you down, he can rip you apart," Devon said. "I saw it at a crime scene once. Nasty."

Kendra, always the quiet one of their friend group, whimpered at their side—the full crew a circle amid the tall trees. "Did you say *rip* apart?"

"I'm afraid so." Devon squared his shoulders.

Dude. Shut up. "It'll be fine." Joel kept his voice level. "We move for the lodge, nice and easy. Solid steps, people." He pinned his gaze on his younger brother. "Jayce, grab the shovel from your pack."

Jayce nodded, snow and ice pellets shaking off his hood.

"Lyle, take his place on the gurney."

Jayce faced the wolf, his shovel tight at his side. "Go. I'll hold it at bay."

Joel froze. A second shadow at their six.

Heath's flashlight followed its movement, the light bouncing off a pair of yellow eyes.

Heath let an expletive slip. "I told you there were wolves. They stay in packs."

And normally don't attack unless provoked.

"Okay, guys," Joel rushed out. "We move for the lodge. It sits at the bottom of this ridge. Watch your balance, and whatever you do, *don't* run. That might engage them."

But . . . what was he missing? He studied the outlines of the animals in the snow. They were poised, pawing the ground, encroaching, but why? "We need someone on our six."

Mia's cries echoed through the hollow below.

"I'll go," Devon said.

"I'll take the gurney if someone can help Mia," Scott said.

"I've got her," Nat said, shifting to Mia's side and hefting her up against her. "We've got this, girl."

Devon pulled the shovel from his pack and strode with purpose to their rear, positioning himself at the edge of the forest between them and the second wolf.

Joel studied where they'd forge a path ahead. He squinted. "Heath, shine your light due west about a hundred yards ahead."

He did so, and the light swept across the abandoned lodge, standing tall in the frozen world.

"The lodge," Heath said, his voice for once upbeat.

Good. They needed spirits lifted. Next to Cassie, Joel feared most for Mia's safety and mood at this point, but they had to press on.

Heath swept the light back to them, revealing the steep slope standing between them and safety.

"All right. Sure, purposeful steps," Joel instructed.

"What about the wolf?" Savannah asked, her voice quivering.

His young cousin had been so quiet, he'd nearly forgotten she was there. Only sixteen—this had to be so terrifying.

"We're covered," he assured them, trusting Jayce and Devon to hold the line.

"Move down at an angle," he said. The sixty-degree slope was a nasty one. He exhaled. *Controlled, focused steps.* If only his weary legs would abide. His left foot skidded out from under him, adrenaline flooding his system. He pressed his weight down into the ground, trying not to teeter. *Please don't let me fall. Please, don't let me drop Cassie.*

His grip on her gurney slipped, his glove easing down his hand.

Catching himself just before the tipping point, he breathed out a whoosh of relief.

Cassie looked up at him through her snow-and-ice-covered lashes.

He nodded. He had her.

Warm from the adrenaline still coursing through him, he took a steady, slow step down.

"One short step after another," he said, and the other three holding the gurney moved in unison as he called out each step. The rest of the party followed.

On a pause, he glanced from Jayce at their three to Devon at their six.

"This guy is getting really agitated," Devon hollered.

What was he missing? It was like they were defending . . . *a den*. "I bet there's a den nearby." Joel scanned his surroundings but couldn't see beyond the edge of the group. And even they were just shapes in the ever-drowning snow.

"What do we do, man?" Brady asked, fear tracking through his voice.

"We keep for the lodge. We don't have a choice."

"And if their den is near it?"

"I pray that's not the case." The lodge meant survival—the elements death.

"Slow, deliberate steps," he repeated.

The group managed their way down a third of the sheer gradient, but exhaustion was taking over. Everyone was hunched for breath or swaying.

He gazed back at the snarling wolves pawing the ground. They needed to move, but any increase in pace could trigger the animals to attack.

He turned his attention back to the lodge. Movement swished twenty yards south of the lodge—a dark shadow silhouetted by white. He squeezed his eyes shut for a breath of a moment. *Another wolf*.

He must have come from their den—his black coat snowless. He stepped farther out from the tree line, and flakes rapidly covered his fur until he blended in.

Joel swallowed. Risk attack by proceeding forward to the lodge, or die of the elements? There was no choice. They had to reach the lodge.

The black wolf edged to their nine o'clock. He and the one to their three were flanking them.

"We need someone on our nine."

"Not more," Amy cried.

"I got it," Heath said, handing Joel his flashlight. He grabbed his avalanche shovel and headed for the infringing wolf.

"They think we're attacking their den. Everyone shift north. We'll go in the back door of the lodge. Maybe that will show them we mean them no harm."

Everyone did as instructed. The black wolf pawed at the ground near Heath.

Heath held the shovel positioned to swing.

"Don't make a move unless they do," Joel said. "They're just testing us out."

"Whatever." Heath sniffed. "I got this."

Heath was the last person they should have put on the line, far too brash. But it was done now.

Joel swallowed, his throat parched. They were surrounded—one behind, two flanking, and the den somewhere ahead. One, at the least, had to be protecting the den and could come at them anytime—encircling them.

He raised his hand to still everyone. Some took longer than others to comply, but soon they all stood fixed in place, the wolves growling but not advancing—at least not yet.

The large black one shifted forward, and Heath swung at it with the shovel. The wolf yelped as the shovel hit its side, then it lunged forward.

"Run!" Heath panicked, turning his back on the wolf.

"No!" Joel screamed, but it was too late. Everyone, save Jayce and Devon, who still held their shovels, raced for the lodge, Amy and Savannah tumbling down the hill.

The black wolf lunged forward with a guttural howl, the others howled in return—their calls echoing in the canyon the lodge nestled in.

Joel glanced at Cassie—her eyes wide. "Nearly there," he assured her.

Snow flew in their wake as they walked, slid, and skidded their way down the slope. The front group reached the lodge, and Joel leapt for the back porch.

"Easy now," Brady said, steadying his grip on the gurney.

"Sorry." Joel reached for the rear door handles. Padlocked. *No!*

"Let's try the side," Brady suggested.

They followed the porch around to the sound of howling wolves and grunts from Jayce and Devon echoing through the hollow.

Joel shifted his full focus to getting inside rather than the commotion behind them. Once Cassie was safely inside, he'd go back to help.

Reaching the side door, they found no padlock.

Thank you, Lord. He turned the handle. *Locked.* He lifted his exhausted right leg and kicked in the door. Safety. Shelter. Finally. Now he prayed for much needed supplies, but first, "I need to get back out there to help. Who can stay with Cassie?"

"Iz and I will," Talbot offered.

He clapped Talbot's shoulder, the contact paining his half-numb hand. "Thanks."

"We've got her. Go on."

He headed out as Heath passed him, dodging into the lodge and slamming the door, his face stricken in panic. Heart of a lion, that one.

Joel rushed back to the melee.

SEVEN

JOEL GRIPPED his shovel as tight as his half-numb hands would allow. Brady followed him. The black wolf stood near, watching their every move no matter how slight, his sideways swath cutting an invisible line between them and the den.

"Everyone move to the right—to the backside of the lodge."

Cries, huffs, and comments flew among the remaining stragglers, but they did as instructed.

"Jayce, Devon, hold your ground. As soon as they see we're in the lodge, staying away from their den, they'll leave."

Devon stood sentry, his shovel out at a diagonal angle. "I sure hope you're right. These guys got some teeth."

"Keep them back long enough to get everyone inside," Joel said, thankful Cassie was already there.

Jayce shifted his legs apart, his position very much like a cop on the riot line. His recent police academy training had kicked in.

Joel assessed the group. "The ladies are too spread out."

Mia hurried, increasing her pace.

"Don't run," he warned, moving to escort her and Nat. He kept his steps as calm as possible while plowing his way through a snowbank.

Mia's pace increased more, bordering on a run.

"Mia, no. Slow down."

She shook her head and, screaming, she broke into a run.

The large black wolf bolted after her, its strong legs doubling the ground she made.

"Stop!" In her panicked state, Joel doubted she even heard him. Another three yards and the wolf was nearly upon her.

"Stay upright!" he warned.

She flailed forward, and the wolf lunged on top of her, baring its teeth.

Jayce raced over, swinging his shovel in the air. "Get off!"

Brady shifted into Jayce's place at their three, providing coverage of the howling white wolf almost blending in with the snow.

The black wolf pawed Mia's back. Nail marks ripped through her snow pants, tearing the thick fabric like butter.

Jayce moved to swing again, and the wolf raced off, then circled back around.

"Inside!" Joel hollered as the remaining members of their group stopped to watch. "Go!"

"I got her," Jayce said, lifting Mia up and moving for the lodge.

Howls rent the air, echoing in the canyon as the group reached the lodge and safety.

My body frozen, I rubbed my arms, trying to ease blood back into them, then stomped my feet to do the same. They all thought they were so safe in the decrepit lodge, but they don't know I'm here—*yet*.

Once his racing heart subsided, Joel surveyed his surroundings. Heath carried an old kerosene lantern, walking down the hall toward them—his shadow looming large on the floral wallpaper, which was unchanged since the last time Joel and his family stayed there years ago.

"No electricity?" Joel frowned.

"Nope." Heath shook his head.

"I thought I saw some light when I was racing back out but must have just been your flashlights." Joel narrowed his eyes. "Speaking of flashlights, why the lantern instead?"

"The lights did come on. Well, they flickered but then went out. Just cut off. Then my flashlight died, and I couldn't find any batteries in this place, but I found a pack of matches with one match left and this"—he held up the lantern—"in one of the bedrooms. Kind of creepy how everything looks frozen in time. But on the plus side, this thing kicks out some serious light for an antique."

And smelled like paint thinner. Joel breathed through his mouth, trying to limit the overbearing odor entering his nostrils. "Where is everyone?"

"In the big room down the hall." Heath gestured in that direction, the light again bouncing shadows off the walls.

Jayce looked at Joel. "The parlor."

They headed for it.

The last time Joel had been here was a half dozen years back, right before they started construction on the new lodge. But as often as he, Jayce, and their cousin Scott had visited over the years, finding his way around was like second nature.

Heath slid the doors to the parlor open, and Joel gazed at the ragtag group, blankets wrapped around the majority of them. Cassie sat in a chair with a blanket draped across her shoulders.

"I should take a better look at your leg." And speaking of legs. "How's Mia doing?"

She laid facedown on the damask sofa that his parents had often chided him to sit still on.

Devon knelt by Mia's side. "I carry a first-aid kit with me. I can handle a few stiches, but as an autopsy assistant, Cassie is better equipped for the sutures, if she's up for it."

"Agreed." Cassie got to her feet and wobbled.

"Whoa!" Joel said, bracing his hands on her hips to steady her. She smiled.

He longed for nothing more than to fully pull her into his arms.

He'd so missed the feel of her in them. "I think you best sit back down."

"I'm fine."

"Of course you are." He shook his head. "I don't think you should put any weight on your leg until I've had a chance to check out your injury."

"Mia's bleeding, I'm not."

"Okay, but at least sit while you do it. Don't try kneeling on it for goodness' sake."

"Fair enough." She nodded.

He helped Cassie to the couch, and she took a seat on the edge beside Mia. "I'll be as gentle as I can." She lifted her chin at Devon. "The first-aid kit?"

"Got it." He handed it to her with a smile and a nod.

"Thanks." She smiled back. "Okay . . ." She directed her attention to Mia. "I'm going to pull your pant leg up and get a good look, okay?"

Mia half nodded, half whimpered.

"We will be rescued, won't we?" Penelope asked in that high-brow inflection of hers.

"Yes. I'm sure our mom and dad have already reported us missing," Izzy assured Talbot's cousin.

"So they'll come soon?" Nat asked.

"Not until the blizzard clears up at least," Joel said.

"At least?" Penelope's brows hiked up.

"He means it depends on how many are missing, where, who needs the most urgent help, how long it takes ski patrol to get in or a rescue copter to fly . . ." Nat rambled on.

Penelope rubbed her arms. "So we could be stuck . . ." She looked around, distaste evident on her brow. "*Here* for an extended time?"

Nat rested her hands on her hips. "Just be happy we're inside and warm."

Penelope shivered. "This place gives me the creeps. It's like some old house in the middle of nowhere where a slasher movie would happen."

"Aww, come on," Brady said, "it's fun."

"How is this fun?" She pinned her disapproving gaze on Talbot. "I'll never understand your friends," she said in her quintessential tone.

"I'd watch out," Heath said. "You know who always goes first in the horror movies—the blond."

Penelope swallowed. "I'm not the only blond," she spluttered. "Mia and Iz are too."

"Still it's a one-in-three-chance." Brady chuckled.

"You two," Cassie said, "knock it off." She looked to Penelope. "Don't let them get to you."

"They aren't. This place is. It's been empty for a while, right?"

"Right." Jayce gave a nod.

"Vagrants stay in abandoned places." She rubbed her arms, her brow indenting into a frown. "How do you know that we are the only ones here?"

EIGHT

"PEN," IZ SAID, moving to her side. "We're safe."

Pen's gaze darted about, pinging from one side of the room to the other. "How do you *know*? Have you checked the house?"

"I'll check the house," Joel said. "I need to take count of the supplies anyway."

"I already did that," Heath said, then shrugged. "For the most part."

"Did you check the cellar?" *Or behind the walls*? Although, he wasn't adding that little tidbit about the lodge now. It'd only freak Penelope out further to know there were passageways built behind the walls. Originally to hide servants from the guests' view until that became an outdated notion, then they just sat empty until he and his siblings terrorized each other playing hide-and-seek in the maze of tunnels.

"Besides the slasher possibility, I'm freezing." Penelope rubbed her arms faster.

Valid point. "Any sign of firewood?" Joel asked, scanning the room.

"Not in here," Heath said, "but we should check the outer buildings. I saw several from the side and back porches."

"Good idea but go out in pairs. We don't want anyone by themselves getting turned around or lost."

"Got it," Heath said. "Here." He handed Joel the lantern. "I'll head out with Devon, and he's got a working flashlight."

"Absolutely." Devon got to his feet.

Brady stood up. "Who's pairing up with me?"

"I'll go," Lyle said, to everyone's surprise.

Joel expected Lyle to weasel out of looking. The guy didn't mix with adventure or even the outdoors. He looked like a bug pincushion every Fourth of July cookout. But he followed close on Brady's heels as they exited the parlor.

"I'll go—" Jayce started.

"Why don't you stay here and keep everyone . . ." *Safe*. "Good."

"Roger that." Jayce took a seat in the chair beside Mia, her leg now sutured up.

"Good job." Joel shoulder-bumped Cassie with a twinge of a smile.

"Thanks." She smiled back.

"What about us?" Talbot asked, indicating himself and Scott.

"You two take the garages on the east side of the house."

"On it." Talbot and Scott nodded in near unison.

"Oh, wait. Hey, guys," Joel yelled, rushing into the hall, grabbing the dudes before they exited. "Watch out for the wolves, especially now you're in lower numbers. And stay on this side of their den."

"Shouldn't be a problem with the shed locations," Devon said.

"You guys be safe. While you're out in them, I'll search inside for supplies."

"And *canoodle* with Cassie," Heath chuckled, using air quotes.

Was the guy twelve or outright mocking him? He and Cassie were clearly not together, as painful as it was to admit. "Excuse me?"

"I saw that look between you two."

What look? Had there been a look when he'd said 'good job'?"

"Let's go." Brady yanked Heath by the jacket collar, and out the door the four guys went.

Joel headed back to the parlor as a bracing draft swooped in upon the guys' exit.

"Close the door. It's freezing, remember?" Penelope gripped a thin throw blanket around her shoulders and sat in the burgundy armchair.

When he was a kid in that very chair, he'd thought he was so grown up at afternoon tea, but his feet couldn't even touch the floor. He'd always wanted to bring Cassie here with it playing such a large part in his childhood adventures, but Stan had built the new lodge before they got together two years ago—a year together and now a year apart, but he couldn't dwell on that. Though once they made it safely out of this—and they would; he'd see to that with everything in him—he had to tell her how he felt. He'd nearly lost her again today. Nearly lost the chance to say *I love you* one last time. Even if nothing had changed on her end . . . he needed to let her know. He wasn't going to live with regrets any longer.

A bang nailed the window by Penelope's head. She swung around on a jump and screamed.

Heath stood at the window with the lantern eerily lighting up his face, and a snarl across his features.

Her scream continued, and Heath cracked up.

"Not cool, dude," Devon hollered from behind him. "Come on, we have a job to do."

"What? It was funny." He waved and stepped off the porch and back into the fierce blizzard.

Cassie stood up, wobbled, but regained her balance.

"What are you doing?" She should be in the chair with her leg propped up.

"Going with you to search the house."

"That's thoughtful of you"—and he'd cherish any alone time with Cassie no matter how it was spent—"but I should check out your leg, then you should rest."

"It's fine. Well . . ." She scrunched her lips in that thinking way of hers. "Not fine, but it's just a twisted knee. It hurts, but if I balance right and hold on to rails, I'll be good to go. It beats just sitting and waiting around."

"All right." Sitting and waiting wasn't in Cassie's wheelhouse. "But let me take a look first."

She exhaled. "Fine."

He smirked at her stubbornness. It should annoy him but, heaven help him, he still found it adorable.

Taking off her boots, he gripped her wet socks. "This isn't good."

"We get a fire going, we can hang them by it. Besides, I'm sure everyone is in the same boat."

He peeled the sock down, expecting terrible frostbite, but there was just the first hint of it.

She leaned forward. "I appreciate your concern, really I do, but until we get a fire going or a way to heat up warm water for our feet, the best thing we can do is keep moving."

He hated to admit it, but she was right, and the smirk on her face said she knew it. Man, she lit a fire in him. He was never more alive than in her presence, but soon this adventure would end, and she'd be back out of his life.

But with her stalker gone . . . Sheriff Gonzales checked in with him often. A weekly call. Fifty-two weeks and no sign of the stalker. She was finally free. Maybe now that fear and stress weren't a part of their daily lives, they could begin again. Had that been it? Because he really had zero clue why she left.

"Ready?" she said, limping for the door.

"Whoa! Let's at least get you something to lean on." He scanned the room. Nothing that would work. "Okay. We'll look for something, but I want you to lean against me until we find you something stable."

"Okay."

Was that a smile on her face?

Entering the shed, I slipped inside—Brady too preoccupied to notice. I waited, observing. Thinking how easily the knife in my hand would slice into him. But only if necessary.

He moved along the work benches. So far, safe. The annoying fool whistled while he worked. What was he, a dwarf?

Trying to block out the noise, I slipped farther back between the two metal shelf racks disguised in darkness. Brady moved, striding mere feet away. People were so oblivious.

Cassie, her ex, and the cops still had no clue how I moved so easily in and out of her place. If you knew a few techniques, it was as easy as slicing pie . . . or Brady, if he got much closer.

My muscles coiled, heat rushing through them.

Brady moved for it.

Don't do it.

The fool lifted the cover off. He'd seen my exit strategy. Night night for Brady.

I stepped from the shadows and moved behind him. They'd said it was hard slitting a throat, but I had it in me. I always had.

NINE

CASSIE HOBBLED behind Joel into what had been an office.

"Stan's dad kept a yardstick in here," Joel said. "The guy was always woodworking and preferred a yardstick to a tape measure. That might work, though a cane or walking stick would be far more stabilizing.

She stepped farther inside the room, taking in the file cabinets with a thick layer of dust on them, the globe on the desk, pictures hanging on the wall. "Why did no one take this stuff to the new lodge?"

Joel poked around in the closet but glanced over his shoulder at her question. "It's kind of a sad story." He straightened and moved for the corner on the right side of the desk, riffling through fishing poles.

"Odd place for those."

"Frank, Stan's dad, was odd."

"Oh."

"When his wife, Mariel, passed away, Frank sort of died too. He wandered around the empty lodge and was really absent-minded."

"Dementia?"

"The docs said no. Apparently when people have been married a long time, it's really hard on the other spouse when one passes. He refused to move out of the lodge and sort of let it fall to ruin. The new lodge was built, but he wouldn't budge. It was really hard on Stan. Anyway, Frank passed not long after, and Stan hasn't had the heart to come deal with all of this yet, so it sits."

"You weren't kidding. That is really sad."

"Here you go," he said, handing her a walking stick. "Like I said, even better than a yardstick. I knew Frank had some around here. The guy loved to hike. Always took a walking stick with him."

She gripped her glove fingers around it. "Thanks."

"You're welcome."

She'd smiled. She loved his scruff-covered, chiseled jaw . . . his strong physique, his even stronger character . . .

"You with me?" he asked, somehow smack-dab in front of her.

She ached with everything in her to be *with* him. But her stalker had given her the gravest ultimatum: walk away from Joel on what was to be their wedding day, or watch Joel die at his hands. Tell Joel and he'd die. So she'd stayed silent. Let the man she loved more than life believe she didn't love him. Not even enough to tell him instead of letting him stand up in front of all their family and friends—*alone*.

"Cas?" Concern creased the corners of Joel's blue eyes.

She blinked. "Yeah. Sorry. My brain is still waking up."

"You sure you don't want to rest in the parlor?"

"I'm sure." She'd take all the time with him she could get while her stalker was far away, because once she was back home, or even back at the cabins, he'd be watching. She'd never be free. But Joel . . . He could have a happy life, find and marry someone new, and go on without her.

His eyes narrowed. "You sure you're okay?"

"Yeah." Maybe if she told him, he'd help again, but he'd worked the case for nearly a year. Worked himself into the ground, but the stalker still eluded them. She wasn't putting Joel back through that either.

It was like the man was invisible—no prints, no fibers, nothing to prove his presence except the letters he left and the hint of Irish Spring.

"I think we should hit the kitchen next," Joel said, thankfully not noticing her delving headlong into her nightmare.

"Sounds like a plan." She forced a smile on her face and followed him into the hall, shadows dancing along the walls above and behind them.

She cringed. The stalker's first message came rushing back with brutal backlash.

I have a little shadow that goes in and out with me.

Your Shadow

A shiver snaked up her spine at the way he twisted one of her favorite childhood poems. Pressure wrapped around her throat. She cough-choked.

Joel turned, the flashlight on her face.

She held up her hand to shield her eyes.

"Sorry," he said with a sheepish smile. He lowered the light. "You okay?"

"Yep," she lied. So many lies between her and the man she loved, but what was she to do? Let the red laser scope on the center of Joel's back in the pic the stalker sent come true? Her stalker wouldn't hesitate to go through with his plans if she "disobeyed." The one time she hadn't listened and went out on that second date with Joel, her dog had nearly died. She'd come home earlier than planned thanks to some bad fish and was able to get Barley to the vet in time to get his stomach pumped, but she hadn't taken any chances after that. She even gave her mom Barley for safekeeping in Montana.

Joel shifted his weight. "What's going on, Cassie?"

She swallowed. "I wanted to tell you . . ." So many things.

"Yeah?"

She bit her bottom lip. "It can wait."

"You sure?"

"Yep. Let's finish checking this place out and then we can chat. We're not going anywhere for a while."

"True," he said quickly, but he studied her eyes slowly.

"What are you two doing?" Nat huffed. "I thought you were searching the inn?"

"We are," Joel ground out.

"You're not getting very far."

"What do you need, Nat?" Joel asked, clearly not trying to keep the impatience from his voice.

"The ladies are asking about facilities."

"Oh."

"Do they still work?"

"Let's find out," Cassie said, and Joel led the way.

Ten minutes and thankfully a surprisingly working restroom later, he and Cassie moved into the kitchen to continue their search.

"How about I take the cupboards working this way . . ." He pointed right. "And you take the drawers working left."

"On it." Cassie nodded.

"Candles," he said, not long into his search.

"Matches," she said, tossing the small matchboxes on the countertop right below the knife block. Five silver handles glinted in the light of Joel's propped-up flashlight.

"Huh."

"What?"

"One knife missing." She shrugged.

He stepped to her side and observed, "Who knows how long ago that went missing."

"True." She tried to force a chuckle, but it wouldn't come. Heath's slasher flick comments were getting to her. But her stalker was *not* here. Unless he was part of the group on the copters, there was no way for him to be out here. And he couldn't be one of their group. A chill washed over her. Could he?

TEN

"NEXT UP . . ." Joel said, handing Cassie the flashlight she'd left on the counter.

"Thanks." She tucked a random slip of hair beneath her flower-patterned stocking cap.

He smiled. He'd always loved that cap. The way it framed her sweet face and the jade lit her green eyes.

"Joel? You still with me?"

"Yep." He coughed. "Let's go this way." He stepped to a narrow corner crook at the rear of the kitchen she'd never have seen if he hadn't taken her there.

A faded door with whitewashed planks and an arched top stood at the end of the alcove nook.

Joel opened the door. It creaked long and low, pricking the nerves along her spine.

"Yikes!"

"I know." He hitched his belt. "Always makes that awful sound. First time I heard it as a kid, I figured it was haunted—mostly because of Jayce's campfire stories. I bolted out of here so fast I ran smack into Mr. Stan."

"I imagine that didn't go over well."

"Stan was great. Still is. Brought me back down here and showed me all the cool stuff he keeps in the cubbies." He pulled his stocking cap off and raked a hand through his mussed hair before sliding the blue cap back on. "Never scared me again."

That must be nice.

"Now," he said, taking the first rickety step and holding out his hand. "If I were Heath, I'd be making a crack about who wants to go down the creepy steps into the dark cellar of the abandoned lodge first."

She chuckled and put her hand in his. Peace sifted through her.

His gaze fixed on her in the tiny confines, their flashlights casting a warm glow.

She swallowed. "Thankfully, you're not Heath."

Joel laughed. "He ain't all bad."

"I know. I just don't see a nice guy like Talbot being friends with the obnoxious guy. Well, obnoxious sometimes. But it's more . . ." She rubbed the back of her neck. "Heath gives me a funky vibe at work sometimes."

Joel narrowed his eyes. "What do you mean?"

"He just hangs around in places I'll be. It's . . . weird."

He raked a hand through his tussled hair again.

Could he be any cuter?

"I didn't know that. I'm sorry, Cass. You've had more than your share of creeps. At least your stalker is gone."

Or so she'd thought.

"Watch your step," Joel said, helping her down one steps. He paused at a missing one.

Her eyes widened at the gap. "What happened there?"

Joel shrugged. "Must have fallen off a while ago."

She swished her flashlight down. It took a moment of searching, but her light found the snapped board lying against the packed dirt floor far from where it originated. "How old is this place?"

"Opened in 1921."

"Whoa. Older than I realized."

Creaks eked out with each step they took to the bottom of the stairwell. Though what could be considered an actual stairwell was far different in her mind.

The space held an earthy vibe, like fresh soil in a garden just before dawn—damp, rich, and something she couldn't place. "So . . . this is the cellar." She swiped her light around, jumping at the deer head on the wall.

He rested his hand on her shoulder, and she jumped again.

"Sorry." He retracted it and took a step back.

"No." She shook her head, ignoring the throbbing through her wrenched knee. "It's not you, it's just . . ."

"Just?"

Pain punctuated his eyes. How could she continue to lie to him? She needed to tell him the truth. Sit him down and tell him, but with her stalker back, she feared for his life. It was a no-win situation. Tell Joel and risk his life. Don't tell him and let him think she never loved him. She needed to tell him when they could sit and talk a minute.

Light flickered by the small window behind Joel's shoulders, and her gaze shot to it.

"What is it?"

"A light." She pointed at the window half sunken in one of those metal half-circle things.

He glanced back.

Her shoulders drooped. "It's gone now."

He shrugged. "Probably someone's flashlight."

"Yep." She shook out her arms. Why was she so jumpy? She was doing exactly what the stalker wanted—letting him terrorize her.

"Let's see if we can find any firewood, flashlight batteries, kerosene lamps, kerosene . . ." Joel said, moving about the space.

"Right." She nodded, her thoughts pinging all over the place. "How about I start on the far end and work my way over?"

"Good plan."

She hobbled for the dark recesses of the cellar, wondering why she'd volunteered for this section. *Lovely, Cass.*

Joel moved in the opposite direction. "I'm going to check the breaker. The lights may have tripped after being dormant so long." He shrugged a shoulder. "It doesn't really make sense, but it's a nice thought and worth a shot. Everything is worth a shot, right?"

Like they were still worth a shot? She swallowed, praying so.

Joel flipped switches. *Click. Click. Click.* "Breakers all look okay. Must be the storm. I'm surprised the lights came to life at all."

"Yeah." Her gaze tracked over each cubby drawer behind the workbench—screws, nails, washers, and so on—her fingers trailing over the odds and ends left strewn across the countertop—the smooth wood of a hammer, the cold metal of a wrench, and the lightweight plastic of a doohickey. "Running water and electricity seem odd for a lodge no longer in use."

"It's a heart project for Stan," he said, leaning back against the bench.

He was so handsome, his strong arms resting behind him on the bench, his deep brown eyes fixed on her. She longed for nothing more than to rush over and kiss him, to run her hand through his tousled hair—he'd always loved when she ran her hands through his hair.

"Something caught your attention?" he asked with a smile.

Man, she loved that smile—so full of life.

And that's how he had to stay. Full of life. Her heart wrested inside her—confliction eating away at her. She shook her head. "Just daydreaming," she said, telling the truth.

"Gotcha. Well, back to work."

"Right." Back to work. Her hand tracked over the next item, and she paused. A dial? She angled the flashlight back down to what her hand was clasping. "Hey, it's a radio." Hope blossomed inside. Maybe they'd get help or, at the very least, could know someone had their position and would be on the way as soon as the dangerous elements settled.

"Let's see." Joel strode to her side, his strong shoulder brushing hers, but it was his inner strength and fortitude that she admired most. So stalwart in an emergency—always had been, and today was no different.

"I haven't worked with one of these since I was a kid, but they're fairly easy. You flip this switch—" He did and nada. He flipped another while she stepped closer. "Probably requires electricity. Some can work on batteries, but—"

"Thank you," she said, leaning sideways against the bench inches from him, shifting the weight off her hurt knee.

He stopped with the switches, his gaze meeting hers.

The rest of the cellar disappeared.

"For what?" A soft smile, a hopeful smile, curled on his lips.

How could she crush a man she loved so? *Because I love him so.* She blinked back the tears burning her dry eyes. "For saving my life today." Hot tears slipped loose, trailing down her cold cheek.

"Hey," he said. His hand moved to cup her cheek, but he paused and pulled it back to his side. "Of course."

Her heart dropped. "Joel, I . . ."

He stepped an inch closer. "Yes?"

"I need to tell you something. . . ." She had to. She'd promised herself if she survived the avalanche, she'd tell him. "Look, I should have told you long ago, but—"

Creeeeakkkk.

Her gaze jumped behind Joel's shoulder at the noise, peering into the darkness.

Evil fled the light. If her stalker was here, if he was one of them, he'd be in the shadows. *Her shadow.* Hadn't he said that all along?

ELEVEN

TEARS STUNG Cassie's eyes. *Please stop letting my fears run away with me.* Releasing a pent-up breath, she turned her attention back to Joel.

Footsteps clamored on the floorboards overhead at the far end of the cellar.

"The guys must be back."

A footstep settled over her head, and dirt sifted down on her nose. Someone was in the kitchen. "Joel! Cassie! You guys around?" Scott called.

They exchanged a glance that held more than she had believed it still could, then Joel cast his gaze toward the stairwell. "Yep. Be right up."

"I found them," Scott yelled, his steps moving for the hall, his voice fading.

Creak. Creaakk.

She turned to the sound emanating behind her. "That sounded like it was down here." A tremble wiggled through her limbs.

Joel swished his flashlight across the dark abyss surrounding them. The creak softened and ceased. "Old buildings make noise."

"Right." She forced a smile.

"You were saying something?" Anticipation held in his gorgeous eyes.

"Uh . . ." She cleared her throat, cast her gaze to her feet and then back on him. "I . . ."

"Are you guys coming?" Kendra called as the light emanated in a shaft down the stairs. Her footsteps followed, the shaft growing wider as she creaked her way down the rickety stairs.

"Yeah, we're—" Cassie began.

Kendra's light blinded her, and she held up her hand.

"We need you."

"We'll be right there." Joel's hand rested on the radio. He reached back and unplugged it.

Kendra's light followed his movement. "Is that a radio?"

"Yeah." Cassie lowered her hand now that a glaring light wasn't in her eyes.

"Awesome." Kendra stepped forward. "Did you try it?"

"Not yet. We were about to when you came down."

"You might need to wait."

Joel frowned. "What could be more important than trying to get help?"

"Brady's missing."

Joel's eyes narrowed. "What do you mean 'missing'?"

"I mean he hasn't come back in."

"Wasn't Heath with him?"

Kendra huffed. "Just come upstairs so you can ask for yourself."

Joel tucked the radio under his arm and gestured for the ladies to head up first.

So close. She'd come so close to telling him the truth. Then Kendra . . .

Brady had to be okay. He was always okay. He was that type of guy. Larger than life. Always raring to go on the next Talbot-and-Izzy adventure they grouped up on.

He probably just got turned around. Joel would find him. He found everyone. Everyone but her stalker. She'd prayed so hard he would, but her shadow had eluded him, eluded everyone.

Reaching the base of the stairs, she turned back one more time, something in her tugging her back down. She passed her flashlight over the space—hitting a masked face bent down in the window.

"Aaaaaa!" She fell back.

"Whoa!" Joel said, diving to catch her.

She landed with a thud on her butt bone, the impact radiating down her leg, throbbing her injured knee. "There . . . there . . . was someone outside."

"Brady?" Kendra asked with enthusiasm.

"He was wearing a mask."

Joel helped her up.

"Are you sure you saw someone? I don't remember any of the guys wearing a mask," Kendra said, hand propped on her little waist.

"Yes, I'm sure. I mean . . . I think . . ." She'd definitely seen a face.

"Probably Heath playing tricks again," Kendra said. "Now come on." She turned and strode up the steps, far more talkative than she'd been since the start of their excursion. Though she tended to go in spurts. Quiet, then a flurry of activity, then back to her quiet self.

"You okay?" Joel asked, his hand on her shoulder.

"Yeah. I just thought . . . Never mind, we better go check on the Brady situation."

His gaze held hers a moment longer than she anticipated, then he shifted it to the stairs.

She stretched over the missing step to reach the next one, then managed to hop-hobble her way back up.

Voices emanated . . . or rather, *roared* from the parlor.

"Whoa," Joel said, setting the radio on the kitchen table. "Better get in there. I'll come back and fiddle with this." He rushed down the hall, and she hurried as best she was able after him.

"What's all the ruckus?" he asked, entering.

She moved right behind him. Raised voices chirped, and accusations flew.

"Brady's missing," Nat said, hands on rounded hips. "That's what all the ruckus is."

Cassie rubbed her arms. The cellar had been even lower in temps, but she hadn't noticed, not with Joel so close. The truth so close on her lips.

She surveyed the room—angry faces; scared, wide eyes; and Devon . . . on the floor? She cocked her head. *Oh*. At the fireplace, now filled with wood. Hallelujah.

He caught her gaze and smiled.

"Should have this ablaze in no time," he said, literally working with two sticks while Heath clutched the kerosene lantern.

"There are matches in the kitchen," she said. "I'll go get you some."

"Awesome. Thanks." Devon tossed the two sticks in with the rest of the logs.

Voices carried as she trekked back to the kitchen, passing the radio on the table, anxiety pulsing through her. As soon as they sorted out Brady's whereabouts, they needed to get on that.

Actually . . . She could take two minutes. She sat her flashlight on the table and flipped it over. Joel said some worked on batteries. Maybe . . . She opened the battery flap. Empty. She mentally went through the items in the cellar. Had there been batteries? Yes. Third drawer from the left. Grabbing her flashlight, she headed back downstairs.

She made it to the right cubby and pulled out a handful of batteries. Turning for the stairs, she paused at the window. She *had* seen a face. It probably was Heath playing another distasteful joke, but she wasn't seeing things, was she?

Hobbling back upstairs, she paused at the landing to catch her breath.

Footsteps creaked along the floor. Deep. Purposeful steps.

"Who's there?" She limped around the corner.

The kitchen door swung, but nobody was there.

Get out of my head. She was making herself crazy.

She dropped the C batteries on the table with a clunk and caught the stray one rolling away.

"Okay." She sat down, then angled her flashlight and took her gloves off for better maneuverability. *Yikes! It's cold.* Pain shot through her hands—the sensation of cold hands dipped in hot water for that first excruciating second. Shaking them for some warmth, she lifted the first battery and slipped it in place. She cupped her hands and breathed on them. *Come on, three to go.* She sped her pace with the second, third, and then she paused. She bent down, angling the flashlight right on the battery well. The spring wire was gone. She traced her finger across where it should've been. It punctured her skin, blood beading on her index finger as she yanked it back. *Great.*

"What's wrong?"

She jumped.

Kendra laughed. "My, aren't you the jumpy one."

She clutched her chest. "You scared me."

"Sorry. Joel told me to come check on you. I guess he worries about you or something." She shrugged.

The words *I can't imagine why* seemed to hang at the tip of her tongue.

"We better get back before he has to come looking for you."

Cass narrowed her eyes. Did Kendra have a problem with her?

For the quiet one, she was being rather sassy. "Is there something wrong?"

"Yes. Brady is missing, and I'm worried about him."

Of course. "I'm so sorry." She stood and rubbed Kendra's arm.

Kendra stiffened.

Cassie pulled her hand back. "I'm sure he's okay." She hobbled to the door. "Let's go find him."

"Thanks." Kendra smiled.

"Oh, wait!" Cassie halted. "I forgot matches for Devon." She grabbed them and caught back up with Kendra in time to enter the buzzing commotion.

TWELVE

"ARE YOU SURE Brady isn't just taking a snooze in one of the rooms?" Joel asked his brother as Cassie leaned against the wall, easing the pressure off her swelling leg.

"I've been in the parlor the whole time," Jayce said. "I see everyone who walks by from the outside. Brady and Lyle went out together to search the first set of buildings. Lyle came back twenty minutes ago but still no Brady. I even checked his beacon, but I'm getting no signal."

"The blizzard must be messing with the reception, or he's too far out," Joel said.

"But everyone knew to switch it on when they went out in the storm." Jayce indicated his hooked by a carabiner to his pocket zipper.

Joel shifted his attention to Lyle. "Where's Brady?"

Lyle shrugged with his hands held out. "I don't know."

"But you two went out together," Jayce jumped in.

"We hit the first shed on the property. Didn't find anything useful there. It was basically empty."

"Okay." Joel shifted his stance to the one he used when he questioned suspects. She'd seen it before.

"And then?" he continued.

"We thought we better come back. The blizzard's fierce. It's a total whiteout. It's a wonder I even made it back." He shivered and rubbed his arms.

"And Brady?" Kendra asked.

Hmm. Cassie sank down on the sofa arm. Maybe Kendra had a thing for Brady she hadn't noticed before.

"I don't know." Lyle sighed. "He followed me out of the shed and then I lost him in the snow. I just figured we'd meet up here."

"It's been too long," Izzy said. "Someone needs to go look for him."

"I will," Jayce offered.

"I'll go with you," Joel said, then cast his gaze at Cassie and mouthed, *You okay?*

Not at all. But she mouthed *Yes* back.

He nodded, but his expression said he knew better.

"We should find a rope or even a twisted sheet, so we don't lose each other," Jayce said.

"Good idea, I'll go get one." Joel disappeared from the room and was back in a flash with two white sheets.

They'd seen them on all the beds in guest rooms. Cassie rubbed her arms as Devon finally got the fire lit. Light and warmth started to penetrate the space, but the room was too large for it to make a big dent.

Joel twisted the sheets together and tied knots in each end.

"If Brady got disoriented in the blizzard, who knows where he is," Izzy said, more than a twinge of panic in her voice.

Of all of them, Brady, Mr. Outdoor-Adventure-Dude, should be the last to get lost out in a storm.

Cassie scanned the room, studying the faces, then realized they were missing one more. "Where's Heath? Is he still out there?"

"Must be," Nat said.

"So we have two out there," Joel said. "I think anyone else who goes anywhere should go in pairs."

"Surely we don't have to go in pairs in the lodge," Nat barked.

"It's not a bad idea. It's dark, the lodge is old, things are rickety, just humor me, okay?"

The majority in the room followed Cassie's lead and nodded at Joel's request.

Joel looked to his brother. "Ready?"

Jayce nodded.

"We'll be right back," Joel said, his words directed at Cassie as he passed by her.

She prayed he would. If anything happened to Joel it would be like losing him all over again. She was probably being ridiculously dramatic, but her emotions were in the agitation session of the washer—jolting back and forth—fear and love warring for her words and actions.

After checking the first shed and finding no trace of Brady, Joel and Jayce swapped their sheets for a strong rope they found in the shed, both tying one end around their waists, then they moved for the second building—heading straight into the driving storm. Snow crested thigh high and continued to pile by the second, it seemed.

"I got it," Jayce hollered over the wind—its howls mixing with the wolves'.

Joel stiffened and reached for his county-issued weapon only to realize he'd done so out of habit. Being a sheriff wasn't just what he did, it was part of who he was. Who God created him to be. His shoulders drooped as a realization struck. He hadn't brought his gun heli-skiing. He should have at least grabbed one of the kitchen knives. Something for a weapon just in case.

"I got it," Jayce said again.

"Got what?"

The rope slacked as his brother walked back to his side. "Brady's beacon signal." Jayce held up the transceiver he'd brought. "We must be in range now."

"Smart, bro."

Jayce studied the instrument. "That can't be right."

"What can't be?" Joel shifted his legs back and forth in a stay-in-place march to keep them warm and the blood flowing.

"It's at the outer bans of the reading capacity. Several hundred feet north, then another fifty or sixty west."

Joel shook his head. "That's way past all the outer buildings."

"What do you think he's doing all the way up there?" Jayce asked.

"We're about to find out." Joel moved forward, the rope gaining tautness between them.

Moving uphill went far too slowly for Joel's liking. Perhaps Brady got turned around and lost in the whiteout. But going so far north didn't line up. Guys like Brady possessed an internal compass, just like he and Jayce.

The pelting frozen mix battered against them like an invisible, unmovable wall in their uphill battle.

"Zeroing in," Jayce hollered, and then the rope went slack.

His chest squeezed. "Jayce?"

"Yeah, I'm here. A dozen feet to your one o'clock. Hang on to the rope and I'll tug you to me."

Joel did so, and soon he was standing by his brother and the oversized oak tree they loved to climb as children when their parents weren't looking. But now as an adult, he couldn't blame them for warning them off it.

Half the boughs hung over the drop-off. It looked bottomless when he was a kid, but it couldn't possibly be as far down as he recalled.

"Where to?" he asked, seeing no sign of Brady.

"I'm afraid *down*," Jayce said, leaning toward the cliff's edge.

Please let Brady be okay.

But his gut screamed otherwise.

THIRTEEN

IT'D SEEMED FOREVER since Joel and Jayce left, but in reality, it'd been less than a half hour, but a half hour in this severe weather and below-freezing temps was pushing it.

And the one fire trying to heat the wide expanse of the room they all huddled in . . . it just wasn't happening.

Cassie sat forward in the chair she was settled in, her leg propped on the ottoman. "I have an idea."

"Okay?" Penelope perked up.

"What is it?" Iz did as well.

"Joel didn't want us separating outside of pairs, but that works perfectly for what we found."

Nat narrowed her eyes. "What did you find?"

"Guest rooms. Nearly half of them have two twins in the room. One bedroom with a double bed, then an adjacent room for the kids, I imagine."

"What are you suggesting?" Mia asked, still lying facedown on the settee, the wolf's claw marks in her snow pants a steadfast reminder of what lurked around outside.

"We pair up. Two per room."

"But the fire . . ." Mia said.

"That's the beautiful part. Each room has a fireplace, and with the rooms being smaller—"

"They'll heat a lot quicker," Devon said. "Smart plan."

"Thanks."

"You start assigning rooms, and me and the guys will get fires going. We piled a ton of wood on the side porch under the overhang, and there is more under the large tarps we found."

"I can go down." Jayce argued against the decision they'd already made.

Ignoring him, Joel tied the rope around the smaller tree trunk that sat beside the large oak. He retied the other end around his waist and cinched it tight. Jayce stood on the cliff's edge, clasping the rope.

"You sure about this?" Jayce said.

"Dude." He cocked his head.

"Okay. You've got it." He tightened his grip on the rope. "I've got you. I'll feed it down as you go."

Joel nodded on an inhale, the frigid air burning his lungs. He put both feet over the edge and rappelled down. Reaching the bottom of the drop, he grasped his flashlight. Swallowing hard, he turned, swiping the light over the snow-covered boulders at the cliff's base.

He stilled as he hit red saturating the snow beneath the overhang. Squeezing his eyes shut on a prayer, he opened them and stepped forward.

Brady lay, arms and legs askew, red-stained snow encircling his head.

Joel's chest compressed. His friend couldn't be dead. Not like this. Not someone so full of life.

"You find him?" Jayce asked.

"Yeah," he hollered up.

"Is he . . . ?"

"Yeah."

"Oh man, what do we do?"

"I'll tie the rope around him," Joel said. "You pull him up, then send the rope back to me."

"Got it."

Joel bent beside his friend's body, snapping pictures of the scene, then trying to determine the best way to lift him. He set the flashlight on the ground, ready to heave him over his shoulder, when something red caught in his flashlight's beam.

He squinted. It couldn't be blood all the way over there. He straightened, and, grabbing his flashlight, headed for it.

What on earth?

A red sled. How had it gotten down there?

"You sending him up?" Jayce asked.

"Yeah." Joel left the sled, got Brady's body secure in the rope, and waited while Jayce hauled him up.

"Oh man." Jayce's voice echoed through the air.

Joel grimaced. It wasn't pretty, but there was no way they were leaving their friend dead at the bottom of the drop-off.

The rope swung back down. Tying it around his waist, Joel climbed up as Jayce pulled.

Reaching the top edge, Jayce yanked him over onto the snow-and-ice-covered ground.

Joel lay on the snow pile he'd flopped on, the cold permeating his snowsuit. Huge flakes fell on his face.

"You okay?" Jayce asked, standing over him.

"Yeah." He got to his feet. "I just can't believe it."

"Me either." Jayce shook his head. "What are we doing with his body until we're rescued? We can't carry him past everyone."

"I know. We'll go in the side door and put him in the first room."

"What do we tell everyone?"

"That he had an accident."

Jayce frowned. "Why'd you say it like he didn't?"

"Take a look at his neck."

Jayce moved for Brady's body and rolled him fully onto his back, then stumbled backward.

"His throat's been slit."

I shifted. The boards in the passageways I discovered creaked far too often, but the liberties the walkways behind the walls afforded was marvelous. I could get anywhere, be anywhere. Soon I was in Cassie's room—standing by her bed, letter in hand. Her face—so angelic—free from the horror about to overtake it.

I stood watch as I always did. Her chest rose and fell in that deep rhythm—up and down, up and down. I set the second letter on the bed, fighting the urge to brush hair from her face. She possessed a fire that fastened me to her.

Soon that sweet face would be stricken with terror. There was no need for it. If she'd just accept the inevitable. We *belonged* together. She just needed to accept it.

I curled and uncurled my fists. Why did she have to be so stubborn? Why couldn't she just accept it, accept *me*? Heat spread through me, burning my limbs as my muscles coiled. Because of *him*. It was all his fault.

It was so clear. *We can't move forward until Joel is out of the equation.* I inhaled and streamed it out. I'd tried so hard to avoid this, to not kill again, but they'd left me no choice. It was on them. If only she'd listened. One way or another, she would come to.

"Good night, my sweet," I whispered.

Checking the hall, I slipped out, ready to head back to the passage entrance.

The door next to me creaked open. "What are you doing?"

Nat.

"I saw you."

"Saw me what?"

"Sneak into Cassie's room."

"Are you sure you're really awake?"

"What?"

"Maybe this is all a nightmare." I stepped toward her, herding her in the direction I chose. *Closer. Closer*. I'd have to be swift. Grab her, muffle her, slice her, before someone saw.

"What are you doing?" She stumbled back, inches from the hidden passageway door.

I grabbed her neck and squeezed, pushing her into the passageway and closing the door. "Finally shutting you up."

Terror bulged wide in her eyes. She was a fighter.

But so was I.

FOURTEEN

CASSIE OPENED her eyes. The ceiling? She jolted upright. She'd fallen asleep? How could she sleep while Joel and Jayce were still out there? She scanned the room. The fire Scott built still blazed in the hearth. But where was Iz? She'd been sitting on the other bed when Cassie said she was just going to rest for a second.

Her heart thundering in her chest, Cassie climbed from the bed and prayed she'd simply slept through Joel and Jayce's return.

She looked at the mirror behind her. Flames danced in the glass. She took off her cap and gloves, running her fingers through her tangled hair.

She stifled a yawn. How long had she been asleep? Having no sense of time left her reeling—like spinning in a storm with nothing solid to hold on to. Joel had always been her solid. And since they'd ended, she'd been listing in the wind. She knew God had her. Well, she thought He did, but it seemed evil was dominating in her case.

She took one last look in the mirror at her messy self and blinked. *Was that . . . ?*

Her entire body went rigid at the sight of the linen envelope on the table beside the hearth. *No. No. No.*

She squeezed her eyes shut.

Please let my eyes be playing terrible tricks on me.

With a deep breath, she opened them. Still there.

She wasn't crazy. He *was* here.

With her breath trapped in her lungs, she eased her way to the envelope, and lifting it with trembling hands, she opened the envelope and slid the letter out.

I saw you two. Have you forgotten the cardinal rule?
Last warning.
Remember, I go in and out with you.

Your Shadow

Tears flowed down her cheeks, rolling off her face.

Stumbling down the hall, she padded her way into the parlor, where Iz took one look at her and yanked her to the side.

"What's going on?" Iz asked.

"I-I . . . I . . ." Cassie studied the faces in the room. Could it really be one of them?

"Let's go back to our room and talk," Iz said. With the gentlest touch, she tugged Cassie out of the parlor by her jacket sleeve. "I'll be right back, hon," she said to Talbot as they passed.

"Joel and Jayce?"

"They should be back soon."

"How long—?"

"You were only asleep about a half hour. They've been gone about forty minutes."

"We should send people to look for them."

"We discussed it, but then we risk losing more in the snow. We'll give them another ten, then rediscuss."

They padded down the hall, a lantern in Izzy's hand.

A shadow loomed large on the side wall.

She stopped short, her chest squeezing.

Izzy held the lantern higher. "Who is it?" she asked, her voice bold as she was.

Heath rounded the corner.

"When did you get back? We thought you were still looking for Brady?"

"A little bit ago." He shrugged.

Iz narrowed her eyes. "We didn't see you in the parlor."

"Because I was rummaging around the kitchen." He frowned. "Why are you looking at me like that?"

"Because Savanah just came from the kitchen and didn't mentioned seeing you. We all thought you were still outside."

"What is this, interrogation hour?" Heath snorted. "I came in the side door after I got turned around in the snow looking for Brady. In case you haven't noticed, there's a blizzard out there." He pushed past them.

"Did you see Brady while you were out there?" Izzy asked.

"Nope." He kept walking away.

"That was weird," Iz said. "He was all on the defensive." She pulled Cassie into the bedroom and shut the door behind them. "Now, what on earth is going on?"

Cassie pointed to the letter she'd left on the bed.

Izzy's wide-eyed gaze fixed on her. "He's back?"

"Apparently, he never left." Tension bubbled over in her, her limbs shaking. She picked up the crumpled paper and sat back on the bed. Something slipped off the pillow beside her elbow. She squeezed her eyes shut. *Please no*.

Her gaze tracked down.

"Another envelope?" Izzy asked, striding forward.

She grabbed it as Iz drew close.

Cassie opened it, and tears welled in her eyes.

Iz's carriage turned stiff. "What did the madman say?"

She cleared her throat and read, "'On second thought, I think you need a stronger reminder. Wait. One is coming soon.'"

Izzy frowned, the firelight casting shadows across her face. "What does that even mean?"

"That he's going to . . ." Her breath hurt. "Or he already has hurt someone."

Izzy's eyes widened. "Do you think he followed you here? But how? How would he know we went heli-skiing? How would he get out here? There wasn't time before the avalanche. . . ."

"Exactly." Iz had just walked them through the logical conclusion. "He's one of us." He'd been there all along.

Her stomach heaved as she slipped the folded letters in her pocket.

"Oh no!" Iz braced her hands on her shoulders. "Come on, let's get you to the bathroom."

They raced down the hall to the closest washroom as fast as she could manage on her bum knee.

Iz rushed inside with her and locked the door behind them.

Cassie dropped her weight on her good knee as she bent. "You can leav—" she said, trying to give Iz a get-out-of-jail-free card before she got sick, but she'd held back too long.

Foreboding wracked her mind as convulsions wracked her body. What did he have in store? And who could it be? The last two years flashed before her eyes—everything struggling for new context.

After an awful few moments, she sat back. The cold sink pedestal behind her back eased the sweat clinging to her.

"You okay?" Iz asked. She brushed back the damp hair fringing Cassie's face.

She shook her head as tears drenched her face.

Iz pulled her into an embrace. "It's going to be okay."

She leaned back. "I know you're just trying to be helpful, but how is it going to be okay? Joel tried the entire year to catch him. Officer Gonzales did too until he determined it a cold case—the culprit either gone or inactive. Like that was supposed to help."

"Yes," Iz said. Her voice was always calm in times of great distress, just like her brothers'. It was a wonder she didn't go into law enforcement too. "But," her florist best friend said, "he's back now."

Cassie narrowed her puffy eyes. "You say that like it's a good thing." She sniffed, her nose swollen shut.

"It is." Iz smiled.

"Come again?"

"Because now they can catch him."

"How?" She sniffed again. "What's changed?"

"Now you have your suspects, and they're all trapped here."

I smiled. She *knew*. It was obvious the second I saw her beautiful, horrified face. But she didn't know it was *me*. How could she not? I mean, who else in this ridiculous group could it be?

At least she knew I was here and I wasn't going anywhere. But she was breaking the cardinal rule—*tsk, tsk, tsk*—she'd told on me. Just like that stupid kid who couldn't keep his mouth shut and got me kicked out of another foster home. Not that I cared. I could handle where they put me. I wasn't soft like some of the other sissies who cried at night in their beds. I've always been tough. Hard. I had no choice, but it's done me well. But that kid—Donnie Brown—he took me from the only person who understood me, so I paid him back and got away with it. I smiled at the delicious memory. Now they'd try to take Cassie from me, but I wouldn't allow it. Instead, they'd pay. Just as Donnie Brown had.

Just as Nat and Brady had. Brady I felt half bad for. The dumb lug was just in the wrong place at the wrong time. Then again, so was Nat, but her death was a long time coming. Always so nosey. Asking questions. Watching.

None of that mattered now. All that mattered was me and Cassie. And we'd be leaving together as soon as I took care of a little business.

I'd be missed, but I wouldn't be away long. We'd made a pledge. Just the two of us—thick as blood. We'd never abandon each other as so many had abandoned us. I'd find her again. I always did, but I *was* leaving here with Cassie.

Too bad she had a thing for Joel. I hated to ruin her happiness of all people, but there was no choice. *Joel Brunswick won't leave this lodge alive*.

FIFTEEN

"WAS THAT THE SIDE DOOR?" Izzy asked at the muffled bang. She leapt to her feet and cracked open the bathroom door.

"Iz, be careful," Cassie said as her bestie opened the door and peered out. He was one of them. He could be any of them. Her mind tracked through each guy in the group—a close-knit group originally made up of smaller cohorts. Her work crew, Iz's friends, Talbot's sports buddies, and their families.

She grappled to her feet, splashing ice-cold water on her face. Frigid temps aside, she needed the smack of clarity it brought.

"It's Joel and Jayce," Iz said, relief in her voice.

"What's going on?"

"Brady," Iz murmured.

"They found him. Oh good."

Izzy shook her head. "It's definitely not good."

Cass wedged in the door crack beside her bestie—her friend who'd stuck by her through thick and thin, even without knowing why she'd left her brother at the altar. Just trusted she had a good reason and one day she'd explain as promised.

Joel carried Brady over his shoulder toward the first room down the hall. It wasn't until he turned to enter the room that she understood Izzy's comment.

Brady's throat was rimmed with blood. She swallowed back the nausea swishing in her gut. "What happened?"

"Let's go find out."

Cassie limped behind Izzy down the hall to the first guest room in the row.

"What's going on?" Penelope asked, popping her head out of the second-to-last room they passed.

"Just going to talk with Joel," Izzy said.

"All right," Penelope said, stifling a yawn, slumber in her eyes. "I'm going to lay back down." She shut her door.

Cassie followed Izzy into the room.

Joel laid Brady on the bed.

"Shut the door," Jayce told Iz in a flurry as he paced the room.

Okay. So not as calm and collected as Cassie assumed, but there was a man with his throat slit mere feet away. Not just a man but a *friend*. Tears welled in her eyes.

He'd done this. Whoever *he* was.

How could he? They were all friends. Or so she'd thought. Her skin crawled. How many times had she been near him? Eaten with him? Gone on one of Iz and Talbot's outdoor adventures with him?

What if it was one of Joel's own family members? Scott? Lyle? Could one of them have done this to their friend?

"Cassie," Joel said, striding over and bracing his hands on her shoulders. "It's okay."

"How can you say that?" She pointed at Brady's lifeless body.

"We'll get through this."

And a stalker bent on killing him? How would they get through that? "You need to get a weapon and fast."

He frowned. "What?"

"Weapons. On it," Iz said, moving for the door. "Jayce, come help me."

Jayce's blond brows shot up. "Huh?"

"Come with me. Cassie needs to talk with Joel."

"We can be here while they talk about Brady."

"Now." Iz tugged Jayce out by his ear, then popped her head back in. *Tell him*, she mouthed.

Joel furrowed his brows, not letting go of her shoulders. "Tell me what?"

"I . . ." Should she risk his life?

She closed her eyes. It seemed too late for that. Would he forgive her for not telling him? Not giving him a chance to fight with her?

"Cassie," he said. His voice hummed barely above a whisper. "Tell me what?"

Izzy and Jayce were back in the parlor, so where were Joel and Cassie? My veins burned through my limbs, causing my left hand to twitch—that old "tell" I loathed, but no one seemed to notice. Except her, and she wouldn't tell anybody. She never did.

I pumped my hands in and out of fists.

They. Were. Going. To. Pay.

I wouldn't hurt Cassie. Well, not to that extent. She was mine, but there's a lot of pain up to the point of death, and if she couldn't listen—wouldn't listen—she'd need to be punished too. Brought in line. They both were going to pay.

I fought the urge to barge right in there. Take Cassie, kill Joel, but I had to be calm. *Focused. Patient.* I knew what I was doing. I just had to remove emotion, but that was never hard. Just separate from my feelings and work the plan that'd been in motion since I found our exit strategy. *Our.* Soon it'd be me and Cassie like it always should have been.

Tears ran down Cassie's sweet face. So much pain.

"Shh," Joel murmured, not anticipating this reaction to Brady's death. It was upsetting. Downright heartbreaking. And he'd shed a few tears on the way back, the moisture freezing the second it left his eye. But she was visibly shaking. Not that she shouldn't care, but she was an autopsy assistant. She lived with dead bodies. At least, in a way. But . . . this was no *body*. This was their friend. He pinched his nose, trying to stall his tears. Now was not the time for sorrow, as heartbreaking as it was. Now was the time for action, and when they were safe, then he'd deal with the grief.

Cassie swallowed back a sob. "I need . . . I need to tell you something," she started again.

"All right." He wiped her tears away with the pad of his thumb.

"He's here." Her voice shook.

Joel frowned. "Who's here?" It took a moment of studying the horror on her face for it to hit home. "Your stalker? You're saying he's back?"

She nodded, tears flowing again.

"How do you know?"

"I dozed off, and he left a letter—actually two letters—in the room with me."

He straightened, his body growing rigid. "He's *here*? As in the lodge? He did this?" He turned and pointed to poor Brady.

The sicko was back to torment the woman he still loved. After the terrorizing year the stalker haunted her, Cassie leaving him at the altar, and the subsequent year apart . . . Through it all and in spite of it all, he loved her still. Her and only her.

"He must have killed Brady." She handed him the letters, her hand shaking. "He said he did it to teach me a lesson."

He gripped hold of the letters. "A lesson?" Flipping the letters open, he read them in succession. He finished and frowned. "What is the cardinal rule?"

"The one I'm breaking now."

"I don't understand." He slipped the letters in his pocket for evidence.

She released a whoosh of air, a fresh wave of tears springing to her eyes. "Telling you."

"Telling me what? That he's back?"

She bit her bottom lip, her gaze drifting down.

He nudged her chin up with the crook of his hand. "Cassie? I know that avoidance glance. What's up?"

"He sent me a picture." She sniffed. "It was a laser scope with the red dot you put on the bullseye, you know? It was centered on you."

"I don't understand."

"The night before we were to get married, he sent me the picture and a message. If I married you, he'd kill you. If I told you, he'd kill you. If I . . ." She heaved on a sob.

"Shhhh," Joel whispered, caressing her cheeck in smooth strokes, aiming to calm her, at least enough to explain. "What are you saying?"

She hiccupped on a sob. "I had to call the wedding off, or he'd kill you."

"You called our wedding off because of him?"

"No." She shook her head. "I called it off to save *you*."

He stepped back, glancing at the door open to the adjacent guest room. He walked into it and sat on the double bed as Iz and Jayce tumbled back into the twin room where Brady lay—their lack of silence always deafening.

Cassie followed him into the double room and shut the connecting door behind them. "I'm so sorry," she said, moving to stand over him. Her arms wrapped around her waist, she swayed side to side in a rhythmic movement.

He looked up at her, not even bothering to hide the hot tears—a mix of frustration and deep, deep love. "You let him rip us apart?"

"I was protecting you."

"By letting me think you didn't love me?" It was anguish—a pain he'd never known, and he'd been shot on the job, for goodness' sake.

Tears rolled down her face. "It was the hardest decision I ever had to make, but I couldn't let him rip you from my life."

"But you did."

"Don't you see?" She shook her head. "You could find someone new, fall in love, live a long, happy life. Be safe as long as you're away from me."

He looked up at her and blinked. "You did it to give me a new life?"

"Yes!"

He exhaled, reached for her hand, and tugged her down on his lap.

Surprise lit her eyes.

He reached up and rubbed her jaw. "Don't you know the only person I want a life with is you?"

"Me?" Her voice came out like on helium. She cleared her throat and tried again. "Want? As in *still* want?"

"As in *always* want." He lowered his lips to hers, forgetting how soft and tender her kisses were. She molded into him as she always had, and suddenly a year of horrific pain evaporated into just a stellar, magnificent, emotion-filled kiss. It was like it'd never happened, but then he opened his eyes. They were still here. Trapped with Cassie's stalker—a killer—and the most crushing moment in Joel's life had happened at *his* hands. The sicko.

She studied his eyes, his face. "You're going after him, aren't you?"

"Of course."

"Let me help."

"All right. We can catch him together like we should have in the first place."

"I'm so sorry. I didn't—"

"I know. If it was the reverse and I thought I had a chance to save your life, I'd take it every time, but this"—he gestured between them—"is going to take some time to wrap our heads around and work out."

"Agreed."

"That is, if you even want to . . ."

"My kiss didn't convince you? If we weren't in the middle of a nightmare, I'd kiss you again."

"Save them up, because after we catch this madman and are finally free of him, we're talking a vacation somewhere—just the two of us to sort this all out."

"Sounds perfect. Just one thing?"

"Yeah?"

"Let's go someplace tropical."

A hint of a smile curled on his lips. "Agreed."

"Now . . . for the sucky part." He tapped her back, and she got up, taking her warmth with her.

He followed her back into the room with Brady's body and his siblings.

Someone among them had killed Brady. Joel shook out his hands. One of their friends, or worse yet, one of their family members was a killer.

He tried to sort it all. This guy knew no limits. Assuming it was a guy, but it had to be, right? Especially with slitting Brady's neck. That took some strength. Some utter commitment to apply the right amount of pressure. Poor Brady. Had he fought?

Joel hadn't seen any signs of a struggle on him. Had he not seen it coming?

Or had he assumed a friend would never hurt him? Whoever the killer was, he wasn't a friend. He was a wolf in sheep's clothing, a murderer masquerading as one of the group. All this time, he'd been right there waiting to strike. When would he strike again?

SIXTEEN

"WE ALL CAUGHT UP?" Iz asked Cassie as the four remained in the room with Brady.

Cass nodded and looked to Joel, who nodded too.

"Why do I feel like I'm the only one out of the loop?" Jayce asked.

"Because you are." Iz ruffled his hair.

"Care to catch me up?" he asked, looking like a little kid waiting for the big reveal.

"Fine." Iz huffed. "But then we need to turn our attention to Brady."

"I'm quick on the uptake," Jayce said.

"Really?" Iz cocked her head.

Jayce rolled his eyes.

"Okay, for the speed lesson," Iz said. "May I?" she asked Cass.

"Be my guest." She didn't have the wherewithal to go through it again.

Iz moved through at the pace of a bullet train—unfortunately, her normal pace—hitting high notes that blasted their ears.

"Only-dogs-can-hear level," Jayce said, rubbing his ear. "Bring it down a notch."

"Sorry." Iz took an actual breath. "You get it?"

"Yeah." Jayce leaned against the far wall. "A friend or family member is not who we believed them to be."

Iz shrugged. "That's it in a nutshell."

"Any idea who?" Jayce asked Cass.

"No. I hadn't considered it being someone close to me. I mean, in the beginning, we went through anyone and everyone, but I settled in to it being someone who obviously knew me but who I didn't really know. However, someone close to me would help explain how he always seems to know where I am. Where I'll be. But who here could be that cruel?" She gestured to Brady.

"Not to get sidetracked," Iz said, pacing the oriental rug on the floor in front of the hearth. "But everyone is going to freak when they realize Brady's dead, and we're effectively trapped in this old lodge with his killer and Cassie's stalker."

"That's why we aren't telling anyone," Joel said.

Cassie frowned. "What?"

"We tell them Brady had an accident. He must have gotten turned around in the storm and took a bad fall."

"Why?" Iz asked. "Never mind. Dumb question. I get it. Prevent mass hysteria."

Joel nodded. "We can watch the guys' faces. See who reacts differently. The person who killed him will know we're lying."

"Double whammie," Iz said. "I like it. Now, what do we do with Brady?"

"I'm going to do an exam." Joel strode toward the bed.

"What for?" Iz stepped back.

"It's a murder investigation. After we're rescued, I want to hand the case off to the cops, knowing I did everything I could to help."

"I'll help too," Cassie said.

"You sure?" Joel asked.

"Positive. It's my job too."

Between Joel's first-on-the-scene details and her minimal autopsy exam—the best she'd be able to do under the circumstances—they'd have a solid start for the cops when this nightmare was over.

"Since I'm not needed . . ." Izzy said, moving for the door.

"Jayce," Joel said over his shoulder. "Go with her."

"And do what?"

"Tell them we found Brady, and we'll be out soon."

"They aren't going to leave it at that, bro."

"You'll think of something." He clapped his brother on the shoulder. "I trust you."

"Thanks." Jayce sighed on a whistle, then locked and shut the door behind him and Iz.

"Okay." Joel cracked his neck and knuckles. "Let's do as much of this by the book that we can. We'll have to find a way to examine him without leaving prints."

"I think we just get as close as we can with our gloves on." She leaned in. One of them would have to hold and position the flashlight just right to get the best pics. "Take zoomed-in pics on your phone, which I'm guessing still has—"

"Zero signal," he confirmed. "The avalanche must have knocked the cell tower out like we thought."

"Or the blizzard. But at least your phone still has power. You can get some good shots for the cops. I'm guessing you got some of where you found him?"

"Yeah." He handed her his phone, and she swiped through them. "Man, poor dude. Looks like he has two wounds based on the blood splatter." She pointed. "His head trauma from the fall, along with his neck in that region, but also lower down . . ."

"Yeah, his lower back . . ." He looked at where the blood pooled in Brady's snowsuit at the back of his left kidney. "If we can determine which cut came first . . ."

"We can recreate what went down."

Someone rapped on the door.

"It's me," Jayce called.

"Hang on." Cassie moved to open the door.

Joel looked up at his bro. "What's up?"

"Most people aren't buying the story. I'm going to head out

and see if I can find where the murder took place. I'll sneak out and check the outer buildings."

Joel clapped him on the shoulder. "Great idea. Use the passageway."

"Will do. I'll be back," Jayce said.

"He's enthusiastic—" A soft smile curled on Cassie's lips.

"That's for sure," he chimed in.

"I was going to say like you."

"Nah. I'm not that revved up."

"When it comes to a case, yes, you are." She shifted. "What passageways are you talking about?"

"They run throughout the lodge. They were built so staff back in the day could move about without bothering guests."

"Oh. No offense, but that sounds creepy."

"Housekeeping has a master key at every hotel you stay at. It's the same thing. There are periodic doors that open up into hallways or bedrooms for cleaning."

"So someone could walk into my bedroom from the wall?"

"Yeah, if one of the doors leads there."

"I bet that's how he's getting around unseen."

"I'll go in and search for him as soon as we complete the autopsy. Well, the best we can do with what we have."

Forty-five minutes later, they wrapped up. Performing an autopsy on a friend was something Cassie had prayed she'd never have to do on the job, and yet here she was. More than a few tears had been shed, and more were sure to come in the days ahead, but for now, they had to focus on staying alive and catching a killer.

Knock. Knock. Knock. Knock.

"For goodness' sake. It's like he's on Red Bull around the clock." Joel opened the door for Jayce.

"What'd you find?"

"I'll tell you, but you got an angry mob coming this way if you don't go in and say something. They're eating up Izzy and Talbot, who are struggling to keep them calm."

"Okay. We got longer than I'd anticipated. Quickly tell me what you found so I can direct the conversation appropriately."

"Brady was killed in the upper shed next to something big. I'm guessing a snowmobile."

"Guessing?" Joel frowned.

"Whatever it was has been moved."

"Why a snowmobile?" Cassie asked.

"The space was large, and the dust had settled around it, leaving an imprint."

"Very smart." Joel typed it into his phone, where he'd put all their other notes and pics.

"I'm thinking the person knifed Brady from behind, then cut his neck."

They'd come to the same conclusion. "Why do you think that?"

"I could be wrong . . ." Jayce shrugged. "But the way the blood was on the floor and the space of the shed. I think Brady's killer came up behind him, knifed him in the back, and then, when he was down or at least hurt, sliced his throat. That's not an easy thing to do. The throat muscles, the ligaments. It's tough, I've read."

"So not something a woman could do?" Joel asked.

Jayce blinked. "A woman? When did we go there?"

"Exactly," Joel said. "We're ruling out half the people in the house without even considering them."

"But the women stayed inside while the guys went out to check the sheds," Jayce said.

Guest room doors started opening and shutting, footsteps tracking down the hall.

"They're coming," Jayce said. "One more thing . . ."

"Yeah?" Joel shifted.

"Someone has been watching you."

"That's a given."

"No, I mean there are footprints at most of the windows. Some are big, but some are small. A woman's size seven if I had to guess."

Cassie widened her eyes. Was he suggesting a woman was involved? That would . . . That didn't seem right. The messages all had a manly vibe to them. Maybe she was wrong. Wrong about it all, but . . . Or maybe he had a helper?

SEVENTEEN

BANG. BANG. BANG. "Joel? Enough. Come out, and let us know what's going on," Heath called.

Joel looked back. "Jayce, stay in here with the door locked. Don't let anyone in or out."

"Me?"

"You're the other cop here. Or soon to be. Do you have someone else in mind?"

"No. I just . . ."

"Wanted to be in the action. I get it. But someone has to protect Brady's body."

Good. Cassie sighed. He couldn't limit their friend to the word *evidence* yet either. Maybe they never should.

Joel opened the door and pushed his way out, pulling Cassie by the hand behind him, and Izzy behind her.

Heath tried to shove his way in, but Iz blocked the door until Jayce got it shut and locked behind them.

Letting out an expletive, Heath shoved into Joel.

"Hey!" Joel roared, shoving off Heath's chest. "Back off."

Cassie held still beside Izzy. One of them was going to give the other dominance. It had to be asserted from the start, and Joel couldn't afford to back down. Would Heath?

"What is going on?" Heath remained in Joel's face.

"I said," Joel bit out, his voice dead calm, "back off."

"Fine, man." Heath took a step back and readjusted his askew coat.

Cassie would have bit back a smile if a roller coaster of emotions hadn't hijacked her. Fear, love, grief, terror. Was there a ride she hadn't been on in the last fifteen hours?

"Just tell us what's going on, please," Scott said.

"Brady had an accident."

"That's what Iz and Jayce said, but . . ." Scott cut himself off as he caught Joel's stare and understanding dawned in his brown eyes.

"Is he going to be okay?" Mia asked.

"Mia, you should be resting," Cassie said.

"I couldn't sleep, and the parlor is empty. I didn't want to be in there alone."

"Is everyone still split up into rooms?" Joel asked as he led the group back to the parlor.

"Yes," Mia confirmed.

"Okay, we got where everyone supposedly is," Heath said. "Now can we talk about Brady? Jayce said he had an accident but wouldn't say if he was going to be okay. What's going on?"

Beaded perspiration lined Heath's brow. That was a trick in this frigid weather . . . though the fire blazed high. He paced and cracked his knuckles.

Cassie wouldn't have pegged him as the one to freak. Or was it an act? He'd claimed to be in the kitchen for a while, but was that where he was the whole time? Had he slipped out unwatched and returned before anyone noticed? She took a deep breath and let it slip out. The crowd needed to be calmed, *then* questions needed to be asked.

Joel cleared his throat, and everyone grew silent, except for Heath's weighted breathing. "I'm sorry to say," Joel continued, "Brady has had an awful accident."

Heath tumbled one hand over another, clearly trying to rush Joel. "We know that. Is he okay?"

"No," Joel said, his voice even. "Sadly, no."

"What are you saying?" Heath's chest rose and fell in rapid fashion. "Is . . . is Brady dead? Is that what you're telling us?"

Joel cleared his throat again. "I'm afraid so."

Rumbles of voices spiraled through the room—gasps, sobs, questions.

"I'll give you the details I have," Joel said, and the room hushed. "Brady didn't come back with Lyle. Who . . . isn't here now, apparently?"

"I'm here," a weak voice said behind him.

"Where were you?"

"Helping Devon on the porch, or I was un—"

"Not now!" Heath said. "Earlier with Brady?"

Lyle stiffened. "We got separated outside. I already told you that."

"Right, they got *separated*." Heath used air quotes.

"We did!" Lyle's squeaky voice rose.

"It took a while for me and Jayce to find him," Joel continued. "He must have gotten turned around in the storm."

"Where'd you find him?" Kendra asked, reentering the room.

"Where were you?" Cass asked.

Kendra cocked her head. "In the bathroom. Why?"

"Shhh," Heath said, "we're finally getting to it."

"Getting to what?" Kendra asked, taking a seat on the couch between Lyle and Scott.

"What happened to Brady," Heath said.

"Okay . . ."

Cass narrowed her eyes. Did the woman seriously just look at her nails?

"Unfortunately, as I said, Brady must have got turned around, and we found him off the side of the overhang."

"Oh no!" Amy sucked in air.

"How'd . . . ?" Mia began, the words getting stuck in her throat.

"Like I said, he must have gotten turned around in the blizzard."

"And took one wrong step," Heath said. "Man, that sucks."

"Where is he now?" Mia cried. "I mean, did you just leave him there?"

"No, of course not," Joel said.

"Then where?" Kendra asked.

"We have him in the last room down the hall."

"Ewwww," Savannah said.

"Savannah," Izzy chided. "The poor guy is dead."

"Exactly," the teen insisted, "a dead body is down the hall from me. I restate my reaction: Ewwww."

"You're gonna have to get past that," Devon said from behind Cass, making her jump.

"Sorry. Didn't mean to scare you."

Her heart racing, she managed a smile. "It's okay. You just startled me. That's all. I didn't hear you come in."

"I didn't want to interrupt Joel." He moved past her and took a seat next to Mia, wrapping an arm around her shoulder. "We need to keep Brady's body until we're rescued, and the Silver Pine medics can handle it . . . him . . . you know what I mean. Right, Joel?"

"Right."

"It's ridiculous to have a dead body in the house," Savannah said.

"He's a cop." Amy pointed at Joel. "And he's a CSI." She pointed to Devon. "I think they'd know best."

"Maybe, though I'm with Savannah," Heath chimed in on the body placement. "But I get it. This life's fickle. One wrong move and . . ." He dipped his finger down with a completely insensitive whistle.

"Heath!" Iz said. "Our friend is dead." Tears rolled down her cheeks. "Have a little compassion."

Heath strode to the leather chair by the hearth and plunked himself in it.

"Life may be fickle," Amy said, her cheeks streaked with tears. "But God's not. Brady was a Christian, so he's with the Lord now."

"Amen," Mia said, sniffing on a sob.

"Whatever," Heath scoffed and stood.

"Where are you going?" Devon asked.

"Back to my room."

Joel shifted. "If we could all just—"

"AAAAHHH!" echoed down the hall.

EIGHTEEN

JOEL RUSHED into the hall, and Cassie was at his side within seconds.

She looked up at him, eyes wide. "Penelope?"

He nodded. They'd all know that screech anywhere. Penelope had screeched like an old barn owl when the group had attempted to watch a horror movie about a month back. Her scream didn't scare him. The reason behind her scream did.

Reaching down, he took Cassie's hand in his, and they bolted down the hall for Pen and Nat's room.

Footsteps clamored down the hall after them. Everyone was coming.

"What's going on?" Jayce hollered from behind the next door over.

"I'll tell you when I know," Iz yelled back.

Joel led Cassie the last few feet into the room.

Penelope stood in the center of it, sobbing and shrieking in spurts.

"What's wrong?" he asked, his gaze tracking to Nat, asleep on the bed. He frowned. How on earth could she sleep through all the commotion?

"I think she's . . . she's dead," Penelope wailed.

"Why do you think that?" Joel asked, wishing they weren't

doing this in front of an audience. It would only elate the killer and scare the rest of them.

"I tried waking her." Penelope hiccupped. "Her eyes are wide and unmoving."

"Okay. Iz . . ." He turned to his sister. "Would you take Penelope to the parlor and sit with her?"

Iz nodded. "Of course." She wrapped her arm around Penelope's quivering shoulders and steered her out of the room.

Joel turned to the remaining crowd. "Could all you head back to the parlor?" he asked. "All except Cassie."

Heath frowned, puffing out his chest like a preening peacock. "Why Cassie?"

"Because she's trained in these things," Devon said.

He knew how to handle a case, being a CSI at the ME's office where he, Cassie, and Heath worked. But, then again, so did Heath, and he acted like he had no clue, but . . . was that just an act to throw them off his scent? Was he more intelligent than he let on? Could he be Cassie's stalker?

"You ready?" she asked, resting her hand on his arm, shaking him from his thoughts.

He turned. Everyone had actually listened and left the two of them alone in the room. Everyone wanted to know what was going on—always did—but no one wanted to see the results, and he couldn't blame them.

With a stiff breath, Joel approached the bed, and Cassie shadowed his steps.

"Ready?" he asked.

She nodded.

Please let Nat just be sleeping.

But he knew better. Bracing himself, he rolled Nat over. Her eyes were wide, her tongue sticking out of the side of her mouth. "Looks like strangulation."

Cassie studied the bruising around her neck. "I concur."

"Poor thing." Joel shook his head, stepped back, and pulled his gloves off.

"Either the killer murdered her in her bed before Penelope entered . . ."

"Or he killed her somewhere else and staged her death here, so she'd appear sleeping, biding him more time. . . ."

"Biding for what?" Her hands shook.

He lifted them in his and ran his fingers across the back of her hand in soothing strokes. "I'm guessing for him to get away, get in the parlor, and be seen there before Penelope figured it out and screamed."

"But why kill Nat?"

"Maybe she caught him doing something," Joel suggested.

"If only Nat could tell us who he is." Cassie exhaled. "This has to stop," she said, stepping back from the bed as he covered Nat with the sheet.

"I think to figure out his identity, we're going to have to go about ruling others out."

"Agreed. So what do we know?"

"Based on the cleanness of the cut on Brady's throat and the large bruises on Nat's neck, I'd say we're definitely dealing with a guy, like we assumed in the first place."

"Agreed. So we have our four possible: Lyle, Heath, Devon, and Scott."

Joel refused to say it out loud, but Talbot had to be in there. He started dating Izzy not long before Cassie's stalker showed up. He'd be shocked if it was him, but he couldn't rule anyone out other than his brother. Jayce would never.

"Jayce has to be removed," Cassie said.

"Agreed."

"And I'd be stunned if it was my cousin Scott. I know him."

"But isn't that the case with everyone here? We know them all—or think we know them. Someone is not who they seem."

NINETEEN

COULD IT BE SCOTT? *Lyle?* Cassie's mind raced. Who made the most sense?

"It can't be Devon," Joel said. "He was back well before he could have taken Brady up to the drop-off. That had to take time. Although . . ."

"Although what?" Cassie narrowed her eyes. "You're making that face."

"What face?"

"The one when you're thinking really hard about something."

He shrugged. "It's just something that's been bugging me."

"What's that?"

"The sled I found."

"Sled?" She frowned.

"The one I found by Brady's body when I rappelled down to lift him back up."

"Of course, the one in your photos. What has you thinking about the sled?"

"I just realized it couldn't have been down there long because it wasn't buried in the snow."

"All right. And what does that make you think?" She started running it through her head—the implications, the possibilities.

"I'd be surprised if a man pulled a body on a sled up to the overhang, but maybe I'm wrong. Although, there is a possibility it could have been a woman. With Brady's size, she'd need the extra help of a sled."

"But you said a woman would have a hard time slitting Brady's throat and strangling Nat."

"She'd have a very hard time, but . . ." He raked a hand through his hair, like he always did when thinking. "We should consider the possibility we could be looking at a pair of them. That would explain the two sets of footprints by the window—one large, one small. It would explain the sled and would give people alibis when they needed it by trading off."

"So what woman was missing long enough to get Brady out to the overhang?" She thought it through. "I don't see Amy as an accomplice, but I could be wrong. I don't know her well, but I can't see a kindergarten teacher dumping Brady's body over the side of a cliff."

"Did Heath hang with any particular women? Though he was so freaked out. Unless it was a really good act."

"He hung with Amy occasionally—which I never could figure out because she's so sweet, and Heath is Heath, but I still can't see her killing anyone or aiding in it. Mia either, plus she hasn't been out of the parlor because of the stitches on her legs."

"Which leaves Penelope, Kendra, and Savannah," Joel said. "We know Iz didn't do it, and Savannah is too sweet natured. No way she's a cold-blooded killer."

"I can't see Penelope doing it. She's too proper to get her hands messy."

"But she was alone in the room with Nat."

"True. And her sleeping took her away from the group for a significant amount of time. What if she discovered the passages too?"

"All right. Penelope or Kendra. Let's attack it this way. Which one entered our group about the same time your stalker letters started?"

"Let's see. Penelope is family, while Devon introduced Kendra."

"Have either Heath or Devon acted strange around you?"

"Strange, no. I mean . . ." She shrugged a shoulder. "They both asked me out. But, then again, so did Lyle."

"They all asked you out after we broke up?"

"Yes. Well, no. Heath and Devon both asked me out before we started dating and then again after we broke up."

Boards creaked behind the wall.

They both turned.

Time to get in there.

Someone was watching.

TWENTY

CASSIE FOLLOWED behind Joel, the boards squeaking beneath them at junctures, foreboding trickling through her at who they might find. Who her stalker was. But whoever it was had disappeared, though clues might remain.

They began in the passageway that wound throughout the lodge—along the bedrooms, out through the kitchen, into halls, down to the cellar, and up to the top floor based on the stairs they passed within it.

The light from their flashlights bounced off the wall as they crept along. She paused to look through a slat into the hallway. Lyle walked by, and she stiffened. As one of Talbot's cousins, they hadn't really considered him deeply, but what if he was her stalker? But her stalker got in and out of her home undetected, always knew every aspect of her life—or so it seemed. He was good. Really good. It was like he had inside knowledge.

She froze.

Devon. CSI.

No. He was a suspect, of course, but of the small group of possibilities, he was her friend. They chatted at work, spent time together. He'd been there for her after she'd had to walk away from Joel. Just as a friend. Only a friend, but what if he viewed it as more?

She stepped back to share with Joel but found herself standing alone in the dark—only her faint flashlight keeping her from being swallowed by it.

Creaking boards sounded upstairs, and she climbed the steps, hoping to find Joel. Instead, she found her way to what was apparently Heath and Devon's room—both their packs rested on the floor. Heath's was white with lightning bolts, mature man that he was. Devon's bag was plain black and streamlined, just like the man. She moved forward, the sensation of being watched crawling up her spine. Turning, she spotted nothing, so she faced back around and moved for the first pack.

I watched her through the register from the other side of the wall. I'd never considered myself a voyeur, but seeing her this way was tantalizing. I wanted her to know me. The *real* me—the one enraptured with her. But, then again, she did know me. I'd poured out my heart and soul in my letters to her. Worked with her daily. Asked her out more than once, but she always turned me down.

Heat seared inside, bitterness biting. She refused me because she was clearly still in love with Joel. I gripped the kitchen knife in my hand, fighting the urge to lash out. To slice Cassie's throat for being unfaithful. But it was Joel who was the problem. If I removed Joel from the picture, that love would cease. Then she'd see how deeply I loved her—the lengths I'd gone to for her. Waiting in the shadows. Always watching. Always there and she never noticed. Always pining after Joel. I gripped the knife harder. I was far superior to Joel. Once he was out of the picture, she wouldn't be able to help but love me.

She moved for Heath's pack. She seriously thought that Neanderthal was her shadow? My skin heated the perspiration clinging to my neck.

I ached to scream out my fury, my love—the two mixing together often. But I wanted her to discover me on her own.

She would. She had to. She was too smart not to realize I was her shadow—glued to her forever. Then she'd appreciate the depth of my love for her, far deeper than Joel Brunswick could muster.

Riffling through Heath's bag, she dumped it out, the items clanging on the wooden floor. She sank back on the bed, confusion on her beautiful face. She hadn't found what she wanted.

Her gaze fixed on my pack, and I rubbed my hands together.

Footsteps sounded in the passageway but on the ground level. Joel had no clue. Poor Sheriff Brunswick, unable to get his man.

Her flashlight flickered, the faint light starting to fade. Soon it would extinguish. And they'd find no batteries. I'd seen to that. Soon it would be just me and her in the dark. A smile tugged at my lips.

Cassie bent over, lifted my pack, and laid it on the bed, her back to me.

This was it—the defining moment of our relationship.

She opened my pack and reached inside. I stepped through the passageway opening and slipped into the room behind her—the cloth soaked with chloroform ready in my hand, but she wouldn't find the bottle of it in my pack. I put it in a bottle labeled lotion. That wouldn't alter what was to come, but my letter materials most certainly would.

She smelled of rosemary and lilacs. A new perfume for a new life.

I longed to smell her neck but refrained. Longed to touch her so very close in front of me, but I restrained. *Discover me.*

She continued riffling through the pockets of my pack. Suddenly, she stilled.

She finally knew. Pulling out the paper and envelopes I'd chosen just for her, she gasped. "No way."

How could she not know it was me after all I've done for her?

She turned. Terror blanketed her face. "You?"

I smiled and reached for her face.

She stumbled back, and I advanced.

"I'm your shadow. With you always. Don't you know me?" I reached to brush the hair away from her face, and she pulled back again. Anger pulsed hot through me. How dare she? "You're *mine*. Don't you understand that?"

"I-I . . ." She widened her mouth to holler, but I grabbed her before it could come out and smothered her nose and mouth with the cloth. It only took a moment, and she acquiesced to the sleep overcoming her. Such a good girl.

I wanted to take Joel out before the escape, but she was in my arms, and I had a way out, so I'd take it. There would be ample opportunity to kill Joel if he followed, and knowing Joel, once the loser figured it out, he'd surely follow.

TWENTY-ONE

NOT FINDING CASSIE in the passageway, Joel exited by the parlor, assuming she'd gone back to the group after getting separated. One minute she was following him. The next, she was gone. He'd searched the lower passageway, where they'd gotten separated, multiple times but no Cassie.

Arguing still roared in the parlor.

He stepped inside. "What's going on?"

"He's keeping us prisoner," Amy said, gesturing to Jayce. "And I have to use the bathroom."

Jayce linked his arms across his chest. "I asked her to wait until you were back. You said not to let anybody leave."

"Thanks," he said to his bro, then shifted his attention to a very impatient, bouncing-in-place Amy. "It's okay. You can go."

"We need to go too," Savannah said, gesturing between her and Kendra.

"Fine." He nodded. With Amy and Savannah with her, Kendra couldn't go anywhere—if she was their culprit.

Plus, their exit would give him time to converse with Jayce about their suspicions of Kendra. He'd question her when she returned, along with Heath, who stood holding up the wall, one foot braced on it behind him. At least Cassie would be safe with Heath stuck in the room with him. Unless it was Devon . . . who was not in the room. He turned to Jayce. "Where's Devon?"

Jayce scanned the room. "He was here." He shook his head. "That's so weird. I didn't even see him leave. Although, I've been chatting with Kendra."

Of course, Kendra. Had Devon slipped out the secret door into the passageway while Kendra had Jayce preoccupied? He needed to find Devon and, more importantly, Cassie.

"AAAAAAHHHH!"

He looked at his brother before bolting into the hall, Jayce's footsteps tracking after him.

"She's dead," Savannah cried, mascara streaks down her face, doubling over, her arms wrapped around her waist, her body heaving with sobs.

"Who is?" he asked, his gaze scanning the hall.

"Amy," she cried.

Kendra. "Did you see what happened?"

"No. There are only two stalls in there, so I was waiting out here. Kendra came out, so I went in and found Amy. Her throat slit. It had to be Kendra. She was the only one in there with Amy."

"Where's Kendra now?"

"I don't know." She hyperventilated, her words coming in spurts. "I rushed back in the hall, and . . . she . . . was . . . gone."

The passageway. He moved for the closest entrance into it when a snowmobile rumbled outside. His muscles coiled, his body freakishly frozen in place. "Cassie." Gathering his momentum, he rushed outside.

A snowmobile raced by him and up the steep incline. Devon with Cassie draped over the front of his lap, his arms around her, steering. Was she unconscious? What had he done to her?

He rushed for the sheds.

"What are you doing?" Jayce asked, hurrying behind him.

"Going to see if there's another snowmobile."

"There is. I saw an old one in the shed when I went to search out Brady's crime scene. I was so distracted with that, I forgot to mention it."

"It's okay. Which shed? The first one?" That's where Brady had been murdered, according to his brother.

"Yeah. It's under the big gray tarp, but it might not run."

"Then we'll have to try and fix it." He entered the dark, cold shed, his breath a white mist in the small shaft of his flashlight's beam. He sat on the snowmobile and turned the key, which, shockingly, was still inside the lock, but no dice—probably why it was still there.

"Could be the spark plugs," Jayce—their family mechanic—said. He checked the engine. "Yep. A spark plug is missing. Hang on, let me look through the tool drawers and shelves."

Joel bounced his leg. "Come on. Come on." He kept trying the key but to no avail. Devon was gaining too much ground at this rate.

"Found one," Jayce said, rushing over. Connecting the spark plug, he stepped back. "Try it now."

Joel turned the ignition, and it roared to life. "Thank you. Now move out of the way," he said, angling for the door.

"You could freeze out there."

"I've got to go."

"I know, but how do you even know where they're headed? I think the snow is falling too fast to follow the tracks."

"He's got to be heading above the avalanche. He's going to try to race the ridge."

"That's suicide. What's he thinking?"

"That he can get back to the lodge and his vehicle, I bet. I've got to catch him before he hits that ridge, or they both could die."

"Be safe," Jayce said.

"Will do." Joel revved the snowmobile. "Find Kendra."

"On it," Jayce said

Joel sped up the mountain in the whiteout, trying to forge ahead in the snow and ice pelting at him.

Please guide me, Father. I can't see anything, but you can see everything. Please direct me to Cassie. Let us get through this.

He'd been saying the same prayer for a year, but for the first time since she left him standing at the altar, he had hope.

Driving blind was crazy, but he had no choice. He couldn't stop until Cassie was safe.

He couldn't see their snowmobile, but finally the roar of its engine revved ahead. Off to his left. If Devon wasn't careful, they could easily fly off the cliff. In this whiteout, it would be impossible to see it until it was too late.

Speeding as fast as the snowmobile would go, he veered toward the echo of the engine, finally catching sight of them.

"Joel!" Cassie yelled, slumber thick in her voice.

"Remember what I taught you," Joel hollered.

They were so close to the cliff. She had to move fast. *Come on, Cassie. Throw that elbow.*

"Taught her what?" Devon mocked, their snowmobile driving ever closer to the cliff.

The fool had no idea of his surroundings.

Cassie swung her elbow back. It collided with his nose.

He released one handle, grasping his nose.

"Now, Cassie!" Joel shouted.

She lunged off the snowmobile, screaming as her leg hit the ground. She ducked into a roll, away from Devon.

"You—" Devon cussed up a storm.

Joel headed straight toward a very distracted Devon. Perfect. He rammed Devon's snowmobile from the side.

Devon rammed back, but Joel regrouped and smashed into Devon—again and again.

Devon fought back, ramming him until Joel sped away.

"That's right," Devon taunted, speeding ahead, completely oblivious.

Joel rounded and sped back, ramming the side of Devon's snowmobile just right—sliding him over the cliff he or Kendra had thrown Brady over.

Devon screamed the entire way down, then an explosion roared up—flames and smoke mixing with the storm.

Joel raced back to Cassie. Stopping the snowmobile, he shut it off and ran to her side, wrapping his arms around her.

She burrowed into him, and he sat there, holding her. The cold vanished—everything vanished, except the feel of the woman he loved in his arms.

TWENTY-TWO

"I CAN'T BELIEVE it was Devon," Cassie said from near the fireplace. She'd been shivering nonstop by the time they made it back to the lodge. "I thought he was my friend."

"He's not your friend." Kendra, who'd been trying to escape through the hidden passageways, laughed.

Jayce had hauled her out of there, Amy's blood still soaking her shirt—and she was laughing?

"You're a passing fantasy," she spat. "Just like the rest."

"The rest?" Joel arched his brows.

Color rushed to her cheeks, and she bit her lip.

Had she spoken out of turn? Did she think Devon would punish her for saying too much? What was their wacky relationship anyway? Was he controlling her in some way, or was she a willing participant? She sat, literally encircled by the remainder of the group. Stuck in the middle of the couch with Lyle on one side and Scott on the other. Heath, Mia, and Penelope sat in a makeshift row of chairs behind her, Jayce in a chair stationed in front of her, and the rest flanked her on the sides.

The lady couldn't get out if she wanted to.

Though *lady* didn't seem appropriate for a killer.

She sat forward, looking past Joel's shoulder.

"Where is he?" Panic filled her eyes. "Where's Devon?"

Joel cleared his throat. "I'm sorry to say he didn't make it."

Kendra narrowed her eyes, but fear anchored there. "You're lying."

"I'm afraid I'm not."

Tears filled Kendra's eyes, and her jaw locked in place, then she lunged at him. "You killed my brother!"

Jayce held her by the waist as she flailed at Joel, trying to kick and scratch him.

"Whoa!" Heath said, trying to help Jayce restrain her.

She swung at him, her fist colliding with his right eye.

He stumbled back, covering it. "Crazy witch!"

Finally, Joel and Jayce managed to force her into a chair, her hands bungeed behind her back.

"You're Devon's sister?" Joel asked.

"For all intents. We grew up in the foster system together. I was little and got picked on, but then he came and protected me," she said with a far-off look in her brown eyes. "Until they made him go away like you just did." She tried to lunge forward again, nearly tipping the chair, but Jayce steadied it.

"Who made him go away?" Joel asked.

"I'm not telling you anything else." Tears rolled from her eyes. "I will pay you back for this! I will pay you all back."

TWO DAYS LATER

Cassie cuddled into Joel on the couch in her cabin, a roaring fire in the hearth. When the main roads finally got cleared, they'd head home and begin their life together again. At least that's what she'd prayed. Everything had been swirling around them a million miles an hour. Helicopters had finally made it in to rescue them from the old lodge. Kendra had been arrested as soon as they'd landed, and Devon's body would be retrieved by local police as soon as it was safe to do so.

She shifted to face him.

"What's up?" He smiled.

"How do you know something is up?"

"I know you."

"I hope you do."

He shifted. "What's running around that beautiful head of yours?"

"With everything happening, we never got a chance to really talk."

He smiled. "We have time now."

"I just want you to know that I never stopped loving you." She shifted to face him better.

"You don't know what a relief that is." He arched a brow. "But?"

"But I see now I should have come to you in the first place. We could have fought this together like we did everything else, but—" Her words evaporated as he cupped her face and moved in for a passionate, over-the-moon kiss.

He kissed her with all the feelings he had been trying to stuff down for a year, and they broke through like the dawn after a long darkness. "Cassie," he breathed, resting his forehead against hers.

Tears continued to roll down her face, but a smile graced her lips.

"Is this okay?" he asked, tracing his lips across her soft, tender ones.

"It's a yearlong dream come true. I love you with all my heart, but I understand if you need more time, or if you don't—"

"How can I kiss you like that and you not know how much I still love you?"

"You do? Even after everything?"

"Would I be here cuddling you, kissing you, if I didn't?"

"No. I just . . . I don't know how you could love me after what I did."

He caressed her face. "You did it to protect me. And, regardless, my love never faltered."

She smiled up at him. "Neither did mine."

"I can't tell you how amazing that is to hear. I never thought . . . I mean, I feared . . ." He swallowed.

She caressed his scruffy cheek.

"I can say it again." She whispered it in his ear, then kissed his cheek, then whispered in his other ear and kissed that cheek, and then pressed her lips fully to his.

EPILOGUE

TWO WEEKS LATER

JOEL APPROACHED Cassie's red door, joy bubbling inside. Their first date. Well, their second first date, but what it officially was he didn't care. As long as he was with her, he was happy. Not to mention the fact that Devon would never bother Cassie again.

Reeling from the loss of close friends and Talbot's cousin, Izzy and Talbot cancelled their large wedding at the resort and instead had a small candlelit ceremony at their local church.

Now, having had more than enough mountains and snow, it was time for him and Cassie. They were planning a trip to the Florida Keys for some tropical time, with Jayce and Mia tagging along. He hadn't seen that coming, but apparently, they'd been spending time together outside of the group. Regardless, it was a new adventure—one that would be spent with long walks on the beach, soaking up the sun and watching beautiful sunsets next to the woman he still loved and who still loved him.

Joel knocked, and Cassie answered in a cheerful yellow sundress.

"Wow!"

She smiled. "I figured I could dress for the islands and bring this"—she grabbed her navy overcoat—"so I don't freeze."

"This is for you." He handed her a canvas bag.

"What is it?"

"Just a little care package for our trip."

She fingered the drawstring. "Can I open it?"

"Of course. We have time. Jayce said he and Mia won't be here for another fifteen. We figured we'd all ride over to the airport together."

"Sounds great. Come on in." She stepped back from the door, and he entered her place for the first time since they'd split. He smiled. Just like coming home.

"So what do I have here? Come, sit down," she said, leading him to the couch.

She reached inside the bag. "Sunglasses. Very nice. And sunscreen. A good essential. A little umbrella." She laughed.

"For those frozen, fruity things you like."

"I see, and . . ." She reached to the bottom of the bag, curiosity dancing across her face. She pulled out the mask and flippers. "Snorkeling gear?"

"I figured it's as adventurous as we'd get on this trip."

"Maybe a little more adventurous." She winked, and his heart fluttered as she lowered her lips to his.

SNOWBOUND SECRETS

LYNETTE EASON

ONE

DESPITE THE DARKNESS that had fallen, the sky was on fire. Green ribbons shimmered above the jagged peaks, twisting and unfurling like celestial streamers in a dance. The auroras had been predicted to appear when the geomagnetic storm hit. And there they were.

Not five minutes later, a sharp crack sounded. The sound grew, building and becoming louder with each passing second, until the mountain shook beneath the weight of it.

Not thunder.

An avalanche.

Ice snapped and splintered with sharp cracks like rifle shots piercing the air. The snow poured down like a tidal wave, its force unstoppable, the sound of its approach deafening.

Terrifying.

Destroying everything in its path. Trees snapped like brittle bones. The impact with the resort was a crashing, shattering force that felt as if the mountain itself was coming apart.

Dr. Maya Sullivan gasped awake, ears ringing, heart thundering. "A dream," she whispered. "Just a dream."

The geomagnetic storm and the avalanche had been two days ago. She'd just arrived at the Silver Pines Ski Resort five hours before the horror began, checked in, found her cabin, and put her stuff away. She'd headed for the main lodge with her laptop, her stomach growling, demanding nourishment.

A mouthwatering chicken salad croissant captured her attention, and she wolfed down the first half without stopping to breathe. With her hunger pangs somewhat appeased, she turned her focus to the reason she was there and opened her laptop. Inheriting her grandfather's ranch—the place where she'd spent her summers—had come as a surprise. The decision to turn it into a place of healing, hope, and peace, however, had been an easy one.

In the middle of emailing her friend Elena Thompson about helping get the ranch operational, the first faint sound reached her. The sounds grew by the second, and in horror, from her seat by the window, thanks to the full moon, she watched part of the mountain slide down in a rolling, rumbling, deadly rush, sweeping past her and dividing the mountain into two sections. Thankfully, ski patrol had recognized the signs and had been able to warn most of the night skiers to get off it before the slab separated and began its descent.

But not all had made it. And who knew how bad the other side of the mountain was, where a heli-skiing group had gone out earlier in the day? And to make matters even more complicated, radios and cell phones didn't work. Even the SOS satellite feature on the newer phones was worthless, thanks to the geomagnetic storm. The resort's repeater station had been taken out as well. They were well and truly cut off from the outside world.

But she couldn't worry about that. All she could do is what she could do. Which was why Maya was sleeping in the chair at the bedside of a victim who hadn't moved fast enough, and dreaming about the massive barrage.

Better than dreaming about Afghanistan.

Or Laura—the best friend she'd lost because Maya hadn't been able to save her. All her efforts had been for naught.

But she could help these people.

She touched the cross at the base of her throat held there by the thin gold chain, then rose to her feet, ran her hands over her hair, and shoved aside the memory of the terror—both of the avalanche and the day Laura had been killed.

She focused on being grateful that no one had died this time. Hurt, yes, but still breathing. Violet, a young woman in her early twenties, had been sideswiped by the flow of the snow and slammed into a tree. Her arm had snapped just above the elbow. Maya had set it as best she could, but without proper tools, she was limited.

The lodge was still standing, but the entrance into the resort was completely packed with ice and snow. The entrance that was also the exit. One way in and one way out.

Neither was an option at the moment.

Since the urgent care clinic was right next to the entrance, it had been buried as well. It would take time to dig their way into it. If they could even do it.

Shortly after the avalanche, Maya had helped set up a temporary medical station behind the lodge, utilizing the large community room where visitors could enjoy a game of Ping-Pong, pool, or cards. Everything had been pulled out to make room for the patients. The maintenance crew worked tirelessly with a single Bobcat to clear a path to the urgent care clinic that held lifesaving drugs and other equipment they could really use.

But progress was slow, so until then . . .

"You okay?" The voice belonged to forty-two-year-old Dr. Delilah Morgan, the ski resort physician. She was a delightful woman with the neatest and tightest cornrows Maya had ever seen. Her dark eyes, that Maya had a feeling normally gleamed with good humor, were shadowed with fatigue and worry.

"I'm all right," Maya said. A trauma surgeon in her everyday world, she'd escaped to Silver Pines for solitude. To hibernate and plan the next steps in her life.

Only that plan was on hold.

Maya had stepped back into her doctor role to patch broken

bones, stitch gashes, and use the AED on a heart attack victim who had survived but definitely needed to be in a hospital.

"It's morning, hon," Del said. "Or almost. Sun will be up soon. You need to get some rest."

"I don't mind staying."

"But you're tired. You need sleep."

She wasn't wrong. Maya let her gaze flick back around the people who needed care. Two other vacationers-turned-medical-workers had things under control. Maybe she could leave for a bit.

Delilah pressed her fingers against her eyes, then shot Maya a smile. "How's Mr. Webb?" Rodney Webb. The heart attack victim.

"He's hanging in there."

"Yeah." Del sighed.

"What about you?"

"I'm good for the next twelve hours or so. We've got more people coming to help." Del quirked a small smile. "Lots of doctors like to ski."

Maya let her lips turn up in response. There were other doctors, but she was the only one qualified to do surgery should someone need it. Then again, it wasn't like she had the tools to do it. "Has it finally quit snowing?"

"Yeah. A few hours ago."

"Thank God. Where do you think the satellite phones went?" she asked.

Del pursed her lips. "There were two in the medical clinic and three in the ski patrol building that got wiped out along with the cell tower. Thankfully, no one was in the ski patrol building, but I can't believe there aren't more phones somewhere. Once we realized the avalanche could hit the clinic, we got so busy evacuating that we didn't grab the phones." She shook her head. "Stupid. All that aside, this place is top of the line. Seems like they'd have more sat phones in different locations readily available for emergency situations." She shrugged. "Then again, cell service isn't usually an issue, so who knows? But I will say, the one at the front desk being gone? That's sketchy if you ask me."

"You think someone took it?"

"I hate to accuse, but yes, I do. It's the only explanation I can come up with and I haven't heard a better one yet."

"Yeah, me either." Maya frowned. "I just don't understand why someone would want to keep us from calling for help."

"Someone up to no good, that's who."

Maya rubbed her forehead. "Okay, well, I guess we'll have to watch our backs and hope it's really just lost." And not because someone had something nefarious up their sleeve.

"Hope all you want. I know what I think."

Unfortunately, Maya was inclined to agree with her but wanted to give the staff the benefit of the doubt. "Maybe one will turn up. On another note, I'm hungry. Before I grab some sleep, I'm going to head over to the lodge to snag a bite to eat. Do you want me to bring you anything?"

"No. I can't believe the gas and power lines are still working. No internet, but I'm not going to complain. The slide was on the opposite side of all of that, so I'll just be grateful for what we do have."

"So will I," Maya said. But she'd still pray for everything else. She suspected Del would too. "Please find a way to get word to me if you need me. I'll be in the café for the next little while, then my cabin."

Since there was no cell phone service, some of the teenagers were acting as messengers. They still hadn't reached anyone outside the resort, so all they could do was hope that someone had noticed the avalanche or had tried to contact a loved one at the resort and failed. The one silver lining was that this would likely prompt a report, and with any luck, someone would come searching.

Hopefully.

She made her way outside, zipping her coat, then pulled on her gloves, and even though the lodge was close by, snow had fallen off the roof and spread onto the usual walking path. Snowplows had made a new one and she set out on it. It was still early morning, the sun just starting to peek above the horizon, which made it a quiet walk, the stillness nice and calming. Like it was just her and nature, but something changed about halfway to the restaurant. She wasn't sure what, but the sensation of being watched slithered up her spine and settled at the base of her neck.

She stopped and scanned the area. Huge piles of snow bracketed the path, so someone could be hiding behind one, but . . . why?

"Hello? Is someone there?"

Silence. Eerie silence. Heavy silence.

A shiver ran through her and she hunched her shoulders. The sun continued to rise, pushing through the darkness, bringing a hint of light to the sky and the path in front of her. Maybe she was just jumpy for no reason.

Three loud pops sounded behind her, and she froze, her mind whirling back to Afghanistan before her platoon was ordered to withdraw. She stood still. "It's not bullets. It's not bullets, it's not bullets." A branch, weighted by the snow from the night before, crashed to the ground.

A man stepped out from behind a pile of snow and right into her path. She yelped and jumped back. He wore a heavy coat like hers and a ski mask. A red scarf was wrapped around his neck. Two more pops sounded. The man gasped and flinched.

"Who are you?" she asked. "Can I help you?"

He didn't speak, just stood there. Frozen. Watching her.

She took another step back.

Run? Or . . . what?

"Hello?" she said. "What do you want?"

Another branch cracked, the sound echoing around them.

He lunged at her, grabbed her arm, and pulled her to the ground.

Gideon Price heard the scream just ahead of him on the snow-packed path to the lodge, and he broke into a run to see a man holding a woman on the ground. "Hey! Let her go!"

The man still thrashed, holding the woman down. Gideon grabbed him and pulled him away from her. And the man still fought. Gideon punched him in the solar plexus and the attacker went down. Then curled into a ball. Gideon ripped the mask off and gasped.

"Vance?" He grabbed the man's arm, but Vance pushed him away, then covered his head with his arms.

"He's having a PTSD episode, I think," the woman said. "Vance, it's okay. It was just snow popping tree limbs. Repeat after me, 'It's a tree. I'm okay. I'm safe.' Say it."

Gideon blinked. He knew that gentle voice.

"It's a tree" came the faint whisper from Vance. He repeated it several times before he stilled, staying frozen in his fetal position.

"Maya Sullivan?"

At the voice behind her, she rose to her knees, turned to him, and gaped. "Gideon Price?"

He had only a brief second to stare at the dark-haired, dark-eyed woman he'd never forgotten before Vance looked up and groaned, then wiped the sweat from his face with the sleeve of his coat.

"Hey, take it easy," Gideon said.

Vance's eyes cleared and widened when he saw Gideon. "Gid? What? How . . ."

"I know. It's a shock to see you too."

Vance rose to his feet.

So did Gideon.

Maya stood gaping at them both. Then she snapped her lips shut and turned her attention to Vance. "Are you all right now?"

The man flushed and his jaw tightened. "Yeah. I'm so sorry. I just sometimes . . . whatever. I've got to go. Ellie is waiting on me." Ellie Harland, Vance's wife.

"Hold up, man. This is amazing we're all here at the same time," Gideon said, then frowned at Vance. "I tried to call you a number of times after you were discharged. Left a few messages, but you never called me back. What's up with that?"

"Uh . . ." Vance blinked and the flush in his cheeks darkened.

Gideon kicked himself and softened his expression. "Oh, sorry, I didn't mean to put you on the spot. I just wondered what happened to you."

Vance scowled, then sighed. "It's a long story. I . . . things happened and I didn't handle them well."

"Yeah, I get it," Gideon said. "I had things happen too."

"We all had things happen," Maya said, her voice soft.

Silence fell for a brief second. "What brought you two here?" Gideon asked, his gaze bouncing between his two former friends.

Vance didn't seem interested in answering, but Maya shrugged. "I have some personal things to work out, and this seemed like the perfect place to do it. Revisit the happy place of my childhood and teen years."

Gideon nodded. "Same."

Vance raised a brow. "The three musketeers back together again?" he asked, his momentary embarrassment over his episode seemingly gone.

"For sure," Gideon said. It was still weird. "How long has it been since we were all here?" he asked, wanting to put Vance at ease with some small talk.

"I don't know," the man said. "A while." Vance shifted like he was ready to bolt once more.

"Senior year of college," Maya said, "just before we all went off and joined the army."

At the mention of the army, Gideon tensed and Vance's nostrils flared. "Where are you living now, Vance?" Gideon asked, needing to change the subject.

After a brief hesitation, Vance's jaw loosened. "Ellie and I moved back to Whitestone about six months ago. We live in town in the old general store. We renovated the upstairs into a living area, and the downstairs is our office. Ellie's an interior designer and I have a security consulting business." He frowned. "Where've you been since—"

"Since I got out?" Gideon wasn't sure what Vance knew about his departure from the army and his life since, but he didn't need him saying too much in front of Maya. Not that he should care. But he did. "Bouncing around from town to town trying to figure out some things. Which is how I ended up here. What about you, Maya?"

"I'm back living on Gramps's ranch. Grandma still lives there, of course, and I commute to a hospital in Nashville where I'm a part-time surgeon."

"Part-time?"

She shrugged. "For now."

"And you're here because . . . ?"

"At the moment, I'm helping in the clinic." She hesitated. "Why not meet for dinner? Take some time to catch up before I have to go relieve Del?"

"Del?" Vance asked.

"One of the resort docs who's stranded here with the rest of us. She and I and some of the others have been taking shifts to care for those who need medical attention."

"I'm going to be helping try to dig out the medical clinic and do whatever else needs to be done," Gideon said. At the flash of disappointment in her eyes, he found himself adding, "But we all have to eat. Sure. That sounds nice. Vance?"

Vance hesitated, then nodded. "All right. I'll let Ellie know."

"It'll be good to see her again," Maya said.

The man paused, then walked over to Gideon and embraced him in a bro hug. "It really is good to see you. I've missed you." He stepped back and looked at Maya. "And you, Maya. I'm sorry about the tackle. I just—"

"It's okay," she said. "You don't have to talk about it."

He gave her a short nod. "Thanks. See you at dinner."

Then he was heading back down the path, pulling the ski mask back over his face. Gideon shivered. The cold this morning was biting. He wouldn't mind a ski mask himself. Or at least a scarf.

"You headed to the lodge?" he asked Maya.

"Yes, I'm starving."

"Same. Do you mind if I walk with you?"

She shot him a smile, and her fingers played with the small cross she'd worn ever since he'd met her. "Don't mind at all," she said. "You can tell me how you've been."

Talking about himself wasn't going to happen. "How'd you know he was having a PTSD moment?"

She raised a brow at him. "Seriously?"

Right. "You too?"

"Yes. I don't have moments like that, but there are things that trigger me."

"Okay." And that was enough said about that. "I'd love to catch up and have some time if you do. I just put in a couple of hours digging, so I won't go back for a while. Everyone who is able is taking two-hour shifts. Most people want out of here, so they're willing to put in the work around the clock." The shifts were short to prevent exhaustion and injuries. It was mostly effective. "I think it's hopeless, to be honest. I know a bit about avalanches, and while the fresh, powdery stuff on top is easy enough to dig through, we've hit the compacted, cement-like stuff at the base. Without proper tools, I'm not sure it's worth the energy or effort. Even the Bobcat isn't strong enough for that stuff."

"That sounds awful."

"Not awful, just tiring—especially when I think it's a waste of time. I'm not the only one who thinks so, but most are still willing to dig because of the desperation of others."

"And that's why you're continuing to help?"

He shrugged. "What else am I going to do? Besides, hope is a powerful thing. If I can offer it in some small measure, then why not? How about you?"

"I had the night shift too."

"Don't you need sleep?"

"I need food more." She laughed and shrugged. "I could use a nap at some point, but the patients mostly slept, so I was able to set my watch alarm and nap in between checking on them."

"How many do you have?"

"Twenty-seven."

"Anyone serious?"

"Heart attack victim could be. He's stable right now but definitely needs a hospital. He needs meds we don't have here, so I'm worried about him. If we could find the sat phone, we could call for a chopper to come haul him out. The others are mostly broken bones, several concussions, lacerations and cuts, a few dislocations—the list goes on. Most we've treated and sent back to their cabins. The more serious ones we're watching."

He helped her around a slippery patch of ice, and his hand on her arm sent shivers coursing through his veins that had nothing to do with the weather. He'd always had a bit of a crush on her, but she'd never seemed to return the attraction, so he hadn't pushed for it. And he definitely wouldn't now.

It wouldn't be right to saddle someone with all his baggage. Especially not after some of the stupid things he'd gone and done. The people he'd gotten involved with. He shuddered and stayed by Maya's side, wishing he'd made different choices in life.

If wishes were nickels . . .

His grandmother's voice echoed in his head and he shoved it away. Nothing he could do about the past. The future . . . yeah, he was working on that one. "Where's the sat phone?"

"We don't know. Some were destroyed—or at least buried—in the avalanche, but the one at the desk? When I asked about it, the staff person looked for it but couldn't find it. She was dumbfounded. Truly shocked that it wasn't in the box where they keep it."

He shot her a frown. "Did someone else have the same idea about calling for help and just didn't return it?"

"Well, help's not here, so I doubt it."

True enough. "And they said the landlines weren't working either."

"To be expected, I suppose."

The Silver Pines lodge came into view. It was an imposing structure that had gone through some recent updates. Not only was the stone chimney and fireplace the centerpiece, they'd added a restaurant off to the side called The Pine Hearth. The addition definitely gave the place an upscale feeling, and mouthwatering aromas came their way as they walked up the steps.

The inside was warm, and they shrugged out of their heavier coats. "The restaurant or the café?" he asked, hanging his coat on the rack just inside the door. Some would say the fact that the power wasn't knocked out was a blessing from God. He wasn't willing to go that far. Sometimes people just got lucky.

"Don't forget, my love, 'every good gift and every perfect gift is from above, coming down from the Father of lights.'"

Again with his grandmother's voice. She wouldn't approve of his straying from the Lord she loved—and had raised him to love. Gideon loved him, he just wasn't sure the affection was returned. He'd made too many bad choices in—

"Gideon?" Maya was waving a hand in front of his face. "You okay?"

He blinked and chuckled, forcing the bad memories away to focus on the good. "Yeah. I was just thinking about my grandmother."

Her face softened. "Well, she's a good one to think about."

"She is. And let's do the restaurant if that's okay with you."

"Perfect." They made their way to the hostess stand and were led to a table. Once they were seated, with the food ordered and drinks in front of them, Maya smiled at him. "Does she still make those amazing chocolate chip cookies with icing?"

"Oh yeah. I stop in and grab a dozen every chance I get." Which wasn't often, because he avoided going home as much as possible. It was too painful, thanks to the distance between him and his parents.

But for his grandmother, he made the effort.

"I miss those cookies," Maya said.

"I miss a lot of things." He swallowed and avoided her gaze.

A small glint of sympathy flashed for a moment, then she nodded. "Maybe one day we'll get to enjoy those cookies together again."

"I'd love that."

TWO

AFTER TWO EGGS over easy, four pieces of bacon, and several bites of expertly cooked hash browns, Maya leaned back in her chair. "Well, I guess we were both hungry since we basically wolfed that down without a word between us."

He laughed. "No kidding. Sorry about that."

"No apologies necessary." The fire crackled in the stone fireplace, giving the wood structure a homey feel. A warmth that she would never get tired of. She definitely approved of the upgrade. Gideon set down his empty orange juice glass and wiped his mouth, giving her a moment to study him. His short blond hair was windblown in a stylish kind of way that she didn't think was on purpose, and his blue eyes took her straight back to her teenage crush that she hoped she hid better than she thought she had. "So, you, Vance, and me here at the same time. That's quite a coincidence."

"Hmm. Quite." He paused. "But not really. This has always been our fun place. Our happy place. Coming here for our annual vacation, all our families together . . . those were the best years. I only have good memories here and I treasure them. Vance too."

She smiled. "Same."

"I didn't realize he was living back in Whitestone. Did you know that?"

Whitestone, Tennessee. Her home. And favorite place on earth.

"I'd heard he was. He and Ellie kind of live like hermits, though. I've never seen them whenever I've been in town. Of course, I've only been back a few times over the years, and I've never been in their office."

He nodded. "How are your parents doing?"

"They're traveling these days. While Grandma is healthy and independent, they're living their best life. Mom can work from anywhere writing her travel blog, and Dad? Well, when you own the company, you can pretty much do as you please if you plan and make it happen." Her father had his own printing company.

"Good for them."

"I was there for Christmas when Gramps passed away. Once I was home, I realized I didn't want to go back to California. I gave notice to the hospital where I was working, applied to the hospital in Nashville, and the rest, as they say, is history."

"You've had a good life, haven't you?"

She shot him a small smile. "I have. For the most part. During my trip home for Christmas, before he died, Gramps talked a lot about what he thought the ranch should be used for. He wanted it to be a place of healing and hope for veterans who needed it. He served in the army and knew what it was like to come home with nightmares and hating fireworks and everything else that PTSD entails. I fell in love with the idea, his vision. Couldn't get it out of my head, in fact." She gave a soft scoff. "I'm a surgeon. I'm good at what I do. I help people who need it most. But . . . this idea to help others who've served and suffer? It sounded great, but I struggled and wrestled with it because I wasn't sure if I was up to the challenge." She drew in a deep breath. "And then I was." She glanced at him. "I have no doubt that's what I'm supposed to do, and God will show me how to do it."

"Your faith has always been strong."

She frowned. "Not always. It's been a process. Seeing what I saw, all the death and—" She looked away. "God and I've been on the outs, but I think we're getting there."

"I know what you mean." He sighed. "I was sorry to hear about your grandfather."

His soft words sent shards of glass across her already wounded heart. "Thanks. It's hard to believe. He was only seventy-six years old. And his death had come out of nowhere. A heart attack. Two months after the doctor had given him a clean bill of health. An autopsy showed he'd died of a heart aneurysm."

"He had no signs?"

"None. That's why it was so shocking. Anyway, that's kind of why I'm here. I need to figure out a plan. He left me the ranch. He actually put me on the deed, so nothing had to go through probate or anything. I want to use the land and buildings on it wisely while adding more to it—also wisely—in order to fulfill the vision in his—and my—head. And heart."

"Of course. What are you thinking? What are you going to do?"

"Good things. Helpful things." A pause. "Healing things. I'm still working through all the details."

"Sounds exciting. Do you mind sharing more?"

"You know Gramps served in the army."

"Yep. I know that was very influential in your own decision to enlist."

"Yeah, it was." She decided to spill everything. This was Gideon. Her teenage crush and friend who'd served in the army as well. He'd even been in Afghanistan the same time as her and Vance. But while they'd been in the same country at the same time, she'd never laid eyes on either man during her service there. And strangely enough, she hadn't seen either of them during all her visits home over the years.

"He was a medic but encouraged me to follow my dream of being a surgeon. Gramps left me just under five hundred acres and everything on it. It's about the only thing in that town that hasn't changed."

The once small town of Whitestone, Tennessee, was no longer small. It had grown up over the years, thanks to the influx of new businesses, tourists, Airbnbs, and more. With its convenient proximity to Nashville, the home she'd loved for most of her life was almost no longer recognizable.

"Grams said neighborhoods are going up all over the place around Mom and Dad's place." He scowled, then shrugged. "But what can you do?"

"Not much, I guess. Progress will be progress, but you grew up in that house. On that land. Are they being pressured to sell to developers?"

"Of course. It's about sixty acres of prime real estate."

"Will they?"

He sighed. "I know they're thinking about it. It's a lot of money to say no to."

She raised a brow. "I don't see them being swayed by money."

"No, but with Jacob gone and just me being left . . ." Jacob, his older brother, had been killed in a car accident when he was only nineteen years old. "Well, let's just say they've lost a lot of their passion for the land. They've been talking about downsizing and enjoying their golden years while they can. This would give them the means to do that. And then some." He hesitated. "And it would allow them to get away from the constant reminder that Jacob isn't there anymore. Not that they'll ever forget, but a change might be nice." He rubbed his chin. "They still have his bedroom exactly like he left it twelve years ago."

"Ohhh . . ."

"I know. It's not healthy. They keep the door shut, but still . . ."

"I can't even imagine how hard that is. Now that you've said that, selling kind of seems like a no-brainer then."

"You would think, but they've offered the place to me—to inherit."

"Do you want it?"

He rubbed a hand over his chin. "I haven't decided, but even though I'm in the construction business, I'm not sure I want to see another subdivision put in either." He frowned. "How did this turn into a conversation about me? Finish what you were saying."

She smiled, then frowned. "I never thought I'd say this, but I may have to sell some acres. Just enough to provide what I need to fund the dream for it. But even with that, I think his vision will live on long after I'm gone. I'll need all kinds of help, of course. With the animals, maintenance, counseling, and so on."

"You think they'll come? Vets with issues?"

She shrugged. "I know PTSD isn't exactly the most talked-about thing. Especially by those of us who have it, but this is something that's needed, and I'm trying to step out of my box of . . . shame . . . I guess, and do something for the men and women who want to do the same and overcome. I think this place can do that."

He blinked. "You said you suffered from it as well. How so?"

"I don't have trouble with gunfire or loud noises like Vance indicated. Mine manifests in dreams. Nightmares that feel so real it's like I've time traveled back to that time and place."

"To what time and place?" Still his voice stayed soft, almost inaudible over the noise in the restaurant.

Maya looked around. She didn't want to tell him there. Or anywhere really, but no one was paying them any attention. "To the place where bullets were flying and bombs were exploding and—" She swallowed hard but forced the words out. "And people I cared about were dying right next to me."

He sucked in a hard breath. "Maya . . ."

"You don't have to say anything. It was horrible and I dream about it. Sometimes in broad daylight with my eyes wide open." There was more, but if she told him about Laura, she might not be able to stem the tears. "I don't really do that at the ranch. Something about being there fills me with peace, dulls the nightmares, the PTSD, and lets me breathe again." She closed her eyes and visualized the rolling green hills. Acres and acres of pastureland, trees, and grazing livestock. When she opened her eyes, Gideon was watching her with such an intent expression that she gulped.

And landed back in the present.

Fatigue hit her. Slammed into her with the force of a raging bull. She signed the bill to charge the meal to her room. "Well, enough about that. Walk with me to my cabin, will you? I'm exhausted and need to get some rest."

"That was fast. Are you all right?"

"I'm fine. Just very tired. It's been a trying two days." In more ways than one. "I'm very concerned about Mr. Webb, the cardiac patient. He really needs to be in a hospital."

"I understand. Then let's go." He signed his bill as well and stood, motioned for her to go before him, then followed her out of the lodge. "I'm still wondering about the landlines," he said. "It seems odd to me that they're not working. At least some of them."

"The workers didn't seem too surprised."

"Maybe they're not supposed to show concern to the visitors."

"Could be."

Resort workers and guest volunteers were doing their best to clear the snow from around the buildings. Most of the snow and ice had ended up at the entrance. And while it wasn't fun to be trapped, there were definitely worse places to be stuck. She was just concerned about those who needed medical care.

"Hey there, Maya, how are you this morning?"

She turned, her mind searching for a name. Bill. Bob. *Ben*. Single father of two boys. One of whom she'd treated for an earache shortly after the avalanche. The youngest. Six-year-old Mitch. "Ben, hi again." She introduced Ben and Gideon, and the two men shook hands. "How's Mitch doing?"

"Much better, thanks. We slept last night at least."

"Good news. I'm happy for you."

"Trust me, we are too." He shuffled his feet and shot a short glance at Gideon, who cleared his throat.

"I'm just going to . . . uh . . . get a coffee to go," Gideon said. "Catch up with you in a minute?"

"Of course."

Gideon walked away and Maya had a sinking feeling in her stomach. She forced another smile. "Well, don't let me keep you. I'm headed back to my cabin to get some rest."

"Right. Right. I was still hoping to convince you to let me buy you dinner sometime while my mom watches the boys."

"That's really kind of you, Ben, but like I told you yesterday, I'm not here for any type of . . . um . . . romantic opportunities."

He raised a brow and looked in the direction Gideon had gone. "I see."

"No, you really don't." Sometimes a woman just had to be a little blunt. "Gideon and I go way back to our teen years. He's a friend."

"Sure. Well, thanks again. I'll be around if you change your mind."

He left, and Gideon reappeared as though he could read her wishful thoughts. "Everything okay?"

"Fine. Yeah. I think he's just a little lonely." Gideon snorted and she frowned at him. "What?"

"The guy is not lonely, Maya. He's like every other man on the planet who knows an attractive woman when he sees one. Trust me." He paused. "And even if he is lonely, that last statement still holds true."

Had he just said she was attractive in a roundabout way? Yes. He definitely had. She tried to ignore the admiring look in his eyes and the heat climbing into her neck. "Well, thanks. I think. Truly, though, the only thing I'm interested in right now is some sleep."

"Then come on. Let's make that happen."

Not all the cabins were within walking distance of the lodge, and visitors had to use the shuttles provided. But hers was. And while it was close in proximity, the ingenious landscaping with trees surrounding it made it feel as if she were the only person on the planet—or at least at the resort.

The tree-lined path led straight to her cabin, and she walked up the three steps to the front door before she turned to Gideon. "It was good to see you again, Gideon."

"You too. So this is yours." He flushed. "Obviously."

"Yes. Why?"

He smiled. "I'm three cabins up the hill."

"Nice." She glanced in the direction of the dark area on the other side of the avalanche slide. "I almost feel guilty that I get to go into this nice warm cabin. I hope no one was over there when all of this happened. If so, they could be in trouble."

"So far, no one's been reported missing, but if they're like us, here alone, who's going to report them?" He frowned and rubbed a hand over his five-o'clock-shadowed chin. "You think Vance is okay?"

"I think he's okay physically," she said. "I'm sure he's embarrassed by the episode, angry that it happened in the first place, but definitely mortified we saw it. The same as you or I would be if it happened to us."

He nodded. "Yeah, true. But I think I'm going to go by his cabin and check on him."

"How do you know which one is his?"

"I'm sure they have a list at the lodge. And if they won't tell me his location, I'll ask them to send a message with one of the teens."

"Let me know if there's anything I can do to help."

"Will do. See you at dinner?"

"I'll be there."

He lingered a moment like he wanted to say something else, then gave her a small salute, turned on his heel in perfect military fashion, and started back down the hill toward the lodge.

Maya swiped her key card, pushed the door open, and gasped. "Gideon!"

At Maya's shout, Gideon stopped in his tracks and turned to hurry back to her side. "What is it?"

She pointed, face pale, jaw set. "Someone broke into my cabin."

He peered around her and smothered his own gasp. "Whoa."

The place had been turned upside down. The half bath just inside the entrance looked untouched, but the French doors leading to the small balcony straight ahead were blocked by the overturned dining chairs. The square table lay on its side and the sofa cushions had been tossed to the floor. The layout was like his, which meant the bedroom was to the right just past the fireplace with the en suite bath next to that.

"The door was locked," she said, "and it didn't look tampered with."

"Let me take a look." He stepped past her.

"I'll report this to security." She snagged her phone and froze. Then rolled her eyes. "Oh, wait. I can't call to report this to security because a stupid avalanche took out the cell tower. You'd think there would be more than one." She caught his concerned gaze and snapped her lips shut. Then pulled in a deep, calming breath. "You don't have to look at me that way. I'm okay, just . . . unnerved. I'll have to walk back down to the lodge."

"I'll go with you, but why don't we take a look around, see if you notice anything missing."

"Fine. I don't suppose it matters if we touch anything. It's not like a crime scene unit can get in here even if we could call one." She paused. "Unless they can parachute in."

"I don't think they're going to do that unless there's a major emergency."

"I know. I just wish we could at least call out."

"Again, my thoughts go to the landlines." That was one thing he didn't understand. He could see the cell phones not working, but the landlines? That was a head-scratcher.

A noise from the back of the cabin stilled them both. Gideon stepped in front of her, his hand going to his hip, reaching for the weapon he no longer carried. "Stay here."

"Gideon—"

"Please, Maya. Stay here." He snagged the poker from the fireplace set for a weapon. "Put your back against the wall."

She frowned but did as he asked while he moved toward the bedroom, poker held in front of him. His heart thudded an adrenaline-induced beat that he'd learned to ignore during his days as a soldier. The only other way out was the bathroom window. If hers was like his, it would be a large stained glass one that opened and closed like a small door. He cleared the bedroom, then headed to the bathroom.

The window was open.

He bolted to it in time to see a fleeing figure dart into the tree line and disappear. Gideon hurried back into the den area, where Maya had moved to the French doors that faced in the same direction as the bathroom window.

"I saw him," she said.

"I'm going after him."

He opened the French door, vaulted over the railing of the small balcony, and raced in the direction he'd seen the man vanish. The tracks led him only so far and then were gone, lost in the undergrowth of the wooded area.

He stopped and blew out a frustrated breath that fogged the air in front of him. With one last glance around, he aimed his steps back toward the cabin. Maya was standing on the porch holding a lamp. He raised a brow and she flushed. "It was this or a frying pan. This was heavier."

He chuckled, then sobered. "Well, you won't need it. He got away." He took the lamp from her and hefted it. She was right. It *was* heavy.

She led him back inside, and he put the lamp where it belonged, then shut and locked her bathroom window. When he rejoined her in the main area, she'd pulled two bottles of water from her refrigerator and passed him one. "How did he get in? That's what I want to know."

"I can think of a few ways," he said. "But with the door not being tampered with, I'm wondering if he swiped a housekeeping key card."

"Management should be able to check the doors and see if someone entered and who the key belonged to."

"What do you think he was looking for?"

"I have no idea. I don't have any jewelry worth stealing here." Her eyes widened. "My laptop."

"Where is it?"

"In the safe." She hurried to the bedroom closet, punched the code in, and opened it. A relieved sigh slipped from her. "It's here." She pulled it and a stack of papers from the interior and shuffled through them. "Everything looks like it's in order. I don't think he got in the safe."

"You have something on the laptop someone wants?"

"Not that I can think of." She frowned. "But it's a high-dollar laptop, and if someone saw me with it in the lodge, they could have decided to snatch it." She glanced at him. "I took it down there for a few hours after I arrived to work near the fireplace. It's the only thing of value that I have." She held up the papers. "These are just plans for the ranch. Notes and whatnot."

"Did you notice anyone paying undue attention to it—or you?"

"No, but I was pretty focused on what I was doing." She returned it and the papers to the safe. "I guess I'd better go let security know. Maybe they have some cameras set up and can figure out who broke in."

"It's worth a try."

Gideon led the way out of the cabin and back down the hill, keeping an eye on the surroundings. The guy may have disappeared into the woods, but that didn't mean he was gone.

The lodge patio was a beehive of activity, the resort's snow-packed entrance far enough away to allow the pretense that vacation was still a go. However, the evidence of the avalanche on the other side of the advanced ski run was in plain view, and glances kept going to it, accompanied by the question of how long it was going to take for someone to realize they needed help and dig them out.

Gideon wondered that himself. The firepit was huge, with picnic table seating around it, the flames warm and welcoming. He wouldn't mind sitting there and having a conversation with Maya once they were finished with the report. They walked up the steps and he held the door for her. She entered the main lobby of the lodge, with Gideon right behind her. They made their way to the registration desk.

"Dr. Sullivan," the woman said. "How can I help you?"

"Hello, Sydney," Maya said, her voice low. "I need to report a break-in in my cabin."

The young woman's eyes went wide before she swallowed hard. "I'm sorry, did you say break-in?"

"Yes. Someone was in my cabin and slipped out the bathroom window. He ran into the trees behind the unit."

"Um, wow. I've never heard of that happening here. Let me get one of the teens to find security and they can take your report."

Maya nodded and looked at Gideon. "I'm going to get a pretzel or something and sit by the fire."

"You're hungry?"

"After that breakfast we had? No. I just stress eat sometimes." She shrugged. "This situation seems to call for a cinnamon-sugar pretzel."

"Okay then, you sit. I'll get you a pretzel."

She smiled and his heart tightened into a hard knot of . . . something. Just like it used to do when they were teens. Seems there were some things one didn't outgrow. He ignored the sensation and looked at Sydney. "We'll be outside on the terrace. Can you ask them to meet us there?"

"Of course."

He nodded and Maya shot him a grateful look. "Thanks." She followed him outside, and he paused to look around for a moment. He couldn't help wondering if one of the guests was her intruder.

And now he didn't want to leave her side.

THREE

SHE SHOT A GLANCE at the door. No security yet. But skiers and snowboarders were on the slopes, so she walked to the railing to watch them while Gideon headed for the walkup window attached to the café.

Her gaze was drawn to the slopes where people zipped down the mountain, kicking up sprays of powder as they slid to a stop at the bottom. The morning sun climbed higher while the cold air nipped at her cheeks.

She tugged her jacket together and zipped it, then shoved her hands into the pockets. A group of teen racers streaked by, their laughter a stark contrast to the anger boiling through her veins. She couldn't expel the sight of her trashed cabin from her mind—or the fear from her heart when she'd realized someone was still in the place she was calling home for the next five days. What if Gideon hadn't been with her?

That was a terrifying thought. Not that she was completely helpless when it came to protecting herself. She'd learned basic self-defense while in the army, had even carried a knife and knew how to hold her own in hand-to-hand combat. Any doctor would be wise to know that. She even had her concealed weapons permit and carried her gun in her car. But her car was at home, along with her weapon. She'd ridden the resort's airport shuttle to the lodge.

A sudden longing hit her for the comfortable weight of it on her hip. Or, right now, in her hand.

The firepit crackled behind her, and the conversation from those enjoying the warmth filtered to her ears. She turned from the view of the slopes and walked to the firepit to hold out her hands, palms facing the dancing flames. Tendrils of smoke spiraled toward the sky. She closed her eyes, soaking in the warmth, and forced herself to relax for a fraction of a moment.

Something slammed into her back, sending her stumbling toward the open fire. Her feet scrambled for traction on the snow-covered deck. For a terrifying instant, she teetered on the edge of the pit, the open fire licking dangerously close.

Then she lost her balance and fell forward. She let out a cry, expecting to feel agonizing pain, just as a strong arm hooked around her waist to yank her back.

"Maya!" Gideon's voice cut through the spiraling terror.

"Gideon. Oh, thank you." She started to hug him when she smelled the burning fabric. The heat spread, and when she looked down, a line of orange flames curled around her sleeve.

Maya swatted at her arm, panic threatening once more, but the glimmer of a thought that she needed to stay calm kept her from full-blown hysteria.

"In the snow!"

Gideon's sharp tone spurred her to action. She dropped to the floor of the terrace and shoved her arm into the white wetness. Gideon knelt beside her and scraped more snow on top.

Steam hissed from where the cold met heat, tendrils of smoke curling away as the flames died a sudden death.

"You okay? Are you burned?" Gideon's breath clouded in the frigid air.

Maya patted her arm and winced at the stinging pain. She raised her gaze to his. "I-I think I'm fine. It burns a little, but . . ." She rolled her sleeve back, revealing stinging reddened skin but no blisters yet. "Just a little singed. And a lot rattled."

Gideon ran his hands over her arm, searching for any other signs of injury. "That was way too close, Maya. You could have been seriously hurt." His low, controlled words couldn't disguise the fear simmering just beneath.

She sat up, brushing wet snow from her burned coat. "Did you see who pushed me?"

"Someone *pushed* you?" Gideon scanned the crowd, his eyes narrowing.

"Yes. I think so." People stood around, concern on their faces. Others moved in and out of the fire's warmth, unaware of what had just happened.

"Whoever it was is gone," he said. "Disappeared into the crowd." He looked up, his gaze scanning the building. "They have cameras. I wonder if we could see the security footage."

"I don't know. It was probably an accident. A dangerous one, but with so many people around, whoever did it may not have even realized it." She pressed on her now-saturated sleeve, the coldness feeling good against her minor burn. "It was definitely weird, though. If it was on purpose . . . why?"

"Could've been an accident for sure." He helped her to her feet, keeping a protective hand on her back. "It's pretty crowded out here. Like you said, maybe someone was just in a hurry, not paying attention, and didn't realize what almost happened."

She shuddered, her mind replaying the moment. "I don't know, Gideon. I don't want to jump to conclusions or act paranoid, but with the break-in at my cabin, I also don't want to brush the incident off. Honestly? It felt deliberate."

Gideon frowned. "But who would do that?"

"I have no idea."

"Let's hope it was just some careless idiot."

He sounded unsure, like he didn't really believe his own words. The break-in? She could write that off as a petty thief looking for an expensive laptop. But that *and* the shove toward the fire?

Coincidence? Or were the two connected? She was definitely

leaning toward connected. And circling back to the one-word question—why? Okay, two one-word questions. Why and who?

They stood there in silence, the firepit crackling behind them, the snow still clinging to Maya's ruined sleeve.

"Security is here," Gideon said, sliding an arm around her shoulders. "I've got your pretzel. That just added more stress to the situation, so I'm assuming you still want it?"

"Absolutely. I might need two."

He motioned to the table where a white bag containing her pretzel sat. "You can eat it and talk to them, then I'll take you back to your cabin and help you clean it up so you can get some sleep."

Maya let out a shaky breath, nodding as they walked back toward the warmth of the lodge.

One thing was for sure.

The more she thought about it and played the incident over in her mind, the more her gut said it wasn't an accident.

Security was very concerned about the break-in and the firepit incident. The two officers who responded introduced themselves as Officers Lila Hawthorne and Ethan Childers. They sat inside the lodge while they talked. Lila wrote everything down while Ethan did most of the questioning.

"He had gloves on," Gideon said. "A ski mask, hoodie, black jeans, black and tan boots."

Ethan raised a brow. "Pretty observant, are you?"

"I'm trained to be."

"Army?"

"Yes."

A new glint of respect entered the officer's gaze, and Gideon appreciated it. "Special ops?"

Gideon smiled. "Yes."

The man nodded. "Me too."

They shook hands. "Always nice to meet a brother."

"Hooah." He cleared his throat.

Gideon was actually impressed at the depth they went into with their questions.

Lila finally shut her notebook and looked at Maya, who'd finished off half the pretzel while she talked. "We'll see if we can get some footage from the cameras. There are two angles aimed right at the firepit. We'd also like to take a look at your cabin, if that's all right?"

"Of course."

Ethan stood. "I'm going to check the door time stamp and see if it was opened shortly before you got there. I'll request the firepit footage as well, then I'll catch up to you."

"Thanks."

Gideon led the way with Maya beside him. She held her arm against her stomach. "You sure your arm is okay?"

She shot him a wry smile. "I think I'd know if it wasn't."

He laughed. "Yeah, I guess so."

The lighthearted moment dissipated when they entered her cabin. It was just as they'd left it.

Trashed. Maya stared at it, shocked once again. "Who would do this? Why?"

"We'll figure it out," Lila said. She pulled out her cell phone and started snapping pictures. She disappeared into the bathroom when a knock sounded on the front door.

Ethan stepped inside. "They're pulling security footage from a few different cameras, and another officer is going to view it and get back to us. I checked on the key card entry. Housekeeping came in around nine o'clock this morning and said everything was fine. That's the only swipe on the door aside from yours—and she still had her key card."

Lila joined them. "You said the guy went out the window. It's a latch you can't open from the outside. Did you leave it unlocked?"

"No. I haven't opened it since being here."

Gideon frowned. "Could someone have piggybacked on housekeeping's key card?"

Ethan shrugged. "Sure, it's possible. Sometimes they flip the latch on the main door so they don't have to keep swiping the card to get in."

"If she was vacuuming, it wouldn't be hard to slip inside without being noticed," Maya said. She walked to the kitchen and opened the hot water closet. Yep, it would be a tight squeeze for the man she'd seen, but he could fit. "Or in here."

"Then waited for her to leave and have free access," Gideon finished.

"Right."

Ethan scratched his head, then made notes in his little notebook. "I don't have access to AFIS right now, but I'll see if I can get some prints off the window for when we're back online."

"All right," Lila said, "let's get this place cleaned up and we'll get out of your hair. Then we'll check a few of the outdoor cameras on the cabins and see if any picked up the guy walking past or whatever. Don't hold your breath. Each cabin is made to feel isolated for a reason, but we'll check anyway."

"Perfect," Gideon said.

"Yes, thank you for everything," Maya said, "but I can get this cleaned up by myself. Now that I take a closer look, nothing's broken, just . . . tossed. It's not as bad as it looked initially."

Ethan nodded. "I'll be in touch about the footage from the outdoor camera and the firepit area if there's anything there."

"Thanks, man," Gideon said. "Oh, quick question. Any progress on getting the landline phones working?"

Ethan and Lila shared a look that Gideon couldn't quite decipher the meaning of. "What?"

"Nothing," Lila said. "Nothing we can share at the moment anyway. But the answer is no. No real progress, but we have someone working on it, so maybe soon."

"Right. Okay then. Thanks."

Gideon and Ethan shook hands once more, and Lila followed her partner out the door.

Gideon returned to the den to find Maya replacing the sofa cushions. He righted the table and chairs and cleaned up the bag of chips that had been knocked off the counter.

Maya raised a brow at him. "Did you catch that look that passed between them when you asked about the phones?"

"I did. You caught it too, huh?"

"Wonder what it meant."

"No idea." But he wanted to find out.

Maya moved to the small desk in the corner, replaced the discarded drawer, and pushed the chair in. Then planted her hands on her hips. "That looks good. I'll put the bed back together in the bedroom and check the bathroom."

She disappeared and Gideon checked his phone. Still no signal. Couldn't even get a text out. He sighed. How much longer would this last? He wasn't complaining but was anxious to let his family know he was all right. Surely they were wondering why he hadn't called or texted by now. Maybe. It was also possible they weren't that concerned. It wasn't like he was a regular visitor. But he did stay in touch. Especially with his grandmother.

And Maya's family? Her parents were probably calling in the National Guard at this point. At least they would have when he knew her as a teen and college kid. From what she said at breakfast, it sounded as if they were still close.

She came out of the bedroom. "All is well. The bathroom window is locked." She walked to the French doors and twisted the dead bolt. "Locked. I'm good for a few hours of sleep."

"Will you really sleep?"

She hesitated, then smiled, but even a blind man could tell it was forced.

"Never mind," he said. "You don't have to answer that. Got an extra blanket and the remote to the television?"

"Yes. The remote's on the end table and the blanket is in the basket by the desk. Why?"

"I'll be on the couch. Go get some sleep."

She bit her lip, looked like she might protest, then sighed. "That sounds really good, but weren't you supposed to go help the digging around the medical clinic?"

"I was, but there are quite a few helpers. This is important. You need your rest so you can help others who need it. Everyone will understand."

One more pause, then a short nod. "Okay, I'll take you up on the offer. Thanks. I just need until lunch, but feel free to leave anytime. You're not stuck here."

"Stop worrying. I'll be fine and I'll be here until you wake up."

She nodded, then walked over to slide her arms around his waist and squeeze. Just a quick hug that punched him to his core. "Thank you, Gideon," she said. "I really appreciate it."

Before he could respond, she walked into the bedroom. It was a full minute before he could get himself together, make sure the front door was locked, grab the blanket, and stretch out on the couch.

He wasn't one bit tired, but instead of turning the television on, he decided to enjoy the moment of stillness even though he kept his ears tuned to any noises that shouldn't be there. It was also a moment to *think*.

Which was what he'd come to Silver Pines to do.

Nowhere in all his plan-making did an avalanche have a place.

Or seeing Maya Sullivan and Vance Harland.

His grandmother would say there were no coincidences, that God had a plan and a reason the two were there. As well as the avalanche. Gideon wasn't so sure. He and God weren't exactly on speaking terms at the moment—frankly because Gideon was a bit angry with the Almighty. Not that he had any right to be. God hadn't done anything wrong.

Gideon had.

So why was he angry with God?

He huffed a sigh and shut his eyes. He was an idiot and should have stayed home.

Thinking was overrated.

FOUR

MAYA WOKE AND FROZE, her ears turned toward the closed door. Silence. That was good, right? The memories washed back into the forefront of her mind, and she sat up. Looked at the clock. She'd been asleep for about three hours.

And she hadn't had a nightmare. Was it because Gideon had been in the next room and she'd subconsciously known she could rest?

Maybe. It was weird, but . . . nice.

She relaxed a fraction. If anything had happened, he would have awakened her.

Then the beautiful and beloved fragrance of coffee triggered her craving, and she hurried to the bathroom. Grateful for his presence, she put herself together before peering out to see her empty couch. Sounds came from the kitchen, and for a moment her heart fluttered and a longing for more than the brew hit her. She wanted this.

With Gideon? Well, yes, she'd always wanted *him*, but *this* in general. Having someone by her side. Someone to wake up to, to share joys and sorrows. Share life. Someone who would watch out for her while she slept. Someone who could make her coffee. She slipped out of the bedroom and walked over to sit in the nearest barstool facing him.

He looked up and smiled. "Feel better?"

"I do. Thank you. I was able to sleep, knowing you were nearby."

"I'm glad." He tilted his head. "Lila came by and said they didn't get anything off the security footage at the firepit. She said you could see the person slam into you, but they were covered up in winter gear. She couldn't tell if it was an accident or not, but they didn't look back. She did notice that."

"Right." She sighed. "I'm not surprised. Disappointed, but not surprised."

"Same." He hesitated, then said, "Can you think of someone who has it out for you? A grudge? Someone you wronged in your past? Anything?"

She shook her head. "I've thought about it, trust me. But no, I can't think of why someone would do this. And we're here. I mean, if someone from my past had it out for me, they would have had to follow me here, right?"

"Yes."

"So, no. I can't fathom it."

Gideon pursed his lips, then sighed after a few seconds. "Well, keep thinking, but in the meantime, this might sound . . . bad . . . in light of things, but do you feel up to a little potential fun today?"

Fun? She raised a brow. "It doesn't sound *bad*. I might feel a little guilty, though. Then again . . ." Sure they were stuck, and they had some injured people to take care of until help could reach them, but there'd been no tragedies. Both she and Gideon were doing their part to help—and more. "What did you have in mind?"

"I thought about the whole feeling-guilty thing, but I don't know . . . we've both done a lot to help. Almost everyone is pitching in. But we need to take care of ourselves too. And that means time off unless there's an emergency." He stopped. "Well, an emergency other than being trapped at a lovely resort that's still mostly functional."

She tilted her head and thought about it. He wasn't wrong. "Okay, as long as no one needs immediate help, I'm game. What did you have in mind?"

"Snowmobiling. Like we used to do when we were kids. If we enjoy it, maybe we can ask Vance and Ellie if they want to go with us tomorrow."

"Yeah. Okay. That does sound fun. On one condition."

"Name it."

"I'd like to run by the clinic and see if they need anything before we go. It feels weird not to be able to just call." She frowned. "In one sense, it's really nice not to be tied to a device. In another, it sure is inconvenient."

"But the teenagers are loving making the extra money with their messenger service."

"True." She smiled. "They're a creative bunch for sure." She sipped the coffee he'd poured for her, relishing the hot brew sliding over her tongue and down her throat. Then she grinned. "Wonder if they've heard about the treasure."

He chuckled. "If they've been coming here for any length of time, they've heard of it."

"I can't believe we fell for that. Believing there were secret tunnels and gold. We searched for hours every day when we weren't on the slopes. Can you believe our parents did that to us?"

"Well, it kept us out of their hair so they could have a little fun and not have us constantly underfoot—or in too much trouble."

"I suppose that was the purpose. Wonder who first made up the story? Started the rumors?"

"A very tired parent."

She laughed. "Probably." She sighed. "I'm hungry again. Wanna grab some sandwiches from the restaurant and take them with us on the snowmobiles?"

"That sounds like a great plan."

Maya headed toward her bedroom and changed into warmer clothes and hiking boots, then grabbed the new heavy coat she'd purchased from the ski shop, hat, and gloves. When she returned to the kitchen, Gideon had shrugged back into his winter gear. He'd also cleaned the kitchen. "You're pretty handy to have around."

His eyes glinted with some kind of emotion she didn't recognize but wondered at. The look disappeared and he nodded to the door. "I'm ready when you are."

"I'm right behind you."

Thirty minutes later, they had their sandwiches, chips, water bottles, and two big slices of chocolate cake packed in a small cooler strapped to the back of Gideon's machine. They also had strict instructions to stay on the snowmobile trails and not to attempt getting to the other side of the avalanche slide. "Ski patrol has been up there, looking for anyone trapped and in need of rescue," the rental manager said. "Brought three people in two hours ago."

"Do they need medical attention?" Maya asked.

"Thankfully, no. They had provisions in a backpack and found shelter in an empty cabin. It's a huge area, and they were closer to this side than the other but didn't get caught up in it. It took some finagling, but we managed to get them across before more snow slid down in a minor avalanche."

"Oh, thank goodness you got them." She frowned. "I didn't hear anything that sounded like another avalanche."

"It was small. Still dangerous to get caught in, but it didn't last long." He shook his head. "It's possible there are people still trapped on the other side, so listen carefully while you're up there, will you?"

"Of course."

He nodded. "All right. You guys be careful. It's safe enough if you stay on the snowmobile runs and away from the problem areas. Everything's marked."

"Thank you."

They mounted the machines, and Maya motioned for him to take the lead. Zigzagging up the mountain on the snow-covered paths and through the woods was exhilarating. Just like when she was a teen, without a care in the world. She crested the top and allowed the machine to slow. Gideon was slightly ahead of her, and she glided to a stop beside him. "That was amazing."

"Look."

She gazed out over the panoramic scene and took in the beauty. "I remember coming up here to watch the sunrises with my dad." She cut her eyes over to him. "You and Vance were always too lazy to get up. Sully, too, when he joined us." Collin Sullivan, a.k.a. Sully, her cousin who was a special agent with the FBI.

He laughed. "I made it a couple of times."

"Hmm. So you say. I never saw you here."

"Well, I did, I promise. How is Sully by the way?"

"Doing well. Loves his job putting the bad guys away. Kinda wish he was here with us right now, to be honest."

"Yeah, that would be nice." He laughed again, and when the laughter faded, there was that look again.

"What are you thinking?" she asked.

"That you haven't changed much."

"Meaning?"

"You were always the one who could make me laugh no matter what was going on in the world—or in my head."

"Me? How so?"

He shrugged. "Back then, it mostly had to do with Jacob and learning to laugh again."

Her heart still hurt when she thought about Jacob. "That was a tough time for everyone."

"After Jacob was killed, Mom was never really the same. She tried to put on a good show for us, but you could tell underneath her exterior, the light was never quite as bright as it was before he died."

"I know," Maya said, her voice soft while she remembered the young man full of life and potential. "Things were never the same for any of us after that. I don't see how they could ever be. But we all learned to laugh and live again. In time."

"Not Mom," Gideon said. "She was really angry with me for going into the army. She ranted and raved for days when I finally told her."

"What? Why?"

"She had already lost one son, and now her other and only remaining son was putting himself in danger. On purpose. She asked me how I could do that to her." He shook his head. "But that was my dream—I've wanted to join the army since I was just a kid playing with the little green army men in the sunroom. And she knew that. I actually talked to a therapist about the whole thing, and he was a very wise person who convinced me that I could not live my life for my mother. That she would come around."

"And did she?"

"I think so. Now that I'm safe and out of the army. For a long time, she would hardly talk to me."

"Your mother? No way."

"Trust me. It was tense." He glanced at her. "When I was home and we all hung out, you were the one who could make me laugh."

She dropped her gaze and tried to ignore the heat climbing into her cheeks. "I'm glad. I didn't like seeing you sad." She shrugged. "But truthfully? I can't see your mom being that way. I'm sorry."

He shot her a tight smile. "That's all in the past. Let's grab the food and eat. I'm starving. How about you?"

So he didn't want to talk about it anymore. Fine. "I can always eat."

They enjoyed the simple meal and surface conversation, which Maya wished would go deeper, but they'd only just reconnected, so keeping it light was probably best. Getting involved with Gideon—assuming he was even interested—was really not the best idea. Not with the scars and baggage she was still dealing with.

He looked at her. "Do you wanna go hiking for a little bit?"

She shook her foot at him. "Why do you think I wore my boots?"

He grinned. "All right, then let's get to the top of that mountain over there so we can have a different view." He returned the cooler to the snowmobile, then took her hand. She hesitated, smiled, then let him lead her to the trail that would take them through more woods and up to the top. There was no way to ride the snowmobiles, so on foot it would be.

"I guess you did come up here," she said. "It's the only way you would know where this trail leads."

"What? You think I would lie?"

"Never. You've always been one of the most honest and transparent people I've ever met. It's one of the things I always admired and really liked about you."

His eyes darkened for a moment, and she wondered what it was she'd said that changed his mood so rapidly.

"What is it?" she asked.

"Nothing."

Maya frowned and let him drop the subject. But she could tell it was definitely something.

An hour later, after more small talk than he could stomach, Gideon followed Maya back down the mountain toward the snowmobiles, replaying her words in his head on an endless loop. *You've always been one of the most honest and transparent people I've ever met. It's one of the things I always admired and really liked about you.*

Unfortunately, if she knew the truth, all of that would change in the blink of an eye. It sobered him. Reminded him his time at the resort was fleeting. A blip in time. He needed to keep his distance and not fall for her again.

And yet . . .

When he looked into her eyes, he saw the concern, the questions, the . . . caring. She'd always cared about him. She just hadn't cared in the way he'd wanted her to. But maybe that could change?

Maybe, but it didn't matter.

In hindsight, it was probably a good thing they hadn't taken their friendship any further. Then again, if she'd been by his side all this time, would he have made the same choices?

Probably. And driven her away in the process.

"Gideon?" Maya hurried after him and placed a hand on his arm. "Wait up. What happened back there? We've talked for an hour without saying anything, and I need to know what it was I said that changed the whole atmosphere between us. Are you okay?"

He stopped next to his machine and pulled his helmet on. "Yeah, I'm okay. It's nothing. Seriously. We should probably get back so I can help in some way."

She planted her hands on her hips and scowled at him. "You're hiding something."

He snorted. "Why don't you tell me what you really think?"

"Someone needs to say what they're really thinking," she shot back.

He forgot how fast she was on her feet when it came to retorts. "Look, Maya, it just occurred to me that I'm not the same person I was when you knew me."

She scoffed. "Neither of us are."

"But I'm—"

"What? Just say it."

"I'm not a good person," he blurted. "And you think I am. So when you tell me how great I am, it just makes me feel like a huge fraud. And that brings up all the regret about some choices I've made."

She blinked. "Okay. So, I triggered you. But why do you think you're not a good person? Because from what I can see, you definitely are. I mean, not so good you don't need God, but good in general."

He bit off a groan. What was wrong with him? And she was right. He did need God. But for now . . .

"I . . . don't know if I can explain. I've just . . ." He swiped a hand down his face, trying to figure out how to word it. "I've made some bad decisions that left me facing the consequences."

"Such as?"

"Such as I'm at a loss right now, okay? I don't have a job or a business or even a family at the moment."

"Wait, stop right there. What do you mean no family? Your parents love you more than life."

"I know. At least I used to know that, but now . . . I'm not sure."

"How could you possibly think that?"

"Because of some of those choices I mentioned. My parents are . . . disappointed and their disappointment guts me. Which means I don't see them. I can't. Much."

"Gideon . . ."

His name in her soft whisper nearly undid him. He sighed. "Don't."

"I'm not. Just tell me."

After a few seconds, he shook his head and looked off into the distance. "I allowed some people who weren't exactly the most honest to invest in my business. They wanted to cut corners. Like a lot of corners. I didn't realize it at the time but figured it out fairly quickly."

"Oh . . . what did you do?"

"Nothing. At first. But I knew I had to do something. Only I waited too long and someone got hurt. I went to the cops and told them what was going on. As a result, there was an investigation into everything. Before long, my reputation, my business, everything, was in question. Most of it was lies, but the part that was true did irreparable damage. A local construction business bought out the company when it went to auction and that was that. I helped the police but told them they had to keep my name out of it. I didn't want any of it reflecting on my family. They kept it as quiet as they could, but . . ." He shrugged and snapped his lips shut. That was way more than he'd planned to say, and she still didn't know the worst of it. "I told you I came here because I needed to think. To figure out a plan, work out the details."

"Details for what?"

"I'm thinking about doing something that could turn everything around or . . . not. It's a huge risk. A new business, a clean slate, and a fresh start. But it would mean putting everything into it. And I do mean everything. It would mean taking out a loan and using every last penny I have." He shrugged. "I just don't know . . ."

For a moment, she didn't speak. Then blew out a low breath. "Oh. Wow. That's intense."

"Yeah."

"I'm just not clear on one thing."

"What?"

"How does that make you a bad person?"

"Because I—" Her eyes were so clear, compassionate. He couldn't bear to see that look change. "It doesn't matter now."

"But you refused to be a part of it. That makes you honorable. Help me understand why you can't see that."

"It doesn't matter. Drop it, okay?" She flinched at his harsh tone, and his heart berated him for it. "Look, Maya, I'm sorr—"

"No, forget it," she said, her voice cool, face impassive. "You said it doesn't matter. I'll respect that. We've just reconnected after years apart. We've acknowledged we're different people on different paths. I can't expect us to go back to the close friendship right off the bat, so I apologize. I'll meet you back at the snowmobile rental."

Before he could respond or attempt to apologize again, she'd snapped on her helmet, hopped on her machine, and started back down the mountain.

Gideon groaned. "You're an idiot, man." He hadn't meant to hurt her feelings, he just hadn't wanted to lose her respect.

But he might have managed to do that anyway.

He mounted his own machine and, when he looked down, noticed footprints in the snow that hadn't been there before.

Footprints that weren't his or Maya's.

He frowned and glanced around. "Anyone here?"

Silence.

He sighed and shook his head, cranked the engine, and followed Maya's tracks. He'd try to apologize again.

And tell her why you snapped?

Maybe.

Probably not.

But he should.

Something in the middle of the avalanche slide snagged his attention as he zipped past. A dip in the snow, something dark—like a hole and a piece of flat wood just below it. He had no time to figure that out and gunned the machine.

He finally caught sight of Maya about halfway down. The slopes to their right were sparsely populated but not empty. Busier than when they'd started out. Maya bounced off the snowmobile trail and onto the ski slope. What was she doing? She wasn't supposed to be there. She whipped around a skier who slid to a stop and yelled something at her, but instead of slowing down, she seemed to go faster. It did look like she was trying to get back onto the trail but was having trouble.

Dread pooled in his belly. There was no way she'd be so careless on the machine, no matter her mood.

Something was wrong.

FIVE

MAYA TRIED the brake again and got the same result as last time.

Nothing.

Panic threatened to choke her. She turned the key to shut off the engine.

And it didn't work.

Her heart hammered. *Think!*

She couldn't stop this machine that was now a lethal weapon. *Oh please, God, don't let me hit anyone! Help me!*

The snowmobile seemed to have a mind of its own and had pulled her off the trail and onto the ski slope. She struggled to keep it on a straight path away from skiers, and thankfully, there weren't many. Relief was fleeting. She still had to figure out what to do and she was running out of time to do it. She managed to get back on the snowmobile run, away from anyone on the slope, but her speed kept inching upward.

The roar of another engine sounded close, and she glanced over her shoulder to see Gideon gaining on her. His helmet covered his face, but she pictured his expression of confusion and worry he had to be wearing. She thought he might have shouted something at her, but she couldn't make it out over the roar of the machines.

He drew closer. ". . . are you doing?"

"I can't stop!"

"Turn it off!"

"I tried! Didn't work!"

Remains of the avalanche came into sight. Piles of densely packed snow and ice loomed high, and an idea formed. It was risky, but she was out of time, and it was the only plan she could think of before she hit someone. She yanked the handlebars, grateful they responded, and aimed for the nearest mountain of snow, praying that the area would create enough drag to slow her down and allow her to jump. She'd have to scrape along the edge or she risked flipping and that would not end well. The problem was controlling the machine. She had no choice. She had to try. It was either that or slam into the lodge at the bottom—where lots of people were gathered.

Please let this work and don't let me die.

It was all she had time to pray before the snowmobile hit the edge of the mound. The momentum jerked her, and she almost lost her grip on the bars. She struggled to stay on the seat and keep it right at the edge of the mound to continue the drag.

She did it and the machine slowed, dragging and rumbling just before it started to roll to the right—away from the remains of the avalanche. Maya pushed off and leaped to the left, straight into the mound, praying she wouldn't be buried—or hit a jagged patch of ice.

She sank for a flash of a second, then landed hard on her shoulder, sending waves of pain ricocheting through her arm and back.

Time ticked past while she fought to suck air into her lungs. Finally, she could breathe and opened her eyes. She was surrounded by snow. Her panic flared, but light filtered to her from above. While she was definitely trapped, she could see the way out. Air reached her. She could breathe. She wouldn't suffocate. Those facts allowed her to control the fear.

Maya reached for the hole, but it was too far. If she could stand . . .

She tried to move her legs and couldn't. Snow and ice held her trapped. Okay, now the panic returned full force.

"Maya!" Gideon's shout sent sweet relief racing through her. "Tell me you're all right!"

The terror in his voice echoed her own. "I'm okay," she whispered. At least she thought she was. She might have sprained her shoulder, but she'd survived. And there was no way he'd heard her soft reassurance. "Dig me out, please?" This time her voice was stronger.

"Already working on it."

She tried to relax. Gideon was here. He wouldn't let anything happen to her. It would be okay. *Oh, please, God, get me out of here. You know I don't like this one bit.* She'd never been a fan of small spaces. She refused to use the word *claustrophobia*, but if it walked like a duck—

"You're going to be okay, Maya."

"I'm counting on it."

"I'm getting there. The ice is the biggest problem. The fresh snow you fell in probably kept you from getting hurt too bad." A pause. "You're really not hurt, right?"

"My arm is aching, but it's not broken. Maybe a sprained shoulder."

"Okay, just keep talking to me. I need to hear your voice."

She needed to hear his too. "Grab someone to help?"

"There's no one around at the moment, so until someone comes along, it's just me because I'm not leaving you."

"Good plan. I'm okay with that plan."

"I'm getting there. Thankfully, you made a hole when you fell, and the snow didn't cave in completely on top of you, but you must have fallen through some ice, because I can't pull you out through that hole you made. It's too deep. I'm going to have to dig down beside you and make another opening."

Getting free was taking way longer than she would have liked, but the comforting sounds of his digging and his running commentary on his progress kept her sane.

Finally, a large chunk of ice fell away from her side, and thankfully, nothing else fell in when that moved. She rolled halfway out of the Maya-sized hole and blinked at the exposure to the light. Then found herself staring into Gideon's eyes.

"Can I pull you the rest of the way out?" he asked.

"Hold on. I need to take inventory." With the space Gideon had managed to give her by taking away the "wall," she could move her legs, then her head slightly to make sure her neck didn't hurt. It did. A little. Probably from hitting the ice so hard, but nothing worrisome. She tested her arms next. The one she landed on protested. "Okay, hold out your hand," she said, "and let me grab onto you. My left arm hurts, but nothing too extreme."

"I'll let you tell me what you need—if I need to pull or just let you do everything on your own."

"Just let me for the moment."

He offered her his hand and she clasped his wrist. Using him as leverage, she wiggled her way out of the opening, and he helped her to stand, keeping a tight grip on her uninjured arm and not touching her aching one.

Her knees wobbled, and she gripped his wrists while she took stock one more time.

"Maya?"

His deep concern touched her. "I'm okay. I think." She moved her sore shoulder, grateful when the stabbing pain eased into a dull throb. She managed a rotation. Not dislocated. "Bruised," she said with relief.

He pulled her into a hug. A gentle one, but one that felt secure and very, very safe. All too soon, he set her back away from him and looked her in the eye. "What happened?"

"The snowmobile wouldn't stop. The kill switch didn't work and neither did the brakes."

"What? How's that possible?"

"I hate to say it, but the only thing I can think of is someone tampered with it."

"But . . . we were with the machines the whole time? When

could someone have—" He stopped. "When we hiked up to the top."

"Yeah."

"And after you left, I noticed footprints around the area."

Maya bit her lip, a cold certainty forming in her gut. "I really think someone is after me, Gideon."

"Unfortunately, I think you're right."

They doubled up the rest of the ride down the mountain, with her arms wrapped around his waist. He took her straight to the clinic to be checked out despite her protests. Three teens hung out nearby, ready to earn a few bucks running messages.

"Got a pen and paper?" he asked the nearest one.

"Sure." The young man handed Gideon an index card and a pen.

Gideon wrote his message and folded it, then handed it along with a five-dollar bill to the guy. "Take this to the nearest cop you can find. It's self-explanatory, but if he or she has a return message, I'll be here at the clinic."

"Got it." The kid took off and Gideon motioned to the door.

She crossed her arms. Carefully. "I'm a doctor, Gideon," she said. "Really, I don't need to go inside. I just want to get a hot cup of coffee and forget this happened."

"I don't think the security officers are going to let you do that. And you know as well as I do that doctors make the worst patients. Please, Maya?"

She groaned and rolled her eyes but followed him inside.

A pretty woman with dark skin and tired eyes walked up to them. "Maya, it's not your turn to take a shift yet."

"She's not here to work," Gideon said. "She jumped off her snowmobile and landed hard. She needs a once-over."

"Goodness, my friend. What in the world?"

Maya held a hand out to the woman. "This is Dr. Delilah Morgan. Del, this is Gideon. My self-appointed protector."

"Nice to meet you," the woman said to him. "But let's circle back to you jumping off a snowmobile. What's that all about?"

Maya grimaced. "The brakes and kill switch didn't work, so it was either jump off or crash into the lodge. I chose the one I thought I—and everyone else—had a better chance of walking away from."

"Hon, come on in here. I know you're perfectly capable of deciding if you're all right, but why don't I take a look just in case there's something you're missing. Adrenaline can cover up a multitude of hurts."

"I know." Maya sighed. "Fine." She shot Gideon a look. "I'll be right back."

"I sent one of our little messengers to let security know to treat that snowmobile as evidence," Gideon said, "and they need to have a qualified mechanic go over to see if it was tampered with."

"That's a good idea." She started to follow the other woman.

"And just for good measure," Gideon said, "I'll send another teen to tell security to meet us here. We'll make a report, and I'm going to ask if they can put a guard on your cabin."

She whipped around to meet his gaze. "A guard?"

"You said it yourself, it looks like someone is after you. Until we can get you out of here, we have to do something to keep you safe." He paused. "I'm not a cop, Maya, but I was in special forces and worked with military police a lot, so I know how an investigation is run. But mostly, I just know how to fight." He looked away for a moment. "Being a soldier was about the only thing I've ever been good at." Much better than being a businessman, that was for sure. He shoved that thought aside. "I have no authority with law enforcement, but I think if we tell them everything that's happened, then they'll see the wisdom of having someone watch out for you. It's not like you can leave to get away from this person, and I really don't like that. So, either the guard or I will be camping out on your doorstep." Another pause. "Not to guilt trip you or anything, but, just in case you haven't noticed, it's cold out here."

Another grimace slipped across her features. "Your *not* guilt trip is kinda mean."

"I know."

She offered him a small smile, then nodded. "Okay then. Fine. I'll go along with a guard if they'll assign one. For now."

He'd take the "for now."

For now.

She disappeared behind a privacy curtain at the back of the room, and he paced from one end of the "lobby" to the other, replaying the break-in. Had the intruder run because Maya hadn't been alone? If she'd been by herself, would he have confronted her? Killed her? The tampering of the snowmobile *should* have killed her. *Could* have killed her and someone else. He shuddered. That was something he'd never be able to forget.

And would probably add to his nightmares. But the two questions foremost in his mind were . . . why and who?

Why had the person trashed her place, and who was doing it? Which raised more questions. What had they been looking for, and what did killing Maya gain them?

That might have been four questions, and he still had more.

It didn't take long for security to arrive, and it was the same officers who'd responded to Maya's cabin break-in, Ethan and Lila. Gideon filled them in.

"We'll bring the snowmobile down and see what we can figure out," Ethan said. He shook his head. "I'm glad she's all right."

"That makes two of us."

"As for the guard," Lila said, "I can do that. I don't mind sleeping on her couch if she doesn't mind me there."

"I don't mind," Maya said, coming from behind the curtain. "I just don't want to put anyone else in danger. I mean, what if the person after me decides to ramp up his attempts?"

Lila cleared her throat. "I *am* a trained officer, ma'am."

"It's Maya."

"All right. Maya. I think we'll be fine."

"But what about your shifts here? If you're watching out for me all night, how will you get any rest?"

"I'll figure it out."

Maya sighed. "Okay, if you're sure. I'm supposed to help out at the clinic, but honestly, unless they're in a state of emergency, I'm going to ask if I have time to catch a few hours of sleep before starting a shift. I have to eat, so I'll still keep my dinner plans at six, so maybe after that?"

"I'll be at your place at nine."

"And she'll be with me until then," Gideon said. He wanted to ask if they'd let him carry a weapon but figured that wouldn't go over too well.

"Okay," Maya said, "I have some work I'd like to do, so I'm going to grab my laptop and some papers from my room and sit in the café where I'm in full view of everyone until it's time for dinner. That should keep me safe enough."

"And I'll be with you too," Gideon said.

She nodded. "That would be nice. I'd like that."

"Come on then," he said, "we'll get your laptop and come on back."

"I'll go with you," Lila said. At his raised brow, she shrugged. "Can't hurt."

"Maya," a voice said behind him. "Everything all right?"

Gideon turned to see the man she'd been talking to earlier. This time he had two young boys with him.

Maya smiled. "Hi, Ben, everything's fine, thank you." She walked over and crouched in front of the kids, who looked enough alike to be twins except for the older boy's height to tell them apart. "Hey, you two." She gave the gentlest tug on the youngest's ear. "How are you feeling, Mitch?"

"Better." He slipped away from his father and wrapped his arms around her neck. "Thank you for taking care of me."

"Oh, sweetie, you're very welcome." She hugged him back with only a slight grimace when she moved her injured arm.

Gideon's heart crashed against his chest wall at the sight of the child in her arms. She looked so natural. So right. She would be a wonderful mother. He swallowed hard. But what kind of father would he be? If he ever got the chance to be one? One with nightmares and who jumped at loud noises, hated fireworks, and carried a weapon with him when he was in the car in case someone pulled up beside him to open fire?

Overwhelming loss nearly pulled him to his knees. He'd never have children because he'd never get married because he couldn't share his baggage. Baggage he'd love to lose and never unpack again. But that meant taking the risk, sharing his secrets, and opening up. Being vulnerable. Trusting.

So, yeah, that wasn't happening. He'd learned the hard way to keep his mouth shut about certain things in his past.

"Gideon?" Maya's voice jerked him back into the present. She was looking at him with a frown on her lips and concern in her eyes. "You okay?"

He drew in a sharp breath. "Yeah, sorry. I was just thinking about something."

"Let me introduce you all. This is Ben and his boys, Mitch and Owen, my new friends. And that's Officer Lila."

Everyone shook hands. Lila's gaze seemed to linger on Ben, and Gideon almost smiled. Then she gave herself a shake and looked away.

"Ben and the boys have asked if I'd have some hot chocolate with them," Maya said to Gideon. "I told them I'd love to if you can join us." Now there was something more in her eyes. Something that said she didn't really want to have hot chocolate but didn't want to disappoint the boys—and their father?—either.

He smiled. "I never turn down hot chocolate. Happy to join you."

She nodded and shot him a relieved look. "Perfect." She turned to Ben. "I have to run to my cabin real quick, then we'll find you in the café."

"Great." Ben's smile looked a bit strained. "I'll go ahead and put the order in, and we'll see you in a few minutes."

After Ben and the boys left, Gideon led the way while Lila hung back, giving them some privacy but close enough to intervene if she needed to.

"Why do I get the feeling you're not real excited about this hot chocolate date?" he asked.

"Because I wanted to work and talk to you, not hang out with them, but—" She shrugged.

No sense in pretending her words didn't thrill him. He cleared his throat. "But you could see how excited little Mitch was at the thought of you joining them."

"I could."

"His brother—"

"Owen."

"Owen didn't seem too upset about the idea either."

She cut him a sideways look. "What are you getting at?"

He shrugged. "Ben has his eye on you for their new mom, and I think he's let them in on the plan."

"Oh stop." Her cheeks turned a deep pink, and he laughed.

"I'm not kidding."

"I'm not either. He's a nice man and I'm always open to making new friends, but I'm not interested in anything more with him."

"Is there someone you *would* be interested in something more with?"

She raised a brow at him, but sadness clouded her gaze. "There hasn't been anyone on the radar in a very long time." She sighed. "To be honest, I feel like I have too much baggage, too many nightmares. Asking someone else to take that on doesn't seem fair to them."

He stopped in his tracks and she did too, looking up at him, her face a question mark.

"Gideon?"

"I . . . It's . . . I just . . ." He shook his head, unable to find the words. Finally, he said, "I know what you mean."

"You do?"

"Yeah." And he left it at that.

She nodded and they continued the trek toward her cabin in silence. Gideon kicked himself the rest of the way. He was an awkward idiot. Once they were inside, she grabbed her laptop and papers from the safe and shoved them in a bag that she slung over her shoulder. "I'm ready."

He opened the door, saw Lila standing on the small porch, and told himself to relax the hypervigilance. He had more important things to focus his attention on.

Like making it clear that Ben needed to look elsewhere for a mother for his boys, because while Gideon didn't have any plans for a romance with Maya, he didn't like that someone else did.

And yes, he realized how stalker creepy that sounded.

He shut the door on the cabin—and his thoughts.

SIX

THE MOMENT she sat down, Ben shot Gideon a frown and Maya figured her insistence that she wasn't there for romance went in one ear and out the other. He was jealous of Gideon and wasn't even being subtle about it.

The truth was, if she hadn't run into Gideon and resurrected old feelings, then maybe she would have been interested in getting to know the single dad a little better. But Gideon *was* here and his presence was the only one she wanted. Which made her frown, because she hadn't been lying when she said romance wasn't a good idea with her issues—or her plans for the future. What if Gideon was interested in her but not in how she wanted to spend the rest of her life? Or if not her life, at least the next several years. Getting involved with him would be setting herself up for a world of hurt. Assuming he was even interested. Which she thought he might be.

Maya set her bag in the chair next to her and paused. It was a table for six. A kernel of an idea wormed its way into her mind. Lila had stationed herself discreetly near an exit, and Maya waved at her to join them. The officer walked over. "Yes?"

"Would you like to sit with us? Ben, would that be all right?"

He smiled. "Of course. The more the merrier."

His smile reached his eyes and Maya relaxed a fraction. He met her gaze and gave a slight good-humored shrug. Lila sat and immediately started talking to the boys, who wanted to know all about being a police officer and if she'd ever put her handcuffs on a bad guy.

She had and they were thrilled.

"So, what brings you to Silver Pines?" Ben asked Maya.

"I used to vacation here as a teen and decided it would be a great spot to do some thinking."

"About?"

"Life." She smiled. "What about you?"

He shrugged. "Like you, we've had good times coming here. It's been a year since I lost my wife to brain cancer and didn't want to spend that anniversary at home. Mom suggested we come here, make some new memories as a new kind of family." He sipped his cocoa. "It was a good idea. We've had a good time in spite of the avalanche excitement."

Lila helped Owen, the oldest boy, put a straw in his cup. She looked up at Ben. "I'm so sorry. I can't imagine how hard that was."

"One of the hardest things I've ever been through." He cleared his throat. "But we're making it."

A small silence fell until little Mitch walked around to Lila's chair and smiled up at her. "I like you."

Lila laughed and brushed his bangs from his eyes. "I like you too, honey."

From there, the atmosphere lightened and talk turned to Ben's career.

"A genetic genealogist?" Gideon asked. "Now, that sounds like an interesting job."

Lila leaned forward. "What exactly does that entail?"

"You really want to know?" Ben asked with a one-sided grin.

"Yes."

He laughed a little self-consciously, but before he could launch into his explanation, Maya placed her hand on his. "I'm sorry, Ben, but Gideon and I have some work we need to do before we have dinner with some friends. Then I need to stop by the clinic to check on a few patients. I hope you won't be offended if we go get started on that?"

He hesitated and frowned, but said, "No, of course not."

"Thank you." Maya looked at Lila. "Feel free to stay here, we'll be within sight."

Lila shot her a grateful look. "Thanks, because I really am interested in hearing what Ben has to say."

Ben looked like he wasn't sure whether to be perturbed or amused. Maya prayed he'd go with amused.

She grabbed her bag, said her goodbyes to everyone, and headed for a larger table in the back corner. She needed the space to spread out.

Gideon followed.

Maya took a seat, then glanced at Lila, Ben, and his boys. They seemed to be happy enough, and she hoped they wouldn't think her rude, but she really did need to figure some stuff out and she was running out of time to do it.

Gideon took a seat opposite her. "I don't think Ben's too happy about this arrangement."

"He'll be fine. Lila likes him."

"I was kind of curious about what a genetic genealogist does."

She scoffed. "Seriously?"

"Yeah. A bit."

She motioned to her computer. "Would you like me to google it for you?" She grimaced. "Oh wait. I can't. No Wi-Fi."

"I'm kidding. I know what one does. It's a cool job. They can work with families, finding lost members, or sometimes work with law enforcement, analyzing DNA and other stuff. It's interesting."

"How do you know all that?"

"I read."

"You read, huh?"

"I do."

"Well, read this." She pulled some papers from her bag and

pushed them across the table in front of him. "What do you think about that?"

He looked down and Maya waited. When he finished, he frowned and met her gaze. "It's an offer to buy the ranch."

"Yes."

"A very good offer."

"I know. As soon as Gramps passed, the vultures started circling."

"Yeah. I'm sorry."

"It's okay. I'm thinking about how to make it work to my advantage. There are three more of those offers. All different amounts, but good ones. That one is the best."

"Wow. But there's no way you want to sell, so how do you plan to work with this?"

"That's the big question. The fact is, I need money to fund this new adventure." She pulled another document from her bag and spread it over the table. "This is a map of the ranch. From border to border." She patted the stack of papers to her left. "These are the offers. If I were to sell off a portion of it, which portion would you pick and who would you offer to sell it to? The one who wants to set up a smaller ranch, the one who wants to create a touristy getaway with a horse farm, or the one who wants to turn it into a wildlife sanctuary and rehabilitation center for injured animals?"

He studied her for a moment, then lowered his gaze to the map. Minutes ticked past as he read each offer, going back and forth between them and the map. "Okay, if I were going to sell, it would be this area and to the wildlife sanctuary and rehabilitation center. It's probably enough land to generate the funds you need, but the business will keep it relatively untouched." He tapped the third offer she'd gotten and pointed to the area on the map that was one hundred acres at the edge of her property line. Without the water source.

She blew out a relieved breath. "Thank you."

"For what?"

"For confirming what I was thinking. It's the best deal for the least amount of land, but it will give me the capital I need to start the nonprofit part of the business. If I sell those hundred acres, it will give me almost a million and a half to start with—to build another bunkhouse, enclose pastures, plant a hayfield, a garden, and more. The ranch itself will be a for-profit business. Vets who come to stay will help with the planting and harvesting of the garden, and we'll dig some wells, run cattle, train and board horses, and so on."

"It all sounds amazing, Maya."

She smiled. "It's exciting, isn't it? And a real answer to prayer." She bit her lip. "But overwhelming too."

"You're going to need good help for sure."

"I have people in mind and I've already put out feelers." She shook her head. "You know, it's wild how my family came to own that land. Years ago, Gramps won the ranch in a poker game."

"Poker? Your grandfather? I didn't take him for a gambler."

"Oh yeah. He was a bit of a scoundrel in his younger days. Before he decided to let the Lord lead him."

"Well, that's the way some people used to do business back then. Over a game of cards."

"Exactly. And he said he never felt right about it. That he had to make it right. He said he went to the man he won the land from a couple of years later and tried to pay him for it."

Gideon blinked. "He did?"

"Yeah. Said he got so he couldn't sleep at night, and every time he tried to pray, he felt like the Lord was impressing it on him to do the right thing."

"So he did."

"He did. Although, he didn't say it was easy. It was a lot of money, and it was more than he had in the bank."

"But he did it anyway," Gideon murmured with a strange look on his face. A look that disappeared so fast she almost wondered if she'd dreamed it. "What happened as a result?"

"Well, he said the man had come to know the Lord by that point as well and told him he'd been foolish and deserved what he'd gotten. But he'd take half the money if my grandfather felt so inclined. Gramps wound up giving it to him over a period of five years so he didn't go broke."

"No way."

"I'm not kidding. Gramps said after the deal was worked out and shook on, that night was the best night's sleep he'd had since the game."

"Because he did the right thing."

"Because he obeyed what the Lord was telling him to do. Which was the right thing, so yes."

Gideon nodded, but he had a faraway look in his eye.

"Gideon?"

He blinked. "Sorry, I was just thinking."

"About what?"

He shot her a small smile. "About what doing the right thing looks like sometimes."

"What do you mean?"

He rubbed his hands together and shook his head. "Never mind. It's not important."

"Okay, well, what about this, then? You're in construction, right?"

"I . . . uh . . . yes. Why?"

"Could you take care of building everything that needs to be built at the ranch?"

He gaped at her a moment and then snapped his lips shut. "Me?"

"Yes. You. I'd sign a contract and so on."

"I . . . I mean . . . why me?"

"Why not you? I need a builder and you're a builder. There's no one I would trust more."

His eyes darkened and he turned away from her. "Excuse me a minute. I'll be right back." He slid out of his chair and headed for the restroom.

Maya watched him go, then snapped her swinging jaw shut. What in the world had just happened?

Gideon rinsed his face, shut off the sink, and took advantage of being the only person in the bathroom to rest his forehead against the mirror. Once again, he was an idiot. Most of the time he was fine and could leave his shameful past where it belonged, but with Maya . . .

She stirred everything up.

He was going to have to either get himself under control or tell her why he didn't deserve her trust, her faith in him. But as soon as he spoke the words, he'd be unable to take them back. Her eyes would cloud with disappointment. Maybe even contain a little shock, and she'd try to figure out what to say but wouldn't be able to find the words. Then she'd finally walk away, and he'd get a text the next day saying it would be better if they went their separate ways.

He sighed. *Get it together, Price.*

He could just tell her and get it over with. Get rid of the whole stress of keeping secrets from her.

But then she might send him away. Refuse to ever want to see him again. And telling her would just put her in danger. While she had someone who possibly wanted her dead, he'd keep his mouth shut and protect her.

After that . . . well . . . that was up to God—a fact that Gideon was just coming to accept. And he supposed keeping Maya safe was also up to God, but maybe he'd use Gideon to do that. Maybe that was why he was here at this particular time. He'd once heard a sermon on "divine appointments," and the preacher had pressed home the point that there were no coincidences with God, that the Almighty had a master plan for each and every person born. If the preacher was right, that meant Gideon was at Silver Pines for a reason.

And he could think of no better reason than to make sure the person after Maya was stopped.

So, he needed to get it together and get back out there. If Lila hadn't been just a few feet away, Gideon wouldn't have left Maya alone. And if his purpose here was to keep her safe, he wouldn't again. He'd make sure she had someone watching out for her at all times. He could do that. *God, I honestly don't know what to say or pray other than it's been a while since we talked. Everything I know about you points to your being willing to listen in spite of my stubbornness. If you've put me here to look out for Maya, then I'm willing. Maybe it will make up for being such a disappointment in other areas of my life. I hope so.* He took a deep breath, then stepped out of the bathroom to walk back over to Maya's table.

He found her talking to Vance Harland.

They both looked up as he approached. Vance smiled. "Looks like great minds think alike. Came down to get some lunch and ran into Maya. I was just explaining that Ellie's got a migraine."

"Oh no," Gideon said, "sorry to hear that. She used to have those when we were younger."

"Yeah. She doesn't get them too often these days, but stress is a trigger. And trust me, she's super stressed about being trapped here with no cell service or internet. She doesn't do well being cut off from the business. She has some part-time help and likes to keep tabs on them a few times a day."

"Please let me know if she'd like me to take a look at her," Maya said. "I do have some pain meds I can give her if she needs them."

"She took some but is running low. I'll let her know you have more if she needs them. Thank you so much." He looked at Gideon. "Maya's got some interesting plans for the ranch. Has she told you about them?"

They'd had the ranch conversation in the five minutes he'd been gone? He glanced at his phone. Okay, ten minutes. It could have happened. "She has. They're amazing plans. Her grandfather would be proud."

"Tell me more," Vance said, "like where are you going to get the people to help work it?"

She shrugged. "I've already put out feelers. I have several friends who are interested. And a few investors. So, that's nice."

"Investors?" Vance asked. "Thought you said you were going to sell off some land."

"I am, but it never hurts to have people who are willing to invest. I don't plan to charge the vets or their families."

"Not charging them?" Vance raised a brow. "So you're going to be a nonprofit?"

"Exactly. And as such, it's going to need a steady influx of donations."

He shook his head. "Better you than me. I don't do anything unless it's for profit."

Gideon frowned. "There are more important things than money."

Vance scoffed. "I can't believe that came out of your mouth. When we were growing up, that's all you talked about. How you were going to have this big construction business and rake in the bucks."

Gideon flinched. He *had* said that. More than once. "Yeah, well, once you grow up a little, your priorities can change."

"Sure, man, if you say so." Vance didn't sound like he believed him, but Gideon didn't really care. He shot his former friend a tight smile, and Vance must have gotten the message, because he nodded to the two of them and held up his bag of food. "I guess I'll get this back to Ellie. Thanks for understanding."

"Of course," Maya said. "See you in the morning. I'll be at the clinic until around six. Can we do breakfast around eight thirty or so?"

"That should be fine. Just know if we don't show, it's because Ellie's not feeling any better and I couldn't find a kid to send a message."

"Got it. Tell her I'm here for her if she needs it."

"Thank you, Maya, appreciate it." He gave them a small salute and walked toward the exit.

Gideon dropped into the seat opposite her. "I'm sorry I stormed off like a brat. There's no excuse other than the fact that I have stuff I'm dealing with. Which is one of the reasons I'm here. To deal. But then the avalanche happened and I haven't had a chance to think, much less deal."

"I can understand that," she said, her voice neutral. No, compassionate. "I don't understand what I said that upset you, though."

He rubbed his chin, thinking. Would it help to talk to her? "I'm seeing a therapist," he finally blurted.

She blinked, but other than that, her expression never changed. "Okay."

"That's it? Just . . . okay?"

"What would you like me to say?"

What *did* he want her to say? "I don't know. I guess I thought you'd be surprised or . . ." He shrugged and looked away.

"Judgmental?"

"No. Maybe." He took a deep breath. "Yeah." He could feel her studying him. Like literally feel her eyes on him. He wanted to squirm.

"What was her name?"

He stilled. Then lifted his gaze to hers. "Jade."

"And what did she say when you told her you were seeing a therapist?"

"That I . . ."

Could he voice it?

Maya simply waited. Not pushing him. Her eyes compassionate and calm.

"It doesn't matter," he finally said.

"Okay."

There was that word in that tone again. He wasn't fooling anyone. It did matter. He rubbed a hand down the side of his face. "She said I was weak."

"She's an idiot."

Maya didn't even hesitate on her response. That fact combined with her simple declaration allowed the tension to release from his shoulders and he laughed.

Actually laughed. Out loud.

She smiled and shrugged. "Sometimes I can be blunt. Sorry."

"No apologies necessary. I can appreciate blunt." His mirth faded. "But that experience with her made me realize that it's not fair to burden others with my . . . uh . . . issues."

"What if it's not considered a burden? What if sharing them makes the weight lighter?"

"Yeah, I don't know about that."

"It's in the Bible, Gideon. We're told to bear one another's burdens. You believe in God, I know you do."

"I believe in him, I'm just not sure I like him very much right now." In spite of the fact that he'd just prayed for God to help him keep this woman safe. And even though he was starting to see that he needed God. That unsettled him. He didn't really want to need anyone.

"Ouch. That's a tough one. Thankfully, God loves you whether you like him or not." She smiled and it took the sting out of her words. There was no rebuke, just a gentle reminder.

He sighed. "I know. And it's not really that I don't like him, I just don't understand some things and need to spend some time figuring those things out."

"Which is why you're here."

"Yes."

"And instead of doing that, you're playing bodyguard." She leaned forward and gripped his hand. "I'm sorry, Gideon. Please, take the time you need to focus on the reason you're here."

"I was thinking about that in the bathroom, and honestly, I think at least one of the reasons I'm here is to help keep you safe. So it's all good. Okay? And . . . I prayed for God's protection, so maybe I like him a little more than I think I do."

She bit her lip, then nodded. "All right, well, if you want to vent or need a sounding board, I'm here."

He did want to. And he didn't. "Thank you." He shook his head. "Enough of this heavy stuff. Want to revisit our childhood and go treasure hunting after I put in an hour or so of digging and you get some work done on the ranch plans?"

"Treasure hunting, huh?"

"Yep. It entails using snowmobiles again, though."

She grimaced. Then shrugged. "It's like falling off a horse. You should get back on, right?"

"Exactly."

"But where?"

"I have a spot in mind. I saw it as we were racing down the mountain."

"What spot?"

"It's in the middle of the avalanche slide."

"Fabulous."

"Exactly. I'll see what Lila thinks about snowmobiling."

SEVEN

MAYA HONESTLY didn't know where she'd left her brain. She should be getting some rest in order to be on call all night if she was needed, but instead, she found herself back on a snowmobile—one she wouldn't let out of her sight this time—and heading back up the mountain beside Gideon. He was to her right, with Lila following. He slowed as they approached the area.

She glanced behind them, grateful to see that they were the only snowmobilers on the slope. She cruised to a stop when he did, climbed off, and pocketed the key. Lila hung back, obviously wanting to keep an eye on the area.

"What do you think you saw?" Maya asked him.

"I'm not sure. It looked like a hole in the snow, and there was a flat piece of wood off to the side. I reported it when I finished doing some digging on the entrance, but they're so busy trying to get us out of here, I'm not sure anyone thought it worthwhile to investigate."

"And you do?"

"I guess. It's weird enough to make me curious. I want to see what it is."

"All right then, let's go."

Skiers whipped past one after the other while she and Gideon made their way to the edge of the avalanche slide. "How did you spot anything in this?"

"Well, I was up a little on the snowmobile and the hole was inside the edge of the slide with the other piece of wood down a bit." He walked along the side with her on his heels, looking for what he could be talking about. "And there it is," he said. "We'll have to climb over all of this. You up for it?"

"Sure. Lead the way."

Gideon climbed over from the smooth section of snow and into the area filled with large slabs of ice and snow, rocks and trees. "Be careful," he said. He offered his hand, and she grabbed it and let him help her over to stand beside him.

She looked around, spotted what he'd seen, and did a double take. "That's not a hole. That's a cave. Or . . . something?"

"No way." He made his way carefully toward the opening. Maya stayed right behind him, stepping where he stepped right up to the "hole." He peered in, then looked back at her, a flash of excitement in his eyes. "You're right. It's a cave."

"Let me guess. You want to go in."

"You don't?"

"Um, not really. It could *cave* in." She smirked.

"I see what you did there, but if the weight of an avalanche didn't collapse it, I would think it would be all right."

She crossed her arms and scowled at him. "I'm trying to stay alive, remember?"

He sighed. "Lila's up there looking at us like she's going to come rescue you."

"I might just let her." But she did kind of want to go in. When had she turned into such a wimp? If they'd found this twenty years ago, she would have been the first one inside. She put a hand on his arm. "What's that?" She pointed to the slab of wood ten yards down.

He pulled his phone out and took a picture, then zoomed in on it. "It's a door, I think. Curved at the top with a black handle and . . . nails."

Maya looked back at the entrance. "The door to the cave. They nailed it shut?"

"That's what it looks like." He tucked his phone away. "Okay," he said, "stay here with Lila. I'm going in."

"I guess I could go with you." She wasn't excited about the idea, and yet a small flame of adventure flickered inside her. Then again, closed dark spaces didn't agree with her.

"Well, now that you've decided to go in, let me do a little recon first. I don't want to ask you to do anything dangerous. I once built a house in a cave. You won't believe all the construction stuff I had to learn to do that and the pros I called in. So let me take a look. You stay put with Lila."

She waved him on. He disappeared into the black hole, phone flashlight on high. Lila walked over to stand next to Maya on the other side of the avalanche edge. "Should we be worried?" she asked.

"Probably."

Lila glanced around. "I don't think anyone followed us. But Ben just went past."

"He's by himself or with the boys?"

"Alone."

"You like him, don't you?"

The pretty officer flushed. "It doesn't matter. He seems to have his heart set on you."

Maya wrinkled her nose at the woman. "Well, my heart isn't set on him, so feel free to charm him."

Lila smiled and shrugged. "I leave stuff like that in the Lord's hands."

"A very good place to leave it." She should probably follow Lila's lead on that. Maya walked to the entrance. "Gideon? You okay in there?" No answer.

She looked back at Lila, who scrambled over the edge to join her at the opening. "Gideon?"

"I'm here!" He sounded far away. "I'll be there in a minute!"

Maya looked at Lila. "Well, doesn't look like this is going to cave in on him, so I guess I'll—"

"Hey, what are you guys doing?"

Ben slid to a professional stop next to the edge.

"Checking out this little cave in the side of the mountain," Maya said. "Gideon went in to make sure it's safe."

He raised a brow. "Interesting. Maybe all those rumors about a hidden treasure are true after all."

She laughed. "Maybe."

"Shouldn't you let ski patrol know about this?"

"Gideon reported it, but Lila can give them more information now."

A gloved hand rubbed his chin. "A cave, huh?"

"Yep."

"Okay, I've got to admit, that's really cool." He stepped out of his skis and planted them straight up in the snow, did the same with his poles, and climbed over into the avalanche chaos to join them.

Maya stepped aside and let him take a look just as Gideon reappeared. When he saw Ben, he pulled up short. "Oh. Hi."

"Hey. Mom's watching the boys, so I decided to get in a few runs. I was skiing past and saw you all out here. Thought I'd be nosy and see what you were up to."

Gideon shrugged. "Just doing a little exploring."

"Is it dangerous?" Lila asked.

"It's actually not a cave. It's a network of tunnels. There were a few places that had collapsed and some tunnels that were blocked, but for the most part, surprisingly, it's pretty solid. I'd love to examine the blueprints of this and see where everything leads—how it was built and when."

"Spoken like a true construction guy," Maya said. "The resort was built in the 1920s if I remember correctly. Looks like they simply put a door on the tunnel, built up the ground beneath to make the run straight and smooth, then packed snow on top. Obviously, the avalanche undid all of that. How fascinating." She looked at Lila. "Ski patrol needs to block all this off before some teens decide it'll be a grand adventure to go exploring."

"I can't call it in, obviously," Lila said, "but as soon as we head down, I'll let someone know."

Gideon nodded. He glanced at Maya. "You want to take a look?"

She shook her head. "I'll admit to a bit of claustrophobia and stay out here after all."

"I wouldn't mind seeing that," Ben said. He looked at Lila. "Interested?"

"Very, but my job is out here at the moment." She glanced at Maya, then the area around them. Skiers and snowboarders whipped past, and Maya could see the workers beyond the roof of the lodge still working on the blocked resort entrance.

Gideon waved Ben to the cave entry. "Help yourself before you lose the opportunity."

Ben laughed and shook his head. "Naw, that's okay. I guess with two boys I shouldn't take any chances." He nodded to the three of them. "Can I help do anything? Like head down and let someone know about the area?"

Lila nodded. "Yeah, actually, that would be super helpful. No one from ski patrol has arrived yet, so I'm a little concerned. Another report won't hurt. Ask for Samantha Davies. She's head of security and will make sure ski patrol is aware and maintenance secures this so no one gets hurt."

"On the way." Within minutes, he had his skis back on and was racing down the mountain to the lodge.

Soon, the three of them were on the snowmobiles and not too far behind. After they turned the machines in, they grabbed coffee and found seats in the café. Lila sat next to Maya. Just as Gideon took the seat opposite them, a teen ran up to them. "Dr. Del said to come find you. She said Mr. Webb was getting worse and she wanted you to take a look at him."

Maya rose. "Of course." She looked at the others. "There are all kinds of doctors here, but not one cardiologist. Apparently, I have the most experience when it comes to that area."

Gideon stood too. "We're coming with you."

She nodded and they all followed the teen out the door.

When Maya walked into the clinic, she spotted Del bent over Mr. Webb doing compressions. She hurried over. "When did this start?"

"Two minutes ago. He's in V-fib and the AED wasn't working. Need someone to find another." The woman's dark eyes met Maya's, but she didn't stop her pumping on the man's chest.

"Where is one?"

"The main lodge or the restaurant. There are a few all over the resort."

"I'll be right back," Gideon said and bolted.

Maya grabbed the mouthpiece from the first aid kit and inserted it between the patient's lips. She gave him breaths until Gideon returned. Working quickly, they got the pads on him and hooked up. Two shocks later and he was back in rhythm.

Del placed her fingers on the man's neck. "Thank you, Lord."

Maya checked. "And he's breathing."

He was still unconscious, but he was alive. For the moment. She looked up to find Gideon, Lila, and the teen watching. "Mr. Webb needs a hospital. We need to get out of here so we can call for help. Now."

Gideon nodded. "That's the new goal. Find a way out or a way to call for help." He sucked in a breath and looked at Lila. "All right, let's head back to the café and we'll see if we can map out a plan."

Maya gripped Del's hand. "You and the others have this?"

"For now. We'll come get you if we need you."

"Okay. Good." She nodded that she was ready, and they made their way out the door, only to run into Vance.

He stopped short. "Oh, hi."

"Hey, man, everything okay?" Gideon asked.

"Uh, yeah. I mean not really. Just coming to see if I can get some more pain meds for Ellie. She's still battling that migraine."

"Let me take a look at her, Vance, please?" Maya asked.

He raked a hand over his head and sighed. "I would love that, but she's convinced it will pass in the next few hours." He shrugged. "She's usually right, but this time has been intense, and it's hard to watch her suffer like this."

"I'll come right now," Maya said.

He hesitated. "No. She's funny about that kind of thing. Let me ask her. I'll get word to you if she agrees."

Maya frowned. "All right, but please reassure her that I don't mind." She was worried it was more than a migraine, but unless the woman consented to an examination, Maya's hands were tied. "Let me see what I can find. We've pooled our resources, and someone had some migraine meds they shared." Desperate times called for desperate measures. "Tell me everything she's allergic to."

"Nothing. No foods, no meds, nothing."

"All right, follow me."

Once Vance had one dose of medicine for Ellie, they made their way back to the café and took their seats.

"So tell us about the tunnels," Lila said.

"It looked like a cave initially," Gideon said, "but once I got inside, I could see it was definitely man-made." He looked around. "There was a maze of tunnels, and while it was hard to keep my sense of direction and stay oriented, I'm pretty sure one of them led this way."

"Then there should be an entrance," Maya said, "right? Or would it be an exit?"

"Guess it depends on which way you went in," Lila said.

Maya laughed. "You know, when we were kids, we looked all over the place for anything that could be used to hide a treasure."

"We didn't go into the employee areas, though."

"True, but I know some kids tried. I never was willing to break the rules." She shrugged. "And now I'm glad, because obviously those who did so didn't find anything either. But from what I remember they sure got in a bunch of trouble."

Lila frowned. "You know, I think I may know what you're looking for."

"What do you mean?"

"I've been here awhile and I've gone through every inch of this resort. I remember seeing a map-type thing tacked to one of the walls in the basement. I had no idea what it was and honestly didn't think anything about it. Just figured it was someone's weird art."

"Where?" Maya asked.

Lila smiled. "You want me to show you?"

Gideon nodded. "Absolutely."

Gideon and Maya followed Lila through the kitchen into a back hallway, and Gideon aimed himself toward the glass door at the end. "Let me take a look here first, will you? I'm curious to see if what I'm thinking is right." He pushed the glass door open. "It's a small alleyway where they dump the trash." He pointed to the dumpster. Then stepped outside and let the frigid wind sweep over him. He shivered but ignored the cold while he took in the scenery. There was a small patio area surrounded by a brick wall. To his right, a wrought-iron gate was cracked open. Gideon walked to it and gave it a push. It swung out and he raised a brow.

Maya stepped up beside him. "What are you doing?"

"Seeing what's out here and if what I'm picturing in my head matches reality." He exited through the gate, and she followed. Lila brought up the rear. He pointed to the avalanche area. "You can't see the tunnel from here, but it's over there. If I remember correctly, I think it runs this way." He pointed toward the lodge.

"How are the tunnels shaped?" Maya asked. "Could one lead us under the slide and out to the road? Like could we use one to escape?"

"That's exactly what I was trying to figure out." He rubbed his chin, thinking. "As I was walking it, it seemed like they make a kind of an M shape. The entrance was straight ahead and then there was a fork in the road, so to speak. I went left, and it had a sharp curve that started taking me back toward the lodge. I don't know where the other curve ends up, but if it's the same as the first, it might take us off the property. There were a couple of other tunnels that branched off the way I went that looked like they went up the mountain, but I can't say for sure." He tracked the area from the tunnel with his eyes, estimating where the opening would be in the lodge.

"The basement," Maya murmured.

"Yes," Lila said, "that's where I was going to take you. It's just a junk-filled storage area, and it's been forever since anyone's been down there. I used to go down just to make sure no one was trying to overstay their welcome at the resort, but I found a way around that nonsense. I finally booby-trapped the door so I could tell if it had been opened or not. It never was."

"Can you get us down there?"

"Of course." She motioned for them to follow and led them to a back room off the kitchen, then to an old door in a hallway. "Look at the bottom."

He looked and saw a piece of black electrical tape that ran horizontally across the crack of the door.

"Still there," she said. "But open it and that's the way down."

"Clever woman."

She shrugged. "I can be. I requested a lock be installed, but no one was worried about anything down there and said it was a waste of money to protect it with a lock. *I* was more worried about someone going down there, hurting themself, then suing the place. But no one else was concerned about that. They said no one knew about the basement anyway. They're not wrong. I still wanted a lock, but we don't always get what we want, so here we are. The map is toward the back on the wall."

He twisted the knob and pulled. Nothing. "It's definitely not locked, but . . ." He jerked harder, and it opened with an earsplitting screech.

Maya jumped and clapped a hand over her mouth to muffle a yelp. He raised a brow at her and she flushed. "Sorry. I guess I'm a little on edge."

"I don't blame you." He tried the light switch on the wall without hope, so when the bulb over the stairs came on, he almost jumped too. "Well, that's good news." Gideon started down the steps, with Maya and Lila right behind him.

Once they reached the bottom, stale air surrounded them. The place was filled to the brim with restaurant and ski equipment. Old furniture and mining tools, safety equipment and dust. *So* much dust. "Talk about a hoarding situation." For the next thirty minutes, they moved stuff to create a path to the back where Lila said the map was.

"Oh wow," Maya said, "look at that." A large intricately hand-drawn map was tacked to the wall. "This has to be it, doesn't it?"

They all stepped closer and Gideon laughed. "No way it can be this easy."

"I think it is actually this easy, thanks to Lila," Maya said.

"You think this is it? Am I right?" Lila asked.

"I really think you are," Gideon said. "Well, it's not an M shape. It's more of a W on top of an M. But I think this is where we are now." He tapped the paper. He looked closer. "I wonder what these little circles are? Ventilation shafts, maybe?"

"No idea," Lila said.

"Guess we know where the rumors came from now," Maya said. "No treasure indicated, but it's a fun thought. Which one of those tunnels leads out? Surely whoever built these wouldn't go to all that trouble without one route off the mountain."

He touched the top one. "This one is a possibility."

Maya placed a finger on another area. "And this one is the area uncovered by the avalanche." She traced it. "So it doesn't go out," she said. "Bummer."

"Is there an entrance to these tunnels from the lodge?" Lila asked. "The map's down here, so it seems like there would be one. Maybe?"

Gideon glanced around the area once more, then returned his gaze to the map. "I would think so. How have we not heard about this map in all the years of coming here?"

Lila shrugged. "The resort's still owned by the original family, but turnover is pretty high, and there aren't any employees that have been here for an extended period of time. And those who were here back in the earlier days have all passed on. So it's no surprise that no one would know about this. And if someone *did* know about it, they wouldn't necessarily have any reason to talk about it. You know how I came to discover it. I haven't thought about it once until you were talking about tunnels."

"Okay," Maya said, pointing to the far wall. "Back there, behind all that stuff and around the corner, is where the door should be." She snapped a picture of the map with her phone, then led the way, dodging items and shoving boxes to the side to make a path. When she rounded the corner, she stopped. "It's a wall, not a door."

Lila tapped it. "Sounds solid."

Maya frowned. "This is the right place, isn't it?" She knocked on the wall next to the area that should be a door.

Gideon rapped as well, then dropped his hand to his side. "Nothing sounds hollow. Huh."

"Well, that's disappointing," Maya muttered. "They must have closed it up."

"Guess we could knock it down," Lila said, "but we'll have to get permission. Of course, I have a feeling the manager would be just fine with that if it meant we could get out and find some help."

"Let's go back to the map," Gideon said. "I know you have a picture on your phone, but I want to see the whole thing again." They followed him to stand in front of the drawing, and he said, "Okay, so here's the entrance that was uncovered by the avalanche." He ran a finger over the lines. "That tunnel doesn't appear to be connected to this side. It's totally separate, but it does lead to another maze of tunnels and this one"—he jabbed the map—"looks like it leads out."

"But it might not be safe. You didn't go that way originally."

"No, we'll have to do a little exploring, but it's our best shot."

Lila nodded. "Let's go tell Grant Paulson. He's the resort general manager." They made their way back up the steps. "He's been here for about two years and does a great job. He's been out there organizing the digging shifts and making sure people stay hydrated and careful not to overexert themselves."

"One thing before we go. What's with the landlines?"

Lila raised a brow. "What do you mean?"

"When I mentioned them before, you and Ethan exchanged a look. Why?"

She sighed. "Okay, yes, it looks like they've been tampered with. I'm not a phone line expert, but even I could see that it's possible someone messed with the wires and stuff. The VoIP cabinet is in the back of the lodge where the main office is. When we first looked, you really couldn't see anything was wrong. But when you traced the primary line feeding into the resort's phone, it was missing. Without one to replace it, there's no way to get the phones working again, even when the internet's restored. Not only that, but security just learned that there was a flash drive inserted into one of the open USB ports. Looks like a jammer that emits a low-level interference signal. Its job is to disrupt any attempts to reestablish communication remotely. Like if anyone tried to reroute calls through a backup system, all they'd get is static."

Maya gaped. Then snapped her lips shut. "Wow. That's clever, but . . . *why*?"

Lila scowled. "I don't know, but it can't be good."

No, it definitely couldn't be good.

EIGHT

MAYA FOLLOWED THEM out of the basement to wind their way through the restaurant, then out into the cold. Snow had started falling again, and Maya suppressed a groan. Snow was the last thing they needed. It would just cause them to have to do more digging.

They climbed into the resort Jeep with four-wheel drive, and Lila transported them to the entrance. Maya got her first up close look at the damage and swallowed a gasp. She had been so involved in helping with the medical clinic that she had left the digging to others. But to see it now . . .

The snow and ice were still piled high, and Maya had to say she agreed with Gideon. Trying to dig out was a hopeless task. At least out any time soon. It was going to take a long time at that rate.

And yet, men and women persevered with tools and gloved hands. Tractors and their operators were doing their best to move the snow and ice, but it was so packed they needed people with shovels, rakes, and other tools to separate it before they could move it. "Have they made any progress at all?" she asked.

"Yeah," Lila said, "believe it or not. They've actually made a good dent in it. But even going at the rate they are, it'll be another couple of days before it's open. At least that's my guess."

She frowned. "I don't think Mr. Webb has another couple of days, Gideon."

"I know."

Ben was working alongside several other men and looked up at their approach. He waved and joined them. "Here to pitch in?"

"Unfortunately, no," Lila said. "Do you know who Grant Paulson is?"

"The resort manager? Sure, he and I were fraternity buddies. He's over there."

Maya spotted him and then saw Vance working as well. "I'm going to ask Vance about Ellie while you talk to Grant," she told Lila and Gideon. She made her way over to Vance, conscious of Lila's gaze following her. The woman took her protector status seriously. Maya could honestly say she appreciated it.

She reached Vance's side. "Hey," she said, "how's Ellie?"

He jammed his shovel into the snow and leaned on it, breathing hard. He wiped the sweat from his forehead with the hem of his sweatshirt. "She's all right. Feeling a bit better after the meds, thanks. Told me to get out here and do my part to dig us out. She really wants to leave." He shrugged. "Either that or she's just tired of my hovering."

She offered him a sympathetic smile. "I understand."

A chopper sounded in the distance, and they all froze as one. Then cheers went up. Tools dropped to the ground, and everyone waited until the helicopter was right overhead to start waving and yelling.

"An army bird," Gideon said, stepping up next to her. "Praise God."

"Yeah," Vance said, "our time being trapped is now much shorter. They'll get us out of here soon." He let his shovel join the others on the ground. "I'm done with this. Someone must have pulled some strings to see why they couldn't get ahold of a loved one, and I could kiss whoever that important person is." He whooped and waved.

The chopper hovered high enough that the wind from the blades was cold, but not overpowering. A line with a large box attached dropped from the open door, and Grant Paulson hurried toward it. He guided it to the ground and opened it. Pulled out an item. "A satellite phone!"

More cheers. The chopper pulled away, the decibels lowering significantly, and the phone rang. Grant answered. "Boy, are we glad to see you guys."

Maya hurried to his side. "Tell them we have a cardiac patient who needs to be airlifted to the nearest hospital ASAP."

He passed on the message. Listened for a moment, then nodded. "They'll have a team here ASAP."

Renewed hope was a wonderful thing. "Please tell me there are medical supplies in that box," Maya said.

He asked and received confirmation, then said, "Basic supplies. First aid kit, splints, tourniquets, pressure bandages, thermal blankets, and some oxygen supplies." He paused. "Over-the-counter pain relievers, insulin, inhalers, and some heart meds."

"Excellent. Heart meds." She could only pray they were the right ones. "If someone can get this down to the clinic, I'll help get it sorted." Gideon and Vance stood there listening and she smiled. "We won't need the tunnels after all."

"Tunnels?" Vance asked.

"Long story, buddy," Gideon said. "You grab one end of the box and I'll get the other. We'll walk Maya over to the tent and let her get started with all of this and then I'll explain."

"Sure." Vance snagged his end and Gideon grabbed his.

With the box between them, they started walking. Maya broke into a light jog with Lila next to her. She heard Grant's voice behind them. "Go enjoy the rest of the time with your families. We'll be out of here soon!"

Another cheer went up, and Maya looked back to see the workers dispersing.

Inside the medical clinic, it didn't take long to get the medical supplies sorted, and Maya gave Mr. Webb one of the meds she'd requested. She patted him on the shoulder, his pale face and shallow breathing a concern. "Glad to see you're back with us. You're headed to the hospital as soon as we can get you there. The next helicopter you hear will be your ride."

"I can't thank you and Dr. Del and the others enough for all you've done for me."

"You're very welcome. Just take care of yourself."

They left, and Maya yawned. Gideon smiled. "I think you need an early night."

"I'm all right. Dinner and a movie sound good, though. You up for some *Pride and Prejudice*? I might have brought the DVD with me, and there's a DVD player in the room." At his raised brow, she shrugged. "Call me old fashioned." He grimaced and she laughed. "Come on, you know you secretly love that movie."

"I can assure you that while I might like it, I do not secretly love it."

"You watched it with me several times when we were younger."

His features softened. "And, trust me, you're the only person I'll ever watch it with."

Okay, she might have just fallen all the way in love with him at that very moment. Hoping to keep her feelings hidden, she linked her arm through his, then studied his face. Mirth now danced in his eyes. "Wait a minute. What?"

He raised a brow. "What?"

"Oh no. You're not innocent. What are you thinking?"

"Have you ever actually made it to the end of that movie when you've watched it at night?"

She blinked. Had she? Saturday or Sunday afternoons? Yes. Nights? "Um . . ."

"Exactly. I won't have to watch much."

Gideon would have watched the whole movie if that's what she wanted, but like he figured, she'd dozed off about an hour into it. This was a different version than the one they'd grown up with and he liked it. A lot. Not that he'd tell her that.

Or maybe one day he'd come clean. Assuming they were still hanging out in the future.

They'd gotten a later start on the movie as they'd waited around until she could help get Mr. Webb into the chopper. Thankfully, a cardiologist had volunteered to do a ride-along, and they could all breathe a little easier knowing Mr. Webb was in good hands and on his way to the nearest hospital with an expert at his side.

She'd fallen asleep with her feet on the coffee table, her head tilted toward him. She'd attempted to stay awake, but he finally pulled her to him to rest her head on his shoulder. At that point, she'd given in and fallen into slumber. The blanket she'd pulled from the back of the couch was tucked under her chin, and he decided she fit just right snuggled up under his arm. He grimaced. The arm that had been in one position too long.

He hated to move, but the cramp had him shifting, pulling her closer to settle her more comfortably for them both. Holding her was like nothing he'd ever experienced before, and it was something he could certainly get used to. The peaceful look on her face had him vowing to stay put as long as she needed him to—in spite of the fact that his arm was once again going to sleep. Minutes ticked past and he found himself drifting off.

He forced his eyes open. He couldn't afford to sleep while someone was after her.

Thankfully, it was only a few minutes before Maya stirred and rubbed her eyes, then looked at the television and laughed. "Okay, you were right."

"Yep. I had no doubts."

She wrinkled her nose at him. "Modest too."

He found himself contemplating kissing her. Her lips were turned up at just the perfect angle. All he had to do was—

A knock on the door startled him, and he pulled his arm from around her, gasping when the blood started flowing again.

"Your arm was asleep, wasn't it?"

"Just a little. It was worth it." He winked and her eyes widened, a flush creeping up from the base of her neck and into her cheeks. The feeling was back in his arm. It was the feeling in his heart that he'd have to figure out what he was going to do with. He made his way to the door. "Who is it?"

"Lila."

He opened the door. "Hey."

"Just wanted to let you know that someone else is taking a shift watching out for Maya tonight." She pointed. "He's parked right there and will be there for four hours, then another officer will take his place."

"Okay, thanks for everything. You've been great."

"It's been fun. In a weird sort of way." Her eyes widened. "Not that I would wish someone threatening Maya's life, of course. Just that the change of pace was, um . . . nice . . . and okay, I'm done now since my words aren't cooperating."

He laughed. "I knew what you meant."

"Thank goodness."

He rubbed his chin. "Do you think I should stay here with her?"

"I don't know. I was going to do that, but she said with all the security, it wasn't necessary." She frowned. "I think she was just worried about putting me out. It wouldn't be an inconvenience, but if you'd rather stay, I understand."

"I know you have to work in the morning. I'll take care of it."

"All right, y'all have a good night."

She left and he shut the door, then walked into the kitchen to find Maya cleaning up the remains of their dinner. "Need any help?"

"No, it's mostly just dumping stuff in the trash." When she was done, she leaned against the counter. "I know you're probably ready to head back to your own cabin, but can I ask you something?"

"I thought I'd stay on the couch if you're okay with that. And sure, you can ask."

"You can stay if you think you need to."

"I think I need to. I'll get more sleep here."

"That's fine. I'll probably sleep better with you here too. So, now that we've got that settled, I'll ask my question. You said you had stuff to work through here, that you came here to think."

"Yes." He frowned.

"I don't think you've had much time to do that."

"No, not really."

"So, what are you thinking about?"

"About my next steps in life."

"Like?"

He sighed, trying to figure out how much to tell her. Part of him wanted to lay it all out there, bare his soul, and take a chance she wouldn't push him out the door, but . . .

He sat on the barstool facing her, the counter between them. "I've made some not-so-great choices since we last saw each other, and it's . . . embarrassing." To say the least. "And while I always want to do the right thing, sometimes it's hard to know what that is."

"We all make mistakes in life, Gideon, it's how we learn. Although, we can only hope and pray those mistakes don't have tragic or deadly consequences. But we still learn."

"Oh, I learned, all right."

"Then that's all that matters, right?"

No, not really.

"What were some of your mistakes?" she asked. "Sometimes sharing them makes the burden lighter, remember?"

"I don't think that's going to work in this case."

"Won't know until you try."

They were so close to being able to leave the resort he could almost taste it. But until they could, she still needed protection. Just because the guy hadn't struck in a while didn't mean he wouldn't. In fact, Gideon had a bad feeling the person was gearing up for something big. And that made his nerves twitch. "All right, but before I go into that, have you come up with anyone who might be after you? Someone you made mad once you got here?"

"No. I'm drawing a complete blank. I really don't think Ben could be behind all of this, and he's the only one who expressed any interest in getting to know me as more than a friend."

"But it could be him."

"I mean, it could be anyone. I just don't think it is."

Just because she didn't think so, didn't make it so.

"Could someone have followed you here?"

She sighed. "Sure. I guess so. But I never noticed anyone. Then again, I wasn't looking either." She rubbed a hand over her eyes. "I'll keep thinking about it. Tell me some of your mistakes."

Ugh. He'd hoped she'd let that go. He should have known better. "After Jacob's death and my mom's descent into depression, I just wanted out. Nothing was going to keep me from doing what I wanted to do, and that was go into the army and serve my country. Make my own way in life and not play second fiddle to the brother who was now elevated to a status I'd never be able to compete with."

"Oh, man, Gideon. I'm so sorry you felt that way."

He shrugged. "I know now my parents never intentionally set out to put that burden on me, but at the time . . . yeah. That's what it felt like. Anyway, I left, did my stint in the military, and realized I wanted more. I love the military, but I also love construction—anything and everything about it—and decided I wanted to have my own company."

"Right. I remember Mom and Dad talking about it and how successful it was."

"*Was* being the operative word."

"What do you mean?"

"It means, I didn't cross all my t's and dot all my i's before I went into business with some people, and as a result, I . . ."

"You what?"

He swallowed the sudden lump in his throat. "I lost everything." There. He said it.

"You indicated that before, but you must have kept those cards close to your chest, because I've not heard even a hint of anything negative about your business."

"Former business, remember. It's not mine anymore." He sighed and raked a hand over his head. "The new owner kept the name."

"Well, if the new owner kept the name, it doesn't sound like all was lost. So why sell it?"

He grimaced. "Mostly because it was related to a bunch of bad memories, and I wanted it gone. I needed a fresh start. That's why I came here. To think. And to pray, even though sometimes I feel like God is far away. And to just figure out what I'm supposed to do next."

"So when I mentioned contracting with you and your business to help with the ranch stuff, that's why you—"

"Stormed off like a petulant child? Yes."

"I'm sorry, Gideon."

"It's okay. Surprisingly, aside from that little moment, I've been more at peace since being trapped in this place than I have in a long time. I don't know what my future holds, but I'm not stressing over it like I was."

"I'd say that's progress."

"Well, I've been a little distracted, but that's all right." He pulled in a deep breath. "I've been avoiding going home because—" What was he *doing*?

"Because?"

"I . . ." He shook his head and sighed. "Never mind. I'm sorry, Maya, I should be keeping my distance, not allowing my attraction to fog my mind."

She blinked. "Your attraction . . . for me?"

He huffed a soft laugh. "Yeah. Surely you noticed."

"I noticed. Surely you noticed it's reciprocated."

"Uh . . ."

"No?"

"I mean, I hoped, but . . ." He grimaced. "Sorry. I'm sending all kinds of mixed signals, aren't I?"

"It's okay. But don't feel bad for not noticing. I got pretty good at hiding my feelings while I was deployed."

"You felt like you should hide them from me?"

"No . . . I mean, yes. I don't know. Maybe."

"Thank you for being so clear on that."

She gave his hand a light punch and sighed. "And, no, I'm the mixed-signal sender. I like you, Gideon. I always have. You were special to me when I was growing up, and even that last trip here before we joined the army, it was all I could do to keep from telling you I was madly in love with you."

Her words sucker punched him. "What? No way."

"Way. Seriously."

"I never knew."

"So maybe I learned to hide my feelings long before the army." She waved a hand. "It doesn't matter. We've both obviously got some things going on that we'd rather not talk about. It's okay. Maybe one day we'll be able to."

He was such a coward. "I'm sorry, Maya, it's not that I don't trust you—"

"But you don't. And that's okay. We've only just reconnected, so it's not something I'll hold against you. I think I'm just lonely. And while it's nothing to be ashamed of, for some reason, I blame myself for that."

"Wait. Why?"

"I lost my best friend, Laura. She and I were surgeons together in Afghanistan. One evening, we got called out to a nearby village. There'd been some fighting and the wounded couldn't be transported. We went and did our best. Two of the six died." She rubbed her eyes, and Gideon almost told her to stop talking, but before he could, she went on. "We were almost back to base when insurgents attacked. It was fast and brutal. Laura and I were in the same vehicle when an IED exploded. Our ride flipped and rolled, and I was thrown out. Gunfire erupted from every direction. Our escorts fought back, and when it was finally over, Laura was . . .

critically injured." Her voice had fallen to a whisper, and Gideon had to strain to hear. "Anyway, shockingly enough, I had no injuries other than the breath knocked out of me. I managed to get to Laura, and she was—she was . . ."

He wanted to stop her, to hold her, tell her that time would heal, but he didn't dare move. She'd chosen to tell him and he'd let her. "I'm so sorry." He said the words so soft that he wasn't sure she heard him.

"I did my best, of course, but all the training in the world wouldn't have been enough to save her. So I held her and lied to her. Told her she was going to be fine, and she smiled at me." Her gaze met his. "She smiled and reassured *me*. Said she would be just fine, and everything was going to be okay. I held her and prayed over her as bullets flew all around us. And then she took her last breath."

"Maya . . ." he whispered.

"So that's what I dream about. I dream about not being able to save the ones I love. About failing. About not living the kind of life I should, having been spared to return home." She swallowed hard. "I just want my life to mean something. And I want it to mean that I did everything I could to help other people."

Her words punched him. Hard. For a moment he couldn't breathe. He could only feel the impact.

"It's better now," she said, "but sometimes, something will trigger that day, and I . . . well, it's bad."

"PTSD."

"Yes. The memories are bad enough, but the full-blown episodes are . . . hard."

"I know."

She met his gaze. "I know you do."

NINE

MAYA LAY IN BED early the next morning, staring at the ceiling, thinking about the conversation from last night. She needed to get up and head over to the clinic, but for a moment, she just wanted to savor waking up and knowing Gideon was in the same space. After she'd confided in him, she kissed his cheek. "I'm going to sleep. Make yourself comfortable."

He nodded, and she'd shut the door to give him some privacy. Time to think. After all, that was why he was here. She hoped he was finished thinking and had concluded she was a safe confidante. She finally got up, took her shower, and put herself together. She could hear Gideon in the kitchen and smelled the blessed scent of fresh coffee.

She walked out of the bedroom and watched him for a moment until he noticed her. Would today be the day that he returned the trust? Told her the parts of his story that he'd left out?

He looked up and met her gaze with a smile. "Good morning."

"Morning. Sleep okay?" she asked.

"Like a baby."

She snorted. "That's not saying much. Some babies don't sleep."

"Well, I slept like one who does. No nightmares, so that's saying something. You?"

"Same. Which is kind of weird, but I'll take it as a gift."

He passed her a cup of coffee, and she took that first sip that always started her day right.

"You think we'll get out of here today?" she asked.

"It's possible, I suppose, but it'll take a while to get the big machines up here to dig us out, so I'd say it's more probable sometime tomorrow."

"That's fine. I'm not really worried about it except for the person trying to kill me."

A sound from the French doors in the den jerked his head up. "Get down," he said. "Right there, behind the counter. Be prepared to run out the front door straight to the officer who's waiting."

She froze for a second, then dropped as he'd ordered. He bolted to the light switch on the wall and plunged them into darkness. She peered around the edge of the cabinet while he made his way over to the doors and stood to the side. He'd automatically reached for the weapon he no longer carried, so once again he snagged the fireplace poker and gripped it while she strangled on the breath in her throat and searched for a weapon.

Maya rose, grabbed the biggest knife from the block, and gripped it. She'd trained with knives, and while bringing a knife to what might be a gun fight wasn't the ideal scenario, she'd take what she could get.

Gideon pushed aside the curtain, and she waited while he scanned the area. "Nothing on the porch," he said, voice low. "An overturned chair." He unlocked the dead bolt and opened the door, leaving the light off. "No snow on the deck, so no prints."

"They clean it off every morning," she murmured, walking up behind him, still gripping the knife. They also scraped the walking path that led to the front of the cabin, so someone could technically come up on the porch and not leave any sign they were there. "Could have been a raccoon or another critter. They're all over the place here."

"I know, but I don't like it. And there's no evidence of a critter in the snow."

"I think we're just jumpy." She stood, working hard to keep her paranoia at bay. "Could have been the wind too."

"Maybe." He motioned her back, and she walked over to the sofa to drop onto it while he stayed by the door. Over the next several minutes, he peered out. While they waited, she picked up her phone and started to text her cousin, Collin, the FBI agent relative who could possibly help with this whole situation, only to remember she couldn't.

She plugged her phone in and paced to the kitchen to return the knife to the block, then back to the fireplace to flip on the gas logs. She was freezing.

Gideon turned from his vigil. "I'm going to step outside to talk to the officer. See if he saw anything or anyone. Stay put, keep the doors locked, and I'll be right back."

She nodded, and he slipped out the front door. A shiver shuddered through her, and she checked the thermostat, then grabbed the fleece blanket from the couch to wrap around her.

A knock on the French door stilled her. She stood for a moment, debating whether to answer, but what criminal knocks?

Maya walked to the door and pushed aside the curtain to peer out—much like Gideon had done just a few minutes before.

Vance Harland stood on the deck. She unlocked the door and cracked it. "Vance? What's going on?"

"Sorry to bother you, but it's Ellie. She's taken a turn for the worse, and I want you to take a look at her whether she likes it or not."

"Oh. Okay. Of course." She stepped back. "Come on in for a minute."

"No, I told Ellie I wouldn't be long. Can you come now? I'm really worried about her." His gloved hands twisted together, then he shoved them into his coat pockets.

"Sure. Let me just grab my coat and tell Gideon, and I'll walk over there with you."

"I'll have one of the kids take Gideon a message where you

are. I don't want to take the time to talk to him. Ellie's in so much pain."

"Vance, it will only take a second. Gideon's just out the front door."

He practically bounced on his toes. "Just leave him a note, then."

"Vance . . ."

"*Please*, Maya. She's really bad!"

Something was going on with him. It might be better to just roll with him than try to deviate from whatever he had in his head.

Maya threw off the blanket, grabbed her coat and gloves and a pen and paper. While Vance hovered, she jotted the message and put it on the table, then got her gloves from the end table in her bedroom. She walked to the front door. She was about to open it when she looked back to see Vance heading toward the French doors. "Where are you going?" she asked.

"It's faster to cut through this way. My cabin's a few doors up from yours. One past Gideon's, as a matter of fact."

"Oh. Right." It *would* be faster than going out the front and backtracking to the path that led from her little back porch. "After you."

He led the way out, and she shut the doors behind her. "Tell me her symptoms."

"She started throwing up and is pretty miserable. She also said she was dizzy and seeing double. And she's slurring her words some." He swallowed hard. "I . . . I think she might be having a stroke or . . . or something."

Maya stopped walking. "Okay, I'm going to need some things from the clinic. I'll have to go there first."

"No, no way. She—she needs you now. I'll get whatever you need and bring it to you. Go in the back door. It's unlocked." He pulled out his phone and handed it to her. "Type what you need into the notes app."

She did so, then Vance headed down the hill while Maya hurried toward Vance and Ellie's cabin. She hated leaving without talking to Gideon in light of everything but prayed he'd get the note and understand. As well as show up.

It didn't take her long to find the right place, and she walked up the back porch steps identical to her own to knock on the French doors.

No response. She twisted the knob and stepped inside. "Ellie? It's Maya. Vance came to get me. He said you were feeling miserable." She paused. "Ellie?"

Still nothing. Maya made her way to the bedroom and stopped. Ellie stood next to the bed, dressed in winter clothes, a hat, scarf, boots, and gloves. The woman lifted her right hand and pointed a gun at Maya's chest. "Thanks for coming."

Gideon tapped the hood of security's SUV and straightened. "Thanks again for keeping an eye on the place and her. I'm planning to hang around too."

"I'm here if you need me," the man said.

Gideon let his gaze roam the area before he turned to head back toward Maya's cabin.

"Hey, Gideon, right?"

Ben approached on the walkway from the back, and Gideon waited, his guard going up because the man just rubbed him the wrong way. "Yes. Help you?"

Ben shoved his gloved hands in his coat pockets and tilted his head. "I'm glad I ran into you."

Gideon remained quiet.

"Right, so anyway," Ben said, "you might have noticed that I was interested in Maya."

"I noticed."

"But she's not one bit interested in me." A small smile curved the man's lips, and Gideon relaxed a fraction.

"I don't know anything about that," Gideon said, then decided not to play. "Okay, you're right. She's not."

Ben's eyes widened, then he laughed. A true chuckle full of good humor. "I can take a hint," he finally said, "but now I won't have to. Thanks for being blunt."

Gideon's neck went hot. "I'm sorry. Sometimes I need to find my filters before I speak. I really didn't mean to be rude."

"It's fine. For real." Ben's eyes clouded slightly. "I'm not sure I'm ready to start dating again anyway. I think I was looking for more of a distraction than an actual romance—and she's an interesting woman." He waved a hand. "But you don't care about that." He shrugged. "Can you just let her know that I won't bother her anymore?"

Okay, now his conscience kicked in. "She never considered you a bother."

"Maybe not, but I have a feeling she's also too polite to say so." He smiled, and Gideon decided he could like the guy now that he wasn't going to be chasing after Maya.

"She might be, but honestly, she's been dealing with other stuff, so I don't think you should take it too personally."

"I don't. And she might be dealing with other stuff, but she also only has eyes for you, so it's all good."

The flush attacked Gideon's neck again. "Dude . . ."

"I'm just saying."

"Well, two can play that game. Seems Lila might have a thing for you."

Ben raised a brow, but a knowing glint sparked in his gaze. "She's a lovely woman."

"She is."

"All right, I'll stay out of your love life if you stay out of mine."

Gideon laughed. "Deal."

The man continued his trek down toward the lodge, and Gideon shook his head. In another time and place, he and Ben might become friends. But for now, he itched to get back to watching over Maya.

He walked up the steps to the front door and knocked. "Hey, it's me."

Nothing.

He tried again. "Maya? Can you open the door?"

Still nothing.

A spot between his shoulders tingled. He walked around the side of the cabin to the back. He tried the knob. The French doors were locked.

He knocked. "Maya! Hey, come on, don't play!"

Even as he said the words, he knew she wouldn't do that. He raced back to the cruiser.

The officer saw him coming and rolled the window down. "What's wrong?"

"Nothing. I hope. But Maya's not coming to the door. Can you let me in?"

"Yeah, sure." He climbed out and unlocked the front door.

Gideon pushed inside. "Maya?" It didn't take long to search the small space and come up empty.

The officer stood in the kitchen with his hands on his hips. "She didn't come out the front. She had to go out the back."

"But why?" He raked a hand over his head. "And why do so without telling me?" He looked around, saw nothing out of place, and his heart settled somewhat. He checked her closet and found her coat gone. He went back to the kitchen. "Her hat and gloves are gone."

"She left," the officer said. "It's the only explanation."

"You're right, but she would have said something. Why go out the back and not the front where she knew we were?" He ran a hand down his cheek. "This doesn't make sense."

"Maybe someone came and got her?"

"But she wouldn't have left without telling me!" He paused. "Unless it was some kind of major medical emergency." He eyed the officer. "I'm going to check the clinic. You mind staying here in case she comes back?"

"No, I don't mind at all. This is where I'm supposed to be

anyway, but can you at least come back and let me know if you found her?"

"Of course." He sighed. "Or I'll be back to get your help looking for her."

He slammed out the front door and headed down the hill.

TEN

MAYA STUMBLED UP the hill, guided by the woman pressing the gun into her back. "Where are we going?"

"Just walk."

She'd been walking.

First out of the cabin with a very healthy Ellie Harland and then into the tree line where they were hidden from any prying eyes. Self-defense moves came to mind, but the woman's finger had been on the trigger the last time Maya had been able to see the weapon. Doing something to cause her finger to twitch didn't seem like a smart idea. So she played along while doing her best to keep her heart rate under control and her panic from flaring.

She'd survived a combat zone. She'd survived losing her best friend. She'd figure out how to survive this. *Please, God, don't let her kill me. And thank you that it's not snowing.*

She rubbed her bare neck and could only pray someone found the necklace and came looking for her. The resort was big, but there weren't that many hiding places. Places where someone could commit murder without screams being heard. And she planned to scream should it come down to it. Gideon should have noticed she was gone by now and would be looking for her. He'd find Vance and demand to know where she was.

"How does Vance fit into all of this?" Maya asked. "He was

so convincing and worried about you. Does he know what you're doing?"

"Of course he knows. We're in this together. He was supposed to grab you the first day we were here but wimped out and had a *stupid* episode over some *stupid* limbs falling." The disgust for her husband rang loud and clear. "He's such a loser."

"Then why stay with him?"

"Because he has money. And with your help, he's going to have more."

"I don't understand. If you're going to kill me, could I please know why?"

The gun dug into her right kidney and Maya winced. "Follow that little path to your right."

Maya did so. "Where—"

"Shut up and just keep walking. You want to know why you have to die? Because Vance comes from a long line of idiots. Men who'd rather gamble their savings and land away rather than take care of their families. Thankfully, his grandmother knew this about her husband and worked around his gambling and wicked ways after he lost the land. She rebuilt their fortune through investments and wise business practices, never letting on she had done so. But she left that money to Vance's mother with a note about how your grandfather took advantage of Vance's grandfather in the poker game."

The light was beginning to come on. "My grandparents' land, the land my grandfather left to me, used to belong to Vance's grandfather."

"It did. And as soon as you write your note of regret, how you learned the land belonged to Vance's grandfather before your thieving grandfather cheated him out of it in the poker game and you have to do the right thing in turning the land back over to Vance . . . Do that, then all will be well."

All would be well for whom? Not Maya, that was for sure. "Even if that would stand up in court," she said, "my grandmother is still alive. She'll never believe that. She and I have had too many conversations about that land and what my grandfather wanted for it."

"I know. Too bad she'll soon die of a broken heart after hearing of your demise at the resort. She'll never know about the letter or that you signed the bill of sale over to Vance."

Chills and panic skittered up Maya's spine. No. This couldn't be happening. "Ellie, my grandfather went to Vance's grandfather—what was his name? Charlie?"

"Yes."

"My grandfather paid Charlie for the land."

"No, he didn't."

"Yes, he really did. I have the receipts, the deed, everything. My grandfather felt horrible about the way he got the land and did his best to make it right."

The woman fell silent. "I don't believe you. Vance told me everything his grandmother told him. Lying won't get you out of this."

"His grandmother was the one lying if she said any different."

"Shut up and stop here."

Maya stopped. "Why have we stopped? Where are we?"

"This wasn't the original plan, but it will have to do for the moment. This is a place for you to hang out and sign the bill of sale I've had drafted."

The gun shoved against her back and Maya stumbled forward. Caught her balance just before she fell into a hole in the ground. She turned. "Ellie—"

"Go down. Now. Walk and remain unhurt or I'll shove you. Your choice."

Maya started down the stone steps backward, keeping her eyes on Ellie. She wouldn't let the woman shoot her in the back. Then again, Ellie still needed her alive. Her right foot slipped midway down, and she landed hard with a pained cry, then rolled to the bottom with a hard thud.

The air left her lungs, and she lay still while she struggled to catch a breath. Finally, she dragged in a ragged one. Now . . . what hurt?

She moved and her knee ached, but after another moment she decided it was just bruised, not broken. And the shoulder she'd injured with her jump from the snowmobile probably had another bruise or two added to it. Other than that, she seemed to be in one piece. She looked up to see Ellie's emotionless face staring down at her from six feet up. Maya stayed put since the woman still aimed the weapon at her.

"Think about your situation," Ellie said. "I have to get back to the cabin before someone realizes I'm missing. I'm sure Gideon has raised the alarm about your disappearance by now. No doubt he'll be knocking on my door asking if you've been by."

"I left a note telling him I was going with Vance to check on you."

A rustling sound reached her and then Ellie held up a piece of paper. "This note? Yeah, we don't need any connection between your disappearance and Vance or me."

So Vance had grabbed it on his way out. But when had he gotten it to Ellie? There'd been no time—

Unless he was up there now and had followed them from the cabin.

"Vance? Are you up there? Vance! You can't be okay with this!"

"Shut up," Ellie snapped.

Maya wanted to bang her head on the ground and wail out her frustration. Instead, she said, "I don't understand. If you need me alive, why try to kill me?"

Ellie's frown deepened. "What are you talking about?"

"By sabotaging my snowmobile and trying to push me into the firepit, for starters."

"I never did that. Vance was just supposed to grab you and bring you here."

"But—"

"But nothing. I've got to go." She tossed the paper down. It fluttered to settle at Maya's feet. She set a flashlight on the top step and started to close the hole covering and paused. "Here's one last thought for you. If you refuse to do as I ask, I'll kill Gideon. Do it, and he'll be fine. I won't touch him."

The door shut and Maya was surrounded by blackness.

She stayed completely still while a bone-deep chill crept through her. A cold not just from the weather but from the betrayal—and fear. Thankful she'd grabbed her winter gear before venturing out on what was supposed to be a mission of care for a friend, she tamped down the desire to have a full-blown panic attack and continued to focus her thoughts on escape. That meant moving, and now that the adrenaline was ebbing, aches and pains were popping up all over her poor body. But standing there looking up at a door that wasn't going to open anytime soon wasn't going to get the job done.

"Okay," she whispered to the darkness, "think. Think. You're in a hole underneath the ground. But there are tunnels around here, remember? So . . . no need to lose it just yet. Time to explore. You're going to find a way out. You have to. And there's a flashlight on the top step. Get it and you'll be fine."

A breeze whipped around her and she shivered. Then froze. If there was a breeze, there was an opening. Right?

Right.

She pulled in a ragged breath and said a short prayer for help. Then decided to keep praying while she looked for a way out. Or rather *felt* her way up the steps to retrieve the light.

Because it was dark in here.

The least the woman could have done was turn the thing on.

The darkness was going to suffocate her. Steal the breath right from her lungs.

"Don't panic," she said aloud. "No need to panic. These tunnels have been here for years. They'll be here for a long time. They have to go somewhere." She closed her eyes and pulled in another breath. Tried to take a step and couldn't make her legs move.

Terror held her captive. Her lungs squeezed. Even knowing there was light not too far away couldn't compel her to move.

Please, God, help me keep it together. And help me find a way out. I don't want my life to end like this. I have too much to do. Too many people to help. And I think I love Gideon. I think I always have. Give me the opportunity to get past my fears and tell him how I feel.

Somehow that now morphed into the motivation to conquer her fear of being trapped in a cold, dark place.

She had to escape and get to Gideon so she could tell him she loved him.

With her hand on the wall to guide her, Maya took a step. Then another. It would be slow going, but at least she was moving. She found the steps she'd fallen down and climbed one at a time. And finally, her fingers wrapped around the flashlight. She pushed the button and the beam lit up the area. There was a pen on the top step. She grabbed it and stuck it in her coat pocket. Then used the flashlight to guide herself back down, where she grabbed the paper and pushed it into her pocket. She'd need it for evidence for when she got out.

And then the light weakened, bit by bit until it was gone and she was in the dark once more. "No! Don't do that! No." She shook the flashlight, clicked the button on and off, but got nothing. "I can't sign your stupid paper if I can't see it, you—"

She closed her eyes and bit her lip, then shoved the flashlight into another pocket. Wasting her breath yelling at someone who couldn't hear her—and wouldn't care if she could—wasn't going to help anyone. Fine. On to plan B. She turned until she faced the moving air and shoved her hand out to the side to place her palm on the nearest rock wall.

Gideon had searched the clinic, the lodge, and the restaurant. And still no sign of Maya. No one had seen her. He stood outside the lodge, feet planted on the snow-covered deck while the flames danced in the firepit. Lila approached. She'd come as soon as she'd heard Maya was missing via paid teenage messenger.

"I need a phone," Gideon said, his voice practically a growl. "We all need phones."

"They're still working as fast as possible to restore service," she said. "The sat phone is in the medical clinic in case they have to call a chopper for another patient."

"We need to call for more sat phones to be dropped so we can stay in touch while we search."

"That's going to take a while."

"I know. I'm not going to stop searching, but we need to at least put the request in."

She nodded. "All right. I'll run over to the clinic and make the call. Where are you going to search from here?"

"Everything all right?" Ben's question came from behind him.

Gideon turned. "No, Maya's missing."

"Missing? Missing how?"

"Meaning we can't find her, and we suspect someone took her," Lila said. "I'm going to put in the request for those sat phones." She hurried off.

Ben frowned at Gideon. "Maya looked fine to me when I saw her talking to that Vance guy outside her cabin a little while ago."

"Out back?"

"Yeah."

"Did she go back in?"

"No, she went up the hill, and I didn't see where Vance went, but he went in the opposite direction.."

Relief nearly unsettled him. "Okay, he probably came to get her to help Ellie. Thanks, man."

"Anything I can do to help?"

"Yeah, go after Lila and let her know I'm heading up to Vance's cabin."

"Sure thing." The man hurried in the direction Lila had gone, and Gideon hesitated.

Two officers sat in a cruiser in their designated parking spot just outside the lodge. He walked over and the driver rolled his window down. "Hey, I'm looking for Dr. Maya Sullivan. Have you heard the history of everything going on with her?"

"We have. Just got word she went missing. Need help?"

"Yeah. I'll take all the help I can get. Can you take me to cabin 42? She may be there helping a friend. I just want to verify it."

"Hop in."

Gideon slid in the back seat.

They arrived much faster to cabin 42 than if he'd tried to hoof it. "Thanks."

"Want us to wait here?"

"That'd be great. Thanks. Hopefully, this won't take long."

Gideon scrambled out of the cruiser and hurried to the front door. He knocked. "Ellie? Vance? It's Gideon." He knocked again. "Ellie?"

The door opened and Ellie stood there in her bathrobe, hand shading her squinted eyes. The woman looked horrible.

"Gideon? What is it?"

"I'm so sorry to bother you, but did Maya come by here?"

"Um, yeah. She did. She just left a few minutes ago. Why?"

His heart rate settled a bit. "Okay, thanks. Did she say where she was going when she finished here?"

"No. She didn't. Um, Gideon, my head is a little better, but I need to lay down." She swayed, then leaned against the wall.

"Of course." He stepped inside and grasped her arm. "Let me help you."

"Um . . . thank you. The couch is fine."

He helped her to the sofa, and she pulled the blanket off the back to wrap it around her shoulders. He looked around. Their cabin was about twice the size of his. "Is Vance here? Someone said they saw him talking to Maya just before she came up to your cabin. I want to ask him if she said anything about where she was going."

"No, he's not here. I'm not sure where he is." Her eyes fluttered and closed, then opened. "I'm sorry. It's the drugs."

"I know. It's okay. I'm going to go now. Feel better."

"Thank you," she whispered.

He turned to head to the door when something winked at him from the floor next to the French doors. He walked over and picked it up, then caught his breath.

A gold cross with a broken chain. And a bent fastener. Like it had been jerked off her neck, not simply come undone.

He turned to face Ellie. And found himself staring down the barrel of a gun. Once the zap of shock faded, he blinked. "You deserve an Oscar."

She smiled. A tight, hard smile that didn't reach her cold blue eyes. "I sure do."

"But why?"

"I've already explained all that to Maya. I'm not going into it again."

"Where is she?"

"Safe for the moment."

"Why should I believe you?"

"I'll take you to her if you like."

"I like."

"Then don't try any funny stuff or she'll die. I won't have to do a thing but just leave her where she is and she'll die. Understood?"

"Understood. One question."

"Just one?"

"At the moment. Why break into her cabin? What were you looking for?"

"Vance saw her working on something at the café. She had papers and the laptop. He thought she'd sold the ranch. I told him no way, but he insisted she had. I told him to find the proof." She rolled her eyes. "And then he had a conversation with her and learned what she was really doing and proved me right. So enough small talk. It's time to go."

She stepped away from him and set the weapon next to her but out of his reach while she shrugged into her coat and gloves. If he moved, she could easily beat him to the gun. Once she was dressed, he allowed her to prod him out the French doors and into the woods behind her cabin.

He could take her down. He had the skills, even with her holding a weapon on him, but he had to know where Maya was. Assuming Ellie was telling the truth about taking him to Maya. But she hadn't put a bullet in him yet. "Does Vance know about all of this?"

"Of course."

"What do you have against Maya? Why do you want her dead?"

"Move."

He moved. "Where's Vance?"

"Don't worry about Vance. He's doing as I've instructed."

Which meant Vance knew where Maya was? So, if he disarmed Ellie, he could find Vance and get him to talk. But what if he wouldn't? Or what if Ellie was lying?

Gideon kept his mouth shut and kept walking. The dense trees closed in around him and the undergrowth snagged at his jeans. Where in the world was she taking—

"Stop."

He stopped and turned to face her. "What now?"

"Open that door." She gestured with the gun, and he almost acted to take it from her, but she had it back up and pointed at him so fast he blinked.

"What . . . ?" He looked down, and it only took him a split second to spot the black handle poking up out of the previously disturbed snow. He leaned over, grasped the handle, twisted it out of the iron hook, and pulled. The door creaked open.

"In you go."

"This is one of the tunnels?"

"It is."

"But where does it lead?"

She smirked. "Nowhere. Now, you can walk down those steps under your own power, or I can shoot you and let you fall in."

In a smooth move, he knocked the weapon from her hand. The gun landed on the snow-covered ground, disappearing in a powdery puff. Ellie screeched and lunged for it, but he caught her arm and threw her to the ground. It didn't take much to subdue her and get her arms behind her with a knee in her lower back. She wiggled and coughed. "Let me up!"

"Not until you tell me where Maya is."

"Let her go!" Vance's shout from the tree line froze him for a split second, then he stood and jerked Ellie to her feet.

She tried to yank away from him and he shook her. "Be still!"

She kicked back and got him in the shin. Pain radiated through his leg and he squeezed her wrists. She shrieked and bucked like a rodeo bronco.

"I said let her go or I'll shoot you!" Vance shouted.

"I'm not letting her go until she tells me where Maya is. Or you do." Gideon kept his voice low and even. "How can you do this, Vance? We were friends!"

"Friendship doesn't make up for what her family did to mine!"

"Says who? Your parents and Maya's were friends!"

"Until my father found out the truth. He found my grandmother's old diary and she outlined exactly how Maya's grandfather stole our land!"

"Vance, shut up, you useless idiot! Make him let me go!" Ellie's raging screech echoed around them, and Vance flinched as though she'd slapped him.

Vance gripped his weapon, complete with a suppressor, and punched it toward Gideon. "Now, Gideon. And I'll tell you where Maya is."

"I don't believe you. Tell me first." But Gideon wouldn't believe that either. "Is she down in that tunnel? Maybe we should all go down and take a look."

Ellie set off on another frenzy of kicking and squirming. "Shoot him, Vance! Don't just stand there! Shoot him!"

"I can't! I might hit you!"

"Shoot him, you worthless loser! Now!"

Time slowed and Gideon watched Vance's eyes narrow, his lips tighten, and his finger twitch.

Gideon dropped.

The gun cracked.

Ellie screamed and fell to the snow, hand pressing her side. "You shot me!"

Vance raced toward her, horror on his face. He looked at her, then Gideon. And swung the weapon toward Gideon.

Gideon dove into the hole as the next bullet sailed over his head. He landed hard on the first step, then scrambled down to the bottom.

"I'm coming for you both, Gideon! After I get Ellie help, I'm coming to kill you!"

The door slammed shut.

ELEVEN

WAS THAT VANCE'S VOICE? And a little bit of reprieve from the darkness. The moments of faint light before the black descended again.

Someone had opened the door.

But why?

She froze and listened. Was it Ellie come to get what she wanted, then finish her off? Maya lifted her chin. "Whatever the case, I won't give her what she wants for sure." Because as soon as she had it, Maya was dead. And if she was to die, she'd go down fighting.

But with what? She had no weapon. Her fingers curled into fists. How could she defend herself in the dark?

Then again, it was Ellie. The woman had bested her once. Maya wouldn't give her that option again. A footfall scraped on the ground.

"Maya! Are you in here?"

She gasped. "Gideon!" She didn't dare move and risk a misstep in the dark in her desire to run to him.

"Maya?"

"Be careful. There are all kinds of rocks and debris on the floor. Ellie left me a flashlight with dead batteries."

"Keep talking, I'll come to you. I have my phone and am using the light."

As soon as he rounded the slight curve, she could see the flashlight.

When he reached her, she hugged him, crushed him to her, and listened to his heartbeat beneath her ear. "What's happening? How did you wind up here?"

"I went looking for you, found Ellie, found your necklace on the floor—"

"You did! I dropped it, hoping someone would find it and you'd realize I left it on purpose."

"When Ellie saw me find it, she knew the game was up, but she got the drop on me. Then told me she'd bring me to you, so I let her. Then Vance showed up and shot Ellie—"

"What!"

"It wasn't too bad a wound, I don't think, but he was going to get help for her. In the meantime, we need to get out of here before they come back."

Her mind reeling, Maya shoved aside all the other questions and focused. "I don't think we can push that door up."

"We can't. There's an iron hook that the handle slides in to. It would be impossible to open from this side. We're going to have to follow the tunnel and see where it leads."

"I felt a draft and was walking into it, feeling my way with the wall, but I've had to go slow so I didn't trip and fall. With your light, we can move faster."

"For as long as it lasts. I have about half a battery."

"Better than nothing."

"Let's go."

They made their way slowly, with Gideon leading the way, shoving aside debris, rocks, spiderwebs, and whatever else blocked their path. Maya held onto his belt and stepped where he stepped, grateful that he'd had the forethought to keep his phone on him. She'd left hers on the charger when she'd gotten up this morning, figuring she'd get it when she learned others finally had a signal. She hadn't even thought about needing the flashlight option. But now that she wasn't in complete darkness, the panic—while still hovering on the edges of her mind—was under control for the moment.

"Do you still feel the breeze?" she asked.

"Yeah, it's—" He stopped and she ran into his back.

He turned to steady her, catching her biceps, phone still held in his left hand. "Oops, sorry. Are you all right?"

"Yes, fine. What is it? Why'd you stop so—"

He shone the light and she gasped. "Oh. Oh no." The path was completely caved in.

Blocked.

They were trapped.

And she was going to have a full-blown panic attack if she didn't distract herself ASAP.

"What are we going to do?" she asked. "Where was the breeze coming from? We didn't pass any openings on our way here. Did we?" Her throat tightened. Her heart raced. Her palms slicked and she thought she might pass out from lack of air. "Gideon, I can't breathe." She tried sucking in more air, but there was none to be had.

Mentally, the doctor in her tried to reassure her panicked self that it was just an attack, she wasn't going to die.

But it sure felt like it.

Gideon's grip tightened. "Maya?"

"Let me sit a moment. It's just a panic attack." She tried another breath, only to have it stop somewhere above her lungs. Even knowing it wouldn't kill her didn't make her feel one bit better.

Gideon helped her to the floor of the tunnel and sat beside her, wrapping an arm around her shoulders and pulling her snug up next to him.

And finally, a full breath expanded her lungs. Her heart slowed. Gideon was here. It was going to be all right. And she needed to pull it together so they could figure a way out. "Thank you," she finally said. "It's easing. I'm okay. Let's keep going."

"You've always hated tight places."

"Dark places mostly, but small places aren't exactly at the top of my 'things to enjoy' list."

"I can relate." He stepped away, leaving her wanting to grab him back and never let go.

She curled her fingers into fists and cleared her throat. "They want my ranch, Gideon. They have papers for me to sign the land over to them and then they plan to kill Grams. I can't let that happen." Tears pricked her eyes just thinking about them being successful.

"That's what this is all about?"

"Yeah." She cleared her throat and blinked the moisture away. "Vance's grandfather lost it in that poker game." She told him everything Ellie had spilled to her, while trying not to breathe the thick air.

A faint draft whispered past them, taunting them with the promise of freedom. "Did you feel that?" she asked.

"Yeah."

"Then there's got to be another way out."

He stepped next to the wall of stone and ran his hand over it. "Okay, here's an idea. You get on the other side and do the same. Feel for the breeze."

She turned toward the opposite wall. "Just don't turn the light off."

"I'm not. Yet. Battery is going down pretty fast, though."

Her stomach clenched. She didn't need to know that. The thought of being in the dark again . . .

Yeah, she couldn't think about that. "Why didn't we feel it on our first pass?"

"I don't know. Maybe the wind stopped blowing as we walked past it. But it's here, somewhere."

They moved together through the narrow tunnel, the stone cold under her palm. She glanced at the light coming from his phone and thought it looked weaker. But dust swirled in the beam. She stopped and pointed. "Wait. Look at that."

Gideon followed her gaze. "Dust?"

"Yeah, it's being pulled toward the wall."

"Something's there." He stepped closer and pressed. "I feel the draft."

"Thank God. How big is the crack?"

"Not big, but I'm going to change that."

A distant sound echoed and Maya froze. "What was that?"

"I think someone just opened the door."

"He's coming," Maya whispered. "Or someone is."

Gideon shone the light on the ground and found one of the many heavy rocks scattered about. "Hold the light on the wall," he told Maya and passed her his phone. "This is going to make noise."

"It's either that or be stuck. See what you can do. It'll take him some time to get back here."

He slammed the rock on the crack and a big chunk of the wall fell backward.

"That sounded like a gunshot," she said. "Weird."

"Must be the acoustics in here." He held the light to examine the area. "It's thin and there's definitely space on the other side."

"Hit it again," she whispered. "I can feel the air stronger now. Hurry."

He bashed it once more, and another large section broke away. Maya slipped her gloves back on, then reached in to grip the edge and pull. Another part separated, and she tossed it to the ground. "It's almost big enough for me to slip through."

Gideon knocked out more and shone his dimming light through the opening. "It's a room with another tunnel directly across from this one."

He motioned for her to go through. She bit her lip, looked at the opening, then back at him. "You won't fit."

"I know, but you will. You may have to go and get help."

"Uh, no way. I don't know where this leads and I'm not leaving without you. Not unless I absolutely have to." She yanked at the edge once more, and while more pieces broke off, they weren't big enough to make a real difference.

Another sound echoed through the tunnel—a footstep. Then another.

Maya's frantic gaze met his. "He has a gun," she whispered. "We have no weapons. And while I'm not too shabby with hand-to-hand combat, I have a bum shoulder and I definitely can't stop a bullet."

"I know." Together, they might be able to take the man down, but he wasn't going to risk it if he didn't have to. An angry, vengeful man with a gun was too unpredictable. "Go on through," he said. "I have an idea."

"What?" She moved to the opening and slipped halfway through, then gasped.

"What is it? Too tight?"

"A little." She wiggled and grimaced.

"You're going to hurt yourself."

"Well, it's either a few scrapes or the possibility of a bullet. I know what my choice is."

She had a point.

With one last grunt, she pushed through. "I'm through and it only took part of my coat and the top layer of skin on my back. If you're going to come through, you're going to have to widen it."

He used the rock once more, his pounding once again sounding like gunshots going off, but finally he managed to add another two inches to the opening. "I think that's as good as it's going to get." He shrugged out of his bulky coat and shivered. He had on a long-sleeved T-shirt and a sweatshirt over that, but the chill still bit. She took his coat from him and he ducked his head through the opening. His shoulders scraped harder than hers had, but he gritted his teeth and pushed on through. Barely.

Pain and a warm sensation traveled down his back, and he figured he'd left a good chunk of skin. But while he was a large man, Vance had thirty pounds on him at least. There was no way he'd make it through. Not without some work to widen the area—which would buy them some time.

"You're hurt." She placed a hand on his back and he turned. She had his coat clamped under her left elbow, one glove clutched in her left hand. She held up her right, and he noted the blood on her palm and the horror in her eyes. "Lift your shirt. I need to take a look."

"It's nothing that won't heal, and like you said, it's not nearly as bad as a bullet." She nodded and he held her hand while he wiped her palm with the hem of his sweatshirt. "I'm fine," he said. "Truly." Okay, it stung like nobody's business, but it wasn't fatal. "Put your glove back on."

She did so, but the worry in her gaze deepened.

"I know you're back here!" Vance's shout echoed around them, and Maya froze.

Gideon pointed to the narrow passage leading off from the cavernous room, and she shoved his coat at him. "Put this on. You're going to need it."

He did so while she disappeared into the passageway.

Vance's footsteps drew closer still. "This place is blocked off. You can't get out. Why don't you just cooperate and this can all be over—"

Curses flowed.

He'd discovered the opening.

"Follow me," Gideon said. "Keep your hand on my belt, and I'll make sure the path is clear with nothing for you to stumble on."

"Okay." She gripped the belt. Tight. "You think he can get through?"

"Depends on how bad he wants to." Gideon aimed the light, noting the low-battery signal on his phone.

"Right." A loud crash made them both jump. "Apparently he wants through pretty bad," she said.

"How'd he get back so fast?" Gideon muttered. "I thought it would have taken him a lot longer to get help for Ellie."

"Who knows? Maybe he dumped her at the clinic and ran."

Or she died. A sense of loss overwhelmed him, and he hated that his childhood friends had come to this.

Greed. Such an ugly vice.

One that he'd been familiar with once upon a time. But no more.

Although he couldn't help but wonder if wanting to live so he could tell Maya about his growing feelings for her could be interpreted as greedy, considering his past mistakes.

Another crash sounded behind them. "I'm coming for you! I don't want that land, and the only way to stop Ellie is if you're dead!"

His thoughts about Maya were for another time. Another place.

"What does he mean by that?" Maya asked, her voice stricken.

"I don't know. We'll figure it out later." He kicked aside more rubble as the light on his phone went out. He stopped in the darkness. "It's dead," he said, stating the obvious.

Her fingers tightened around his belt. "I assumed. But just before it went out, I thought I saw the tunnel tilting upward a bit."

"And the air seems a little fresher, doesn't it?"

"Maybe."

"Stay close and feel before you step. I'll do my best, but I'm going blind here."

"I'm right behind you." A crash, then a frustrated scream sounded, echoing around them. "But go. He's determined to follow, so we've not got a lot of time to find a way out."

Gideon stopped. "You go. Be careful. I'm going to stay and fight him off if he gets this far."

"And take a chance on getting shot?"

"I've done it before," he muttered.

"In a war where you were equally armed and not at a disadvantage."

She had a point. If he was alone, he would chance it. Or if they wound up trapped with no other option.

But for now, he pushed forward, shuffling his feet along the floor, shoving aside anything that might trip her up. The narrow passage sloped upward even more, and cold air gusted across his face. "We're getting close to something," he said.

Behind them, the sound of pursuit was faint but growing louder. "He's through, Gideon."

"I know."

"You're going to have to move faster," she whispered.

"I can't see anything. I don't want to chance stepping into a hole or something." He pushed out a foot, feeling in front of him, terrified at some point the ground wouldn't be there and he'd fall, pulling her with him. He shuddered at the mental picture. "How are you doing back there?"

"Trying not to panic and to keep breathing. So far I'm managing. Holding on to you is grounding me. Keeping me from losing it."

"Then don't let go."

Please, God, help me keep her safe.

TWELVE

IN SPITE OF HER WORDS of reassurance to Gideon, if she didn't get out of the dark tunnel, she was going to start screaming. The only thing holding her together was her grip on Gideon's belt—and wondering what Vance meant about not wanting the ranch. She followed him around a sharp curve and gasped at the faint light shining from above. "It's a cavern."

"Correction. It's a ventilation shaft," he said. "About three hundred feet to the top." Almost the length of a football field.

"Which means up is out." The light above was very faint, but it was there, and it spilled down to them so they could at least see each other's outline and a little bit of their surroundings.

"We need more light," he said. "I want a good look around us."

"Try turning your phone on again. Sometimes you can get it back on for a few seconds after it shuts off."

He tried and it powered up. He pressed the flashlight icon and quickly shone the light around.

Maya spied a rusted ladder bolted to the wall. It looked ancient, its rungs corroded and bent, but still . . . "That's our way out," she said.

Gideon powered down the phone once more just in case he needed to save what little juice was left. He grabbed two rungs of the ladder and pulled. It groaned but stayed attached.

Maya moved close enough to be able to see him. "Will it hold you? Us?"

"Yeah, I think so." He tested each rung he could reach and one broke off in his hand. "I suppose I should be glad it's only one."

"Only one of those you can reach," she said.

"True." He paused and listened. "Do you hear anything?"

She stilled. "No."

"That worries me."

"Let's just get out of here."

A flashlight beam bounced on the far wall. "He's in the tunnel and coming this way," Gideon said, his voice low, hushed. "How's your shoulder?"

"Sore, but nothing that will keep me from climbing. How's your back?"

"Same. Okay then, it's time to go. Normally, I'd say you go first, but I want to make sure the rungs are safe. I believe it will hold both our weights, but we're going to be strategic about this. I'm going to climb more to the left and you stay over to the right. That way if something falls, it won't hit you."

"Fine. Got it. Climb."

"Yes, ma'am." He gripped the first one and started climbing. Maya waited a moment, then followed, staying to the right as he'd asked. It was more awkward this way, but it was better than having a rusting steel bar land on her head.

Footsteps thudded below her, drawing closer.

The ladder shuddered and Maya clung tightly. The higher they climbed the lighter it grew. But the ladder shook and the top left-hand bar pulled from the wall. She gasped and lost her grip with one hand—the one attached to the arm with the sore shoulder.

"Maya, hold on tight."

"I am. What about you? I know this has to hurt your back."

"I'm fine. How's your shoulder?"

Not necessarily fine, but she'd manage. "It's okay. Keep going."

He moved up three more steps, grabbed the next rung, and it came off in his hand.

His feet slipped and Maya gasped. "Gideon!"

His right foot found the nearest rung and Maya could breathe again.

"I've got it," he said. "Just be careful."

Gideon continued his climb, and Maya stayed right behind him while Vance's footsteps grew closer. They were about halfway to the top when the first shot rang out, the bullet striking the wall near Maya's foot. Rust and concrete fragments showered down, the metallic tang of corroded steel mixing with the damp, musty air of the shaft. She jerked, nearly losing her grip.

"Vance! Stop! You don't want to do this!"

"Come back down and I'll stop shooting!"

Once a liar, always a liar. Maya didn't believe that for one second. "You just told me you wanted me dead!"

"I don't want the land, but Ellie won't listen to reason."

"So, I'm supposed to die?"

"Don't look down," Gideon said. "Keep going." The shaft walls glistened with condensation, decades of moisture having eaten away at both concrete and metal. Each breath came out in visible puffs in the frigid air. Now that she could see, she almost didn't want to.

The next rung he tested broke free with a metallic snap that echoed through the shaft. "Give me that," Maya said. "Hurry."

He passed it to her, and she turned, looked down to see Vance taking aim again. She bit her lip, held on with her left hand, shoulder protesting, and threw the piece of metal at the man she'd once considered a friend. He cursed and ducked. She climbed faster. They were almost there. Her breaths came in frigid pants, and she kept expecting to feel the bite of a bullet in some part of her body.

"This is all her," Vance shouted. "Everything! . . . Well, almost everything. Not the phones. That was me. All me. Cut off communications, straight from the manual, right? Improvise. Modify, and adjust. Outsmart the enemy." He mumbled something about the snowmobile accident that she didn't catch but figured he'd been behind the sabotage. "That was supposed to land you dead or in the clinic. Easy access. She kills you and is arrested and I'm free!" More mumbling about achieving his mission. Then an odd laugh.

"I'm not sure I understand that plan," Maya said.

Gideon huffed and moved to the next rung. "Doesn't make any sense to me. He's sounding unhinged."

The ladder groaned, the sound of metal scraping against concrete sending shivers down her spine. Another shot echoed through the shaft, closer this time. She glanced over her shoulder to see Vance climbing as well. At least his aim was off with trying to climb and shoot at the same time. She dug into the pocket of her coat and snagged the flashlight.

Curled her fingers around it and paused. Turned to see Vance aiming again.

She let the flashlight fly and it clipped his head. He screamed and fumbled with the weapon. She held her breath, praying the gun would fall to the floor, but he caught it.

"Almost there," Gideon said. His hands reached the edge of the ventilation opening where winter sunlight filtered through, casting long shadows down the shaft. Snow had drifted into the opening, creating patches of ice on the upper rungs. He pulled himself up, stretched out a hand, and shoved at the wire covering. Maya breathed a sigh of relief when it gave way with a loud protest. He looked down and his eyes flared a fraction before meeting her gaze. "As soon as I'm out, reach up and I'll pull you up. Hurry."

She nodded and watched him disappear through the opening. Vance had stopped shooting, and she looked back one more time. He was climbing fast and gaining on them. His proximity explained Gideon's look. She had to get out before Vance reached her or she was dead. She scrambled upward.

The ladder lurched with a screech of tearing metal, pulling

away from the wall. Maya screamed as she fell backward, the shaft spinning around below her.

Vance's cry reached her as well.

"Maya!" Gideon lunged, catching her wrist in a tight grip.

Pain raced up her arm, panic flowed, and she slammed back against the ladder. She waited for the drop, the terrifying freefall that would lead to her death at the bottom of the shaft, but the other side held as well as the bolts just below her. *Thank you, God.*

"I got you," he said.

"Let go of my wrist. I need my hand."

He released her, and she clamped her fist around the rung and moved upward once more. Vance's flashlight beam found them, and she looked back to see him taking aim.

As soon as her hand clamped on the concrete side, Gideon locked a hand around her wrist again. She placed a foot on the wall and pushed upward. The momentum propelled her forward as Gideon pulled her through the opening.

The gun cracked once more, and the bullet whizzed past her ear just as Gideon hauled her out of the shaft. The distance from the top of the shaft to the snow-covered ground was only about three feet, but the hard landing stunned her for a brief moment.

"You okay?" Gideon asked.

She nodded and sucked in a lungful of crisp mountain air.

The cold had never felt so good. The shaft opening was located in a small clearing, encircled by trees. The sky was gray above them.

She had no idea which way led to safety, but they were out—and Vance was closing in. "He's going to be coming out of there as long as the ladder holds him," she said.

"I know," Gideon whispered. "That's why I'm going to stop him."

"He'll have the gun." She kept her words soft as well.

"I know that too. Run for the trees and hide. I need you to leave your footprints running in that direction. Weave back and forth. Try to make it look like I'm with you."

"You have a plan?"

"Yeah. As soon as he goes after you, I'll go after him. But you're going to give me the element of surprise."

"Got it." To their left through sparser trees, the main ski slope stretched down the mountain, dotted with late afternoon skiers living their best lives, unaware there was a killer in their midst. To Maya's right were the dense trees that offered a hiding place. She took off toward the trees.

Gideon dropped to cozy up to the side of the concrete shaft. Maya made it to the tree line and ducked behind a large fir. Gideon had his eyes on the opening, looking up from his crouched position.

She peered through a gap in the branches and saw Vance's head come into view. He paused to look around, saw the footprints, and pushed himself out, his right hand clutching the weapon. He dropped to the ground. Gideon popped out from his hiding place and swept a foot into Vance's. Vance hit the ground hard but brought the gun around to aim it at Gideon.

Gideon clamped a hand around the man's wrist and held it so the weapon was aimed at the sky.

Then Gideon stumbled and the men went down together. Maya raced toward them.

Gideon flipped Vance onto his back but lost his grip on the hand with the weapon. Vance aimed it at his head. Maya drew back her leg and planted a hard kick on his wrist. Vance screamed and the gun flew from his grip to land in the snow.

Maya swooped in, snagged it, and aimed it at the raging man. "Vance! Stop or I'll shoot! Stop now!"

"No, you stop!" a voice said from the edge of the trees about fifty yards away.

A crack sounded and a burning pain shot through Maya's bruised shoulder.

At the gunshot, Vance froze and Gideon took advantage to land a vicious punch on the man's temple, knocking him out.

Another gunshot sounded and Gideon flinched, then rolled to see Maya ducking near the shaft's concrete structure. While Vance was unconscious and the other shooter was taking cover, he ran to Maya. "Into the woods. Go."

"Here." She gave him the weapon and led the way. "There's a maintenance shed just ahead."

The shooter's gun barked again. The bullet whizzed past his head.

She grabbed Gideon's arm and pulled him toward the tree line opposite from where the bullets were coming from. He spotted what she was talking about and wondered how she'd even seen the thing. The wooden structure's dark green paint almost camouflaged it against the pines. "Maybe there's something—"

Another bullet missed him by inches, striking a pine tree and sending bark flying. He turned to shoot back, but the sun broke through the clouds and silhouetted the shooter, making the person harder to target.

Gideon shoved Maya behind a snowbank and aimed his weapon once more. Bullets struck the packed snow and ice crystals sprayed the air. He ducked. "Get to the shed," he said. "I'll cover you. If it's locked, go around to the other side and use it for cover."

She hesitated. "But—"

"Go, Maya, please!"

Maya sprinted for the shed, her boots crunching in the crusty snow. He waited for the shooter to open fire again, but no more bullets came his way. The sun broke through the clouds again, casting a shadow from the ventilation shaft and a figure outlined on one side. He fired in the direction of the shooter once more, making sure his bullet hit the concrete hiding place. He wanted to know where every bullet he shot landed. He glanced back to see Maya yank the metal door open and bolted to join her. He slammed the door shut behind them and drew in a ragged breath.

The musty interior smelled of motor oil and old wood, and while the building was solid, constructed of metal and wood, he wasn't confident it would stop bullets.

A sound caught his ear. "Do you hear that?"

"Security sirens?"

"Yeah." They didn't sound like police sirens, but they were music to his ears nonetheless. "No doubt someone heard the gunshots and reported them." He glanced out the small window to see a figure hurrying away from the ventilation shaft area. "It's Ellie," he said.

"She must not have been hurt too bad, then."

"No, I guarantee you Vance didn't take her down to the medical area. He probably patched her up as best he could, and they hatched this little plan and came after us."

"I don't understand why he'd gone along with this whole thing so far. He doesn't want the land, but he wants Ellie blamed for my death."

"Sounds like it."

"What now?" She winced and looked down at her arm.

"What is it? Are you hit?" He bolted to her.

"Grazed, I think."

"Let me see."

She shot him an amused look. "I'm the doctor here. I'll let you know if I need anything. In the meantime, what about Ellie?"

"Thinking about how to handle her. Hang on a sec and let me take care of this." He shrugged out of his outerwear and ripped part of his T-shirt into a long strip that he tied around her upper arm.

"At least it's the same arm that I hurt earlier." She raised her right hand. "Still have one good one."

"Okay, I have a plan. It's not a good plan, but it's the only one I have at the moment. You stay here."

"What are you going to do?"

He pinched the bridge of his nose. "I'm going after her."

"Then I'm coming with you."

"Maya, you're hurt—"

"It's nothing. I'm not staying behind. And besides, we have to catch her to keep Vance in line. He's probably awake by now and no doubt looking for Ellie—and us. You have his gun, but Ellie has hers."

True enough on both counts. Gideon could only hope the man had a raging headache. He and Maya made their way through the wooded area and came out at the back of one of the cabins.

Vance and Ellie's cabin.

With fresh footsteps too big to be Ellie's leading to the sliding glass doors. "He's in there."

"Yes, but where's Ellie? Is she in there too?"

"There are only his prints leading into the house, but she could have gone in the front door, I guess."

"I'll look," Maya said. "You stay here in case they come out that way."

"And if they come out the front?"

"I'll be hidden. And I'll scream if I need to."

"Maya—"

"Seriously. I'm prepared now. I know what she's capable of. Both of them. I won't hesitate to defend myself."

"Remember the bum shoulder? No, I don't like it."

"I know, but the sirens are getting louder. There's no way they're going to be able to find us unless we can signal where we are."

"I'll figure it out, but you need to stay here."

"If I stay here, Ellie may escape." She raised on tiptoes to kiss him, her soft lips grazing his and leaving him wanting more. She pulled back and met his gaze, conflicting feelings turning her dark eyes stormy. She cleared her throat. "Sorry, I hope that was okay."

Gideon cleared his throat. "More than okay. Let's revisit that once this is all over." Assuming they lived through it. She took off before he could protest again.

Please, God, let us live through it.

THIRTEEN

SHE'D KISSED HIM. Something she'd dreamed about doing for years. And he hadn't seemed to mind one bit. It might have been a selfish move, especially if he wasn't interested, but deep down she knew he was. And kissing him, even that light brush of butterfly wings, had been the stuff of dreams. Now she wanted to live to see if they could have more.

Be more.

Together. And she had a glimmer of an idea how to move things in the right direction to make sure they could explore that option.

But before that could happen, they had to find Ellie and Vance and stop them. If she didn't, her dreams were dust.

She hurried around to the front of the condo, looking for fresh prints. None.

A shot rang out from the back. "Gideon!" Maya darted along the cabin wall, staying close to the rough wood. At the corner, she cautiously peered around and her heart squeezed. Using the tree line for cover, Ellie had her weapon trained on Gideon, who was near the stack of firewood and facing the cabin's French doors.

Before Maya could get Gideon's attention, Ellie's gaze snapped to her, and the gun swung in her direction. Maya pulled back and bullets splintered the cabin beside her, sending wooden shrapnel raining into the snow. When the shooting stopped, she looked around again, praying she didn't get a bullet in the head. She caught Gideon's eye just as the French doors swung open and Vance bolted out of the cabin.

He spotted Gideon and never slowed. He ran down the steps of the porch, through the icy snow, slipping and sliding, with no weapon that she could see. But she knew what a good fighter he was. He could kill a man with his hands, and that seemed to be his intent as he reached the woodpile.

Maya stood still, watching, as did Ellie. The man dove over the stack of wood and landed on top of Gideon. Gideon grunted and the two men rolled down the slight hill away from the wood and into the open.

Ellie's gun barked once more in Maya's direction.

"Ellie, Vance, stop! It's over!" Maya yelled.

The sirens were closer, but they wouldn't be able to see what was going on, thanks to the privacy of the cabin's location. Not unless they were watching the security cameras.

"It's not over!" Ellie shouted. "We may never get to claim the land now, but you're not going back to it! Ever! *You've ruined everything!*" The high-pitched screech echoed through the air, and Maya breathed a prayer for divine help.

She couldn't see Gideon and Vance now. They'd rolled back behind the woodpile. But the sounds of their fight came through loud and clear. She had to do something to distract Ellie and help Gideon. She could only pray the men were evenly matched, with Vance's head wound hampering his strength. "Security is on the way!"

For a moment Ellie had her weapon aimed at Vance and Gideon. Obviously trying to hit Gideon.

"No, no, no," Maya whispered. Using Ellie's distraction to her advantage, Maya darted for the woodpile, praying she could get there before Ellie could refocus her aim.

A bullet whipped over her head, and she slid to her knees behind the wood. From her vantage point, she had a good look at Gideon and Vance.

And it was not going well for Gideon.

Gideon struggled under Vance's weight. His back dug into the icy underlayer of the snow, sending shards of pain rippling through him while he tried to find some kind of leverage to get the guy off him. The man's massive hands were wrapped around his throat and closing like a vise. Vance's eyes were wide open, but he was lost in another time, another place, another battle, his PTSD set off by his wife's gunfire.

"Vance!" Gideon's gasp came out on a whisper. Another crack followed, then another, Ellie's shots echoing off the mountainside like firecrackers. And very close to their heads. One more pop from another direction, someone screamed, and then the shooting stopped.

Vance's grip loosened and his body trembled. Gideon gasped in a full breath, bucked Vance to the side, and threw a punch to the man's chin. It just grazed him, and Vance came back at him, his fist aimed at Gideon's face. Gideon ducked and Vance's punch landed on the ground. A howl came from his throat, and Gideon rolled, but the man reared back and came at him once more with a chunk of ice gripped in his right hand.

"Vance, no!" Maya's shout came just before she swung a log into Vance's upper shoulders.

Vance turned to look up just as she swung again and connected with his head.

Vance cried out and slumped over. Unconscious. On top of Gideon.

Gideon didn't move, simply lay there, trying to regain his breath, knowing he needed to protect Maya. Screams came from his left.

"Maya!"

He started to push Vance off once more.

"Everyone stay down!" Lila's voice rang out, and Gideon froze for a brief second, then he lifted his head. The last gunshot he'd noticed coming from a different direction had been Lila's, and her bullet had caught Ellie in the shoulder. The woman lay writhing on the ground, her screams still echoing around them. *Her* screams. Not Maya's.

Oh, thank you, God.

Ellie's weapon lay next to her, but even in her pain with two gunshot wounds, she still fought back, her fingers grasping for the butt of the gun. Maya ran over and kicked it away while Lila got the squirming woman under control and pulled her arms behind her. She zip-tied them in spite of the wound in her shoulder.

"Stop!" Ellie's screech was earsplitting. "You're hurting me! I need help!" Her cries would have been heartbreaking if she hadn't just tried to kill him and Maya.

Gideon grunted and shoved Vance off him and onto the snow. The man was out cold. Gideon drew in ragged breaths, his throat aching. Maya's hands were on his face, checking him over. "I'm okay," he managed to rasp.

"Nice swing you got there," Lila said to Maya, not taking her eyes off Ellie. "When I saw what was happening, I waited for an opening. Didn't want to risk hitting any of you in the scuffle."

More sirens were almost on them now. Vance remained unconscious, a momentary reprieve from his life and what was to come.

Maya moved from Gideon to kneel beside Vance. She checked him over, then looked up. "He has a pretty severe head wound. He needs medical attention immediately." She chewed her lip and a tear slipped out. Just as Gideon started to go to her to pull her into his arms, she swiped the tear away and sniffed. "I didn't mean to hit him in the head, but he moved and—"

"It's not your fault," Gideon said, his voice sounding hoarse and rough. He could only pray Vance hadn't done any lasting damage to his vocal cords. But he'd worry about that later. "He brought this on himself."

"I know, but still . . ." She shook her head and cupped a hand over her shoulder with a grimace. "He and Ellie both need a hospital, but let's get them to the clinic where I can treat them as best as I can. Then we can get a chopper on the way to transport them to the nearest hospital." She raked a hand over her hair. "And I suppose we'll have to alert the authorities and make statements and all that."

"Sounds about right," Gideon said. He retrieved the weapon he'd taken off Vance and passed it to one of the other officers.

"They've managed to dig through the entrance," Lila said, still holding on to the more subdued Ellie. "Anyone who wants to leave can get out now. And local police can get in. You can give your statements to them, and we can get Mr. and Mrs. Harland to a hospital."

Gideon nodded and finally couldn't stop himself. He went to Maya and pulled her close.

It was over.

Thank you, Lord.

FOURTEEN

FOUR MONTHS LATER

MAYA STEPPED OUTSIDE onto the deck that overlooked the rolling hills for miles. The mountains in the distance sent her memories back in time to the weekends when she and her grandfather, along with her cousins Sully, Miles, Trent, and Deb, went hiking. She loved this time of year. While she enjoyed winter and the snowy winter sports, summer never came soon enough for her. The warm days were here to stay for a while, and she was all for it.

The past four months since she and Gideon had escaped the mountain tunnel had been healing and productive. The ranch was now fully staffed and ready for its first vet.

Thank you, God.

A prayer she couldn't seem to stop saying.

A rumble in the distance caught her attention. A different kind of rumble than an avalanche, thank goodness. Gideon's truck needed a new muffler, and it was starting to be an inside joke with them. Something that warmed her right to her very soul.

Like Gideon's presence in her life. And yet . . . something held her back. Something they needed to talk about.

He parked and joined her on the deck, leaning over to claim a kiss that left her a little breathless.

"Well, that was nice," she said.

He raised a brow. "Nice? I must be losing my touch."

She laughed. "Never."

Gideon took a seat in the rocker next to hers. "Are you going to share with me what's going on?"

She slanted a look at him. "So, you're a mind reader now?"

"No, I've just known you forever, Maya. I can tell when something's bothering you."

She sighed and nodded. "Yeah. So . . ."

"So . . ."

Another laugh slipped from her. "I love that when I'm with you, I always have something to smile or laugh about."

He curled his hand around hers but stayed quiet. He was in listening mode.

"These past four months have been pretty amazing. So busy neither one of us has really had time to breathe, much less have a heart-to-heart talk."

"True."

"But now it's time, isn't it?"

"I'd say so."

"I'm scared, Gideon. Scared of loving you and losing you. My love for Laura was very different, of course, but losing her scraped away a part of me I don't know how I'll ever get back. And then there's the nightmares that still plague me every so often. They're awful and I don't want to inflict those on anyone else."

She fell silent, her arguments sounding weak now that she'd voiced them. But they still had a hold on her, so . . .

"I think my biggest fear is that I'm not whole enough to be the kind of person you need. The kind of—" She snapped her lips shut. She didn't want to jump the gun if he wasn't thinking along the same lines she was.

"Wife?"

Okay, so maybe they *were* on the same page.

"Well, yes. If it were to get to that point." She hoped the heat she could feel creeping up into her neck didn't show in her cheeks.

"I was kind of hoping it would," he said.

Oh boy. She swallowed. "I'm not going to lie and say I haven't thought about it."

"Well, that's a relief."

She huffed a laugh once more. "Okay." She frowned. "I didn't think that was on your radar, though."

"It wasn't. And then this whole being trapped by an avalanche and chased by killers happened and seeing you in danger, feeling helpless to do anything about it . . . well, let's just say I have a different perspective."

"Which is?"

"Life is short, Maya. Too short to let the past rule the future. God allowed us to be born, and he has a purpose for our lives. Sometimes we go through seasons. Good and bad. Sometimes those seasons are a result of our own choices. I made some really bad choices that resulted in some really bad consequences and one really awful season. The worst one since Jacob's death. At least I didn't have anything to do with that. But these past four months have given me time to reflect on a lot of things."

"Like what?" Maya asked. Her heart thumped a little faster at the intensity in his gaze.

"Like consequences. My bad choices caused a good buddy of mine to do something he thought I'd be okay with."

"What did he do?"

"Cut a lot of corners on a project to pocket the profit. I wasn't okay with it, but I'd skirted the edge of ethics myself, and he knew that. I told you some of the people who invested in the business were . . . unsavory . . . to put it mildly. Anyway, as you also know, I walked away. He didn't and now he's in prison."

"I'm so sorry," she said, her voice low, "but you did the right thing."

He nodded. "Eventually. But I also know that I had influence over Pete, and he made decisions he might not have otherwise made."

"So that's what you meant when you said you'd lost everything."

"Yeah."

"I'm proud of you."

He blinked. "What? How?"

She shrugged. "You did the right thing," she said again. "You chose to right your wrongs. To sacrifice in order to be honorable. That shows integrity and I'm proud of you."

He sighed and rubbed his chin. "It was a low point in my life, Maya. I regret it with everything in me."

"And if you've asked for forgiveness, then you're forgiven."

"I have. I've also made things right with the company I wronged. I overcharged them and cut a few corners. Not like Pete did, but enough. That was the project that Pete worked with me on, and when the next project came along, he decided he'd prove he could do better. Cut more corners, make more money." He shook his head. "Someone got hurt when the side of a building collapsed. It made the news. Everyone in town knew it was my business, and ever since then, I've been running from God because I figured I'd disappointed him. And if I disappointed him, then I sure didn't deserve happiness or any blessings he might want to give me."

"Oh, Gideon," she whispered. She frowned. "How did I not know this?"

He shrugged. "I don't know. Seems like everyone did."

"Grams and Gramps never said a word."

"Really?"

"Really."

"Huh. How about that? I mean, it happened on the other side of the country, but I thought . . . well, I guess I figured everyone would know and judge me."

"I don't think people in Whitestone do know," she said. "Or if they heard about it, they didn't connect it with you."

"I guess not." He raked a hand over his head. "Well, I'm glad you didn't know, but it did make telling you hard."

"Past mistakes are difficult to admit when we don't know the reaction we're going to get. I understand."

"Exactly. Anyway, initially, I threw myself into my construction business because physical labor was easier than dealing with the emotional pain of losing Jacob. I pushed my parents away because their grief was my grief and I didn't want to face it." He looked her in the eye. "And most of all, I've been fighting my feelings for you because I've been afraid of messing up. That if we were to become a couple, I'd somehow hurt you—or you'd be hurt by my . . . reputation." He swallowed hard and pulled in a deep breath. "And hurting you is one thing I never want to do."

"Gideon, you—"

"Shh." He laid a finger over her lips. "Let me finish."

She nodded.

"Anyway, after all we've been through—like almost dying—after a lot of prayer and hard conversations with God, I'm ready to face my fears if you are. I don't want to let another day go by without telling you how I feel."

Could her heart beat any faster? Should she say something? What could she say?

"While I've been working on getting everything ready for you, I've also been thinking about the ranch and about how you need someone to oversee the building projects and the maintenance. You may even want to expand someday."

"Yes, that's the vision."

"I know construction. I know how to manage crews, handle contracts, build things that last. And I'd like to do that here. With you."

Maya blinked away the tears that wanted to blind her. "But what about rebuilding your business? I thought that was your dream."

"Initially. Maybe. But dreams can change. Or morph into something better. Something you never thought of until you're planning and are in a place to envision it. I'm choosing to go with the something better." He rubbed a hand over his lips. "When we were in that tunnel and pretty much facing death, I thought about a lot of things—mostly escaping with both of us alive—but also about choices and ones I regretted." He pulled her to her feet and leaned over to kiss her. Gently. Sweetly. "I don't want to have any regrets when it comes to going forward. I wish I'd told you how I felt about you years ago. I love you, Maya. I think I've always loved you."

"I love you too," she said, pushing the words past the lump in her throat. "But the nightmares—"

"We'll face them together and we'll beat them. Just like we did Vance and Ellie. Together. Whatever comes next, we're a team. And we have God, so that really makes us an unbeatable trio."

"I like the sound of that." A tear slipped down her cheek. Could she put aside all her insecurities and fears to spend a lifetime with this man?

She gave herself a mental slap. Why was she even questioning that?

She could do it because the alternative wasn't an option. She closed her eyes, relishing the feel of his arms around her. Standing in this moment, this place. Then her mind slid back to what they'd been through, and she looked up at him. "I can't believe Vance really thought he could use Ellie wanting to kill me as a way to get away from her. I believe in fighting for your marriage, but when your spouse is deadly . . . well, that's a whole different situation."

"I have no doubt he was afraid she'd kill him too, if he didn't do what she wanted." He paused. "I wonder if that bullet he hit her with was meant to kill her."

She shook her head. "I don't know. He had the chance to kill her when he was supposedly taking her to get help, but he didn't. Maybe deep down he just couldn't do it."

"But, in the end, he could kill us."

"Yeah." She sighed. "He sure used that avalanche to his advantage. Ellie had ranted and told him her plans to get rid of me, so he piggybacked on that. I'm sure if the avalanche hadn't happened, he would have figured out how to work everything so Ellie took the fall and he came out as the grieving husband with the murderous wife. It's hard to wrap my mind around it."

"Then don't. Wrap your mind around something else."

"Happy to. Why are we even rehashing this? What should I wrap my mind around now?"

"This." He dropped to one knee, pulling something from his pocket.

Maya sucked in a breath. *Oh, God, please don't let me pass out.*

He looked up and she looked down. Their eyes met. "I've been thinking about this for a while, waiting for the right moment and this is it. Right here on the porch, just us, with a beautiful view, perfect weather, and, well, frankly, I don't want to wait any longer."

"I agree. Don't wait any longer." She gave a breathless little laugh, and he grinned.

"All right then." He held the ring up to her. "Maya Sullivan, will you marry me? Will you let me help you run this ranch, build our future, and trust God to heal whatever needs healing—together?"

With a trembling hand, Maya reached for the simple ring. A beautiful solitaire diamond set in white gold. Then she looked into the face of the man she'd loved for what seemed like forever. The fears were still there, just small and less significant.

"Yes," she said. "Yes to all of the above." He slipped the ring on her finger and she cupped his face. "I love you, Gideon Price."

He stood and kissed her, long and slow, tender and demanding. A kiss that said he cherished her and desired her. That she was finally home.

He pulled back and hugged her. She'd never felt so secure, so safe. So unafraid. "Gideon?"

"Yeah?"

"Call your parents. Today, okay? Life's too short not to reconcile."

He pressed his forehead to hers. "I already did that this morning. Dad's going to help me draw up the plans for the new veterinary clinic you're wanting to build."

Maya laughed and wound her arms around his neck. "I think this is what Gramps always dreamed of for this place. For it to be a place of healing. For all living creatures—animals and people."

"Yeah. It's going to be exciting to see that come to life."

"Oh, there's one more thing that needs healing," she said.

He frowned. "What?"

"Your muffler."

He snorted, then laughed. "Right. It's on my list."

"A list that can wait," Maya said, pulling him down for another kiss. "For now, I just want to stay here and plan our future."

"I'd say that's the perfect way to spend the day as long as it involves lots of kisses."

She grinned. "I think that can be arranged."

For more from

LYNETTE EASON,

read on for an excerpt from

TWILIGHT TACTICS

A remote ranch for healing veterans becomes a battleground when FBI agent Collin Sullivan arrives with a teenager who witnessed a mob hit. Survival instructor Elena Thompson's peaceful haven is shattered when the ranch is cut off from help by tech skills superior to their own. Collin and Elena must fight to keep everyone alive as secrets and danger close in.

Available Summer 2026.

ONE

NOVEMBER

FBI SPECIAL AGENT Collin Sullivan—a.k.a. Sully—gripped the wheel and glanced in the rearview mirror once more. The silver sedan was still there, following at a discreet distance, but it was enough to set his teeth on edge.

His partner, Piper Whitaker, sat in the passenger seat, her jaw set, brow furrowed. She shot him a quick glance. "You see it too?"

"Yeah."

"See what?" Ollie Callahan, the fourteen-year-old foster child and murder witness, had hearing like a bat. Sully had thought she was asleep. "The car behind us?"

No sense in lying. "Yes. You recognize it?"

"I can't see it very well. It's too far back." She gazed out the rear window.

"Turn around," Sully said. "Don't let him know you've seen him."

"Oh. Sorry." She faced front again and lowered her gaze to her hands, but not before he caught the sheen of tears in her eyes.

Remorse kicked him. "It's okay. I should have prefaced my question with 'Don't turn around.'" The teen was a good kid as far as he could tell. She'd just been in the wrong place at the wrong time. And it was his and Piper's responsibility to make sure nothing happened to her.

Like death.

A bullet pinged off the back bumper. Ollie screamed and flattened herself against the seat, her seatbelt still around her. Piper pulled her weapon and rolled her window down while Sully pressed the gas, the speedometer inching up past sixty, then seventy. Tennessee's winter wind whooshed through the window. The poor heater had been fighting a losing battle almost since he'd cranked the vehicle at six o'clock this morning.

"There are two of them now," Piper said. "Black SUV coming up on my side. Silver sedan hanging back on the left. Passenger of the SUV is the one who shot."

"Hold on."

Sully pressed the accelerator, and the engine roared as they wound through the rolling farmland dotted with patches of dense woods. The Smoky Mountains loomed in the distance. He glanced back at Ollie. She lay still on the seat, quiet as a statue.

The road narrowed. Weathered fence posts whipped past. Fields of dried cornstalks offered no cover or escape. His hands tightened on the wheel while his brain searched for options.

Broken Chains Ranch was less than ten miles ahead, but they'd never make it before their pursuers caught them. And besides, he didn't want to take the bad guys right to his cousin's doorstep.

Another shot took out the passenger side mirror.

Ollie screamed.

Piper climbed in the backseat and lowered the window. "I got this," she said to Sully. "Let them pull up a little."

Sully did as instructed and used the rearview mirror to keep track of the SUV and the sedan.

"Use the curve, Sully."

"Got it." It was a good plan. He turned into the curve, and the sedan fell back, but the SUV gained. Piper fired.

Shattered a window. They never slowed down.

"Ugh," she said. "Let's try that again."

Sully winced. She was a good shot, but trying to hit a target in this situation was difficult if not downright impossible.

Ollie whimpered, and his heart clenched for the child. No kid should have to go through what she had unintentionally found herself in the middle of. "Ollie, hang in there, hon."

"I'm hanging, Sully." Her voice shook. She was terrified, of course, but she was also one of the bravest people he'd ever met. He needed to tell her that as soon as they got out of this mess.

The black SUV surged forward, right on their tail, then pulled up beside them. Piper gasped. "Is he positioning for a PIT maneuver?"

Sure looked like it to him.

With impact imminent, Sully accelerated and steered slightly toward the shoulder of the road.

When the hit came, his SUV spun, but because of his counter measures, he was able to gain control after a 360 that left him slightly dizzy. Somehow, he was still on the road and heading in the direction of the ranch with the black SUV falling behind them.

Piper looked behind her. "Ollie, you okay?"

He heard a small but sure voice from the back seat. "Still in one piece."

The wind from the open windows whipped around them, and Sully's mind raced. They couldn't outrun them much longer. Whoever *they* were, *they* had fast cars. And knew how to execute PIT maneuvers.

That worried him. He glanced in the rearview mirror once more. "We passed an old barn a while back. With the overgrown access road."

"Yeah," Piper said, "I saw it. About a quarter of a mile back."

"I have an idea. Hang on." He slowed and did a quick U-turn. The sedan shot past with a squeal of brakes.

"I don't know about this, Sully," Piper said. "They could split up and cut us off."

"Maybe. Or they'll just follow us."

"What are you thinking?"

"Flash-bangs are in the back, right?"

"Yes."

"Then I've got a plan."

"All right, then. Let me know my part when it's time."

Ollie sat up, and her slender fingers pressed into his shoulder. "Sully—"

"Not now, kiddo. Get back down and stay there, okay?"

She did as he said. "I'm scared."

"I am too, but we're going to fight our way out of this and be just fine. Got it?"

"Sure." Her dubious tone conveyed what she really thought.

But she didn't know everything that was going through Sully's head right now, the mantra that he could not fail. *Would* not fail.

Not this time.

Please, God, let this work.

"Sully's really good at this," Piper said. "He won't let anything happen to us. My daughter, Hannah, thinks he's a superhero in disguise."

"How old is Hannah again?"

"Sixteen."

"A little old for that kind of belief, isn't she?"

Piper's chuckle was tight, but she'd managed to distract Ollie, and that was all that mattered.

The black SUV edged closer once more, but Sully was ready. He had one chance to get this right. Movement caught his attention—the second vehicle had dropped back.

He glanced at Piper. "As soon as I stop, I'll pop the back. You grab the bag, and hightail it back."

"Got it." She rolled the window up.

Sully sucked in a breath, said a quick prayer, and cranked the wheel hard left.

Gravel sprayed as he whipped the SUV onto the overgrown

access road. Tree branches slapped against the hood, leaves and twigs snapped and sprayed across the windshield.

Nothing like leaving a trail a blind man could follow.

The abandoned barn loomed ahead, the weathered boards having seen better days. But it would do for what he needed.

Piper looked back. "Splitting up like I thought they would."

"It's okay." He pressed the accelerator and aimed for the barn's gaping doors. He slammed on the brakes and spun the wheel hard once more. The SUV slid sideways into the barn in a shower of dirt and rotted wood.

Piper was already out of the vehicle, and he popped the hatch. Less than five seconds later, she was back in her seat. She shoved the go bag on the floor and snagged a flashbang. "Ready."

"Here he comes," Sully said.

"And the sedan?"

"Don't know." He frowned. "Hands over your ears and close your eyes, Ollie. Got it?"

"Yes!"

He nodded to Piper, who waited. Seconds ticked past, and the black SUV roared into sight. It slammed to a stop, and Piper tossed the weapon under the vehicle. She yanked her door shut, ducked her head, and clamped her arms over her ears.

Sully did the same.

The flash and bang came, expected, but jarring all the same.

He threw the vehicle into reverse and shot through the back wall of the barn.

"The sedan!"

Piper's cry alerted him to the vehicle he was almost on top of. The driver overcorrected, seeking to avoid hitting Sully, and slammed into an old, rusted tractor.

"Go!" Piper's urgency fueled his own, and he accelerated toward the road, taking the path he'd created on his mad dash to the barn.

"Ollie! Still okay?"

"I'm okay," she said, sounding breathless.

Sully allowed a moment of relief to sweep over him. And gratitude. They were safe. For now.

However, relaxing wasn't an option. He swept his gaze between the mirrors, looking for movement, any sign that their pursuers were still on their tail somewhere. Piper did the same. She was a good partner, and he was glad she had his back. "We bought some time," he said, "but they're not done. They'll regroup, replan, and come back."

Piper shot him a tight smile. "Let's hope Maya's security is as good as she says it is."

"It is. David and I helped her come up with it." David Broussard, Maya's head of security at the ranch, was also one of Sully's childhood buddies. The man had been looking for something different and approached Sully about any job recommendations. He'd sent the guy to Maya, and she'd hired him a few months ago. "David and Maya discussed us using the ranch as a safe house," he said. "And they agreed Ollie would be safe there. She's got top-notch tech out there."

"Well then, that makes me feel so much better. Security by David and Sully. What could go wrong?"

A soft chuckle came from the backseat, and he found a smile curving his own lips. He enjoyed sparring with Piper, and apparently Ollie liked it too. She sat up and met his gaze in the rearview mirror. "Will they find us at the ranch?"

"I can't promise they won't, but I *can* promise that the ranch is a special place with special people, and you'll be as safe as possible there."

She nodded, and he glanced toward heaven. *Please, God, let us be safe there.*

The roar of the engine coming up the dirt driveway caught Elena Thompson's attention. She was outside the barn with four of the ranch's occupants, teaching them how to make a solar water distiller. A simple enough process with only a few materials needed, but it was something none of them had ever seen before so she had a captive audience.

The SUV sped along, dust flying behind it.

Maya Sullivan Price, the owner of the Broken Chains Ranch and good friend to Elena, joined her in watching the approach. "Who's that?" Elena asked.

"My cousin."

"Oh yes. We've met. Mr. FBI Special Agent Collin Sullivan."

"Sully to most. Pain in the neck to others," Maya murmured.

Elena laughed. "I've always found him pleasant enough." More than. But she kept that to herself. "Who's with him?"

Maya pulled Elena to the side, out of hearing range of the others. "I'm just letting you in on this because I have permission. He has his new partner, Piper Whitaker, and a young girl who witnessed a murder with him. Her name is Olivia Callahan."

Elena's laughter faded. "Oh, how terrible."

"Yeah. Sully and David used to work together in some capacity at the bureau. David and I talked about it and agreed to let them hide out here until the trial." She waved her phone. "Sully called and said they were attacked on the way but managed to get away."

"Attacked! By whom?"

"The people who want his protectee dead, I would assume."

"Poor girl."

"They were working a case, and the murder she witnessed was in conjunction with that. It's turned into a RICO investigation starting before the murder that Ollie witnessed. There were two or three before that. Anyway, it's a big thing involving the mob and all that. She's a foster kid. Been in and out of the system almost as long as she's been alive."

The words kicked Elena in the gut. "Life can be so unfair." She knew that better than most. Maya's dark eyes glistened with a compassion that Elena knew was reflected in her own gaze. "But," Elena said, "if she's coming here, we'll take care of her."

"We?"

"Yep." She gave a decisive nod. "We."

Maya hugged her and looked back at the others. "I don't want them to know or worry about this. I hesitated to say yes when Sully asked if he could bring her here. But David and Sully felt like this was the best place for her." She shrugged. "I'm still not sure, to be honest. The ranch is supposed to be a place of calm and healing, not a hideout for people on the run. But the girl . . ." She chewed her bottom lip. "I had a hard time saying no to this one."

"There is no way to say no to that," Elena said. She glanced at Frank. "You should let Frank in on it. He was special ops and is completely trustworthy—in spite of his scruffy appearance." His black beard curved around his chin, and his bushy brows could use a good trim, but he had the kindest heart of anyone Elena had ever met.

"Maybe. I'll have to run that by Sully. Right now, all anyone knows is that my cousin, his 'sister'—also my cousin—and her 'daughter'—my niece—are coming to visit."

"Right."

Maya bit her lip. "I pray I'm making the right decision," she said, her voice low and soft.

"You've said over and over that you want this ranch to be a refuge. A place of restoration. Well, there you go. If that girl has seen a murder, she's going to need us to be her village."

Maya's worry faded from her features. "I knew you'd say that. With your certification in wilderness therapy and trauma counseling, it may be you who'll be able to help Ollie the most."

"I'm happy to help her any way I can, you know that, but Rachel's the trained counselor." Rachel Evans, their art therapist, was a former military chaplain. She had her own counseling practice and split her time between her in-town office and the office at the ranch.

"We'll just see what she needs, then make the judgement as to who can help her the most."'

"That works." Elena nodded to Adam. "He was in the system a few years and from what little he's shared, it's not a fun place to be. In some ways I think his wounds from that are worse than the ones he got in combat." She shot a pointed look at his titanium leg attached to what remained of his thigh.

"Yeah," Maya whispered. And then there was no more time to chat. The SUV pulled to a stop in front of the house about fifty yards away from the barn. "All right," Maya said. "I'm going to get everyone settled."

"I'm right behind you," Elena said.

"Thanks. They need to meet everyone as soon as possible so they can be familiar with who belongs here."

And so they could also know if someone *didn't* belong.

Elena dismissed her class with promises to finish the project in their next session, then followed Maya to the main house. She let her gaze scan the area behind it in the direction of the mountains that hid . . . a lot.

"You okay?" Maya asked.

"Yes, why?"

"You've seemed a bit preoccupied lately."

Ouch. She'd been that transparent? "I just saw someone in town the other day who reminded me of my childhood."

"Your childhood? With the cult?" A snort slipped out.

"Preppers." Elena said the word with a mild tone and small smile. The argument was a familiar one.

"Cult."

She wasn't convinced they were an actual cult, but she wasn't convinced they weren't either. They hadn't started out that way in Virginia, but when they'd left the group in Virginia to join the one here in Tennessee . . . Yeah, it was very different, so maybe cult was the right label. It hurt to think so. She still cared about people up on that mountain in the distance. "Okay, whatever. But yeah."

"Who?"

She sighed. "It doesn't matter. It was just a glimpse. I'm probably seeing things." But she didn't think so. "Let's focus on your company."

"Fine, but you're spilling the tea later."

Elena should have known better than to try to hide anything from the person who knew her best.

The main house was set on a ranch that spanned about five thousand square acres. In the main house, Elena lived in the lower-level apartment while Maya and her husband, Gideon, had the top space. Elena's small living area, complete with two bedrooms, a den, and a tiny kitchen was all she needed—and more. She was the only worker who lived in the big home, and she paid a modicum of rent because she didn't feel right mooching off her friend.

Although to hear Maya tell it, Elena was the one doing the favor.

The tall man who'd just exited the vehicle was Collin Sullivan. Elena had met him a few times over the past six months she'd been there. And Maya had told her all about the cousin she adored, so Elena felt like she knew him. Maybe. He favored Maya in looks. Dark hair, dark eyes, deeply tanned skin even in November. Five o'clock shadow. A couple of inches over six feet.

He caught her staring and held her gaze, a hint of amusement coloring his eyes. "Hi."

Busted. "Hi. Good to see you again." Thankfully, her voice was steady, no hint of her rapid pulse. And with her turtleneck and hoodie on, there was no way for him to see the heat climbing into her neck. Hopefully it would stop before it could reach her cheeks.

"You too," he said.

The back door opened, and he turned his attention to the teenager climbing out.

The witness. Poor girl.

The front passenger door opened, and a woman with pretty features that were set in a hard expression emerged. Her eyes scanned the area, then swept back to the house.

Maya went to Sully and hugged her cousin. "Welcome. We'll get you all set up. I've got a four-bedroom cabin available that's not too far from the house, but it's secluded so you can easily see if anyone approaches. It's set pretty close to the lake and has an updated security system. It's called Serenity."

Sully nodded. "That sounds perfect."

Maya smiled. "Let's hope it can live up to its name."

"Definitely." He frowned. "Where's David?"

"In town checking on a client." While David was in charge of security for the ranch, he and his team also had private clients who hired them on a regular basis. "He should be back sometime tomorrow, I believe."

"I can't thank you enough for being willing to take us in at the last minute like this. Our last three places were compromised, and we've been running out of options. ASAC Winters suggested I find a place and keep it secret. This place came to mind."

Elena raised a brow. "Sounds like you're trusting someone you shouldn't."

His gaze collided with hers, and it was like a physical impact smack in her gut. She swallowed. Weird.

"I don't want to think it," he said, "but can't say it hasn't crossed my mind." He gestured to the tall woman still standing by the car. "This is Piper Whitaker, my partner, a.k.a. my sister and cousin to Maya." Piper was only about three inches shorter than Sully. And she was very pretty. The woman nodded and offered a smile. "And this brave young lady," Sully continued, "is Olivia—better known as Ollie—Callahan, 'my niece.'"

Once the introductions were made, Maya held out a key to Elena. "Do you mind showing them the cabin and giving them the code to the alarm system as well as the door code? I don't think they'll have any trouble, but here's a backup key in case. I have a phone call I need to make."

Elena took the ring and curled her fingers around it, letting the jagged edge dig into her skin and keep her grounded. Now wasn't the time to be mooning about Collin Sullivan—Sully. Not that there was ever a good time for that.

Focus.

"Of course," she said, forcing a smile. What she needed to do was figure out what this weird attraction arcing between her and Sully was, but that would have to wait. She climbed into the SUV, and within ninety seconds, they pulled into the horseshoe-shaped dirt drive. The cabin was the biggest one on the property and most would call it a house, but all of the structures around the lake and up the hill into the woods were known as cabins.

She unlocked the door with the code and waited for them to grab their things. Ollie, who still hadn't said a word, slung a backpack over her shoulder and pulled her rolling carry-on inside. Elena met her gaze and offered her a reassuring smile. The girl's lips never twitched.

Elena drew in a breath and motioned to the area in front of her. "The kitchen, dining area, then the great room are one big open area, which you can see from here. To the right are two bedrooms. On the basement level there are two more bedrooms. You access the stairs though the great room. I think Ollie should have the bedroom on this level next to the stairs. It's safest, and there's no door leading out to the porch."

"Perfect." Sully nodded to Piper. "Why don't you get Ollie settled. I'll be fine with whatever—even the couch at night so we can all be on the same floor. In the meantime, I'm going to check over the security system."

Piper nodded and led Ollie through the kitchen and dining area, then made a right and disappeared into the hallway. The agent had placed herself between the far windows and Ollie. Smart. But something about the agent's movements seemed off. Stiff, like she was . . . mad? Worried? "She doesn't agree that this is the best place for Ollie?" she asked Sully.

He quirked a small smile. "I'm impressed. And annoyed. How'd you guess?"

Elena shrugged. "Body language. Some people are easier to read than others. Why would you be annoyed?"

"Because you read her that easily."

"Oh." She smiled and nodded to the wall in the kitchen. "The security panel's over here." He followed her. "You'll find it in good shape." She tilted her head at him. "Or did you do this one too?"

"No, I didn't."

"Oh, well, Maya must have taken direction from what you did with her home because this one has the motion sensors, infrared cameras, and more."

"Good to know." She stilled. He was right behind her. Close enough to breathe in his musky scent. "You know a lot about the security setup," he said, taking a step back and giving her some breathing room.

She cleared her throat. "All of the staff do, but Maya and David know I have relevant experience, so they're smart enough to put that to good use and let me give the introductory tours."

She reached for the panel, but Sully's hand shot out, catching her wrist. Her pulse flared and she tensed. "What are you doing?"

"You have blood—there."

"What?" She looked down. Then opened her hand. Thanks to the keyring she still gripped, a small trail of blood had traveled from her palm to her wrist. She'd squeezed the little piece of metal too tight. "Oh, for crying—it's nothing." She pulled away, uncomfortable with his powers of observation—and how much she liked the feel of his hand on hers. She cleared her throat. "This is the panel. Obviously. I should probably, um, go do . . . something. Like clean up."

Wow. Awkward much? Heat climbed into her neck for the second time that day.

She turned to leave and stopped when she spotted Ollie in the doorway, eyes now on Elena's wrist. Something flickered in her expression. Recognition? Understanding?

"You've hurt yourself," Ollie said.

"It's nothing. Just squeezed the key too tight."

"It's your way to stay focused, not let yourself think about other things, isn't it?"

Elena's breath caught, and Sully went still. "Um, I didn't mean to. It was an accident." But she *did* have her coping mechanisms. Not that she needed to air that dirty laundry.

"Sometimes," Ollie said, "I add numbers up in my head. Hard numbers. It helps clear my mind of everything else and makes stuff fade into the background."

Elena walked to the teen who'd seen too much. Who'd learned too young how to cope with those things. "I could teach you other ways," she said. "Maybe not better, but possibly. If you wanted. I mean if it's okay with Sully and Piper, er, Agent Whitaker."

Ollie's eyes widened, and Piper, who'd stepped up behind the girl, made a sound that might have been a protest. Then she said, "Piper's fine."

Sully's quiet "thank you" made Elena realize she might have crossed a line she wasn't aware was there. Well, if so, whatever. She straightened, nodded to the others, and headed out the door. She was halfway back to the main house, desperately trying to keep past memories, feelings, and fears at bay, when she heard footsteps behind her.

"Elena, wait."

She looked back to see Sully gaining on her. She tried to push the memories of her family's compound from her head. Along with everything she'd been programmed to believe—and later had to unlearn. She took a steadying breath. "Yes?" Thank goodness the word came out low and calm.

He stopped next to her, eyes kind. Concerned. Compassionate. "You mentioned some ways to help Ollie. Did someone teach them to you?"

She huffed. "That's what you want to know?"

He shrugged. "Yes."

"Then no. No one taught me. I had to figure a lot of things out alone." She met his gaze. "But that's why I'm here now. So others don't have to do the same."

"I see."

"Do you?" He probably did, and that made her want to squirm. "I've got stuff to take care of," she said. "A class to finish tomorrow so I need to make sure I'm prepared." She was, but it never hurt to double-check. "Talk to you later."

She hurried into the barn, where her students had put all of the pieces of the still. Just being in the barn and planning what she was going to do tomorrow grounded her. She had a solar still to finish building so she could demonstrate it. Simple. Practical. And one more tool in her belt of those kind of survival skills.

The other kind—the ones Ollie needed—would come later. For now, she just had to ignore the way Mr. Big Shot FBI Special Agent Collin Sullivan seemed to see right through her carefully constructed walls.

And pray she hadn't made a huge mistake by giving him a glimpse of what lay behind them.

For more from

DANI PETTREY,

read on for an excerpt from

ONE WRONG MOVE

Making amends for his criminal past, Christian O'Brady has become one of the country's top security experts. But a string of heists brings attention from Andi Forester, an insurance investigator with her own checkered past. The two of them are drawn into a dangerous game with an opponent bent on revenge, and one wrong move could be the death of them both.

Available now wherever books are sold.

ONE

"WAIT HERE," Cyrus ordered.

"Why?" Casey asked—though pawn suited him better. As much as it galled him, Cyrus needed the insipid man. Needed his skills. For now. But when they were done, so was he. "Why?" he asked again.

Cyrus gritted his teeth. So incessant. He shook out his fists. Only a handful of locations to go and the questions would cease. *He* would cease. "It doesn't take two of us to get what we came for," he said, hoping Casey would accept the answer and let it drop, but he doubted it. "I've got this. Two of us will only draw more attention."

"Fine." Casey slumped back against the van's passenger seat.

The imbecile was pouting like a girl. And, that knee. Cyrus wanted to break it. Always bouncing in that annoying, jittery way. The seat squeaked with the rapid, persistent motion. He shook his head on a grunted exhale. If Casey didn't settle . . . if he blew their plans. Cyrus squeezed his fists tight, blood throbbing through his fingers. Too much was at stake. His own neck was on the line.

He turned his attention to the task at hand. "I won't be long," he said, surveying the space one last time before opening the van door. The lot behind them was dead, the building still. He climbed out, his breath a vapor in the cold night air. He glanced back at their van, barely visible in the pitch-black alley.

Shockingly, Casey remained in the passenger seat, his knee still bouncing high.

He shut the van door as eagerness coursed through him. The thrill and rush of the score mere minutes away. Just one quick job and then it was finally time.

He slipped his gloved hands into his pockets. A deeper rush nestled hot inside him, adrenaline searing his limbs. His fervency was for the kill.

He moved toward the rear of the restaurant, where the rental rooms' entrance sat. His gloved fingers brushed the garrote in his right pocket, and he shifted his other hand to rest on the hilt of his gun. Which way would it go? Garrote or gun? Anticipation shot through him. Rounding the back of the building, he hung in the shadows and then stepped to the door and picked the lock—so simple a child could have done it. But what had he expected of a rent-by-the-hour-or-day establishment?

Opening the door, he stepped inside the minuscule foyer and studied the two doors on the ground level. Nothing but silence. He found the light switch and flipped off the ceiling bulb illuminating the stairwell, then crept up the stairs, pausing as one creaked. He held still, his back flush with the wall, once again shadowed in darkness. Nothing stirred.

Reaching her room, he picked the lock, stepped inside, and shut the door, locking it behind him.

She was asleep on the shoddy sofa, a ratty blanket draped across her. Getting rid of her now might be easier, but what fun was it killing someone while they slept? And he needed to make sure she had the items.

He stood a moment, watching her chest rise and fall with what would be her final breaths, then he knocked her feet with his elbow.

Her eyes flashed open as she lurched to a seated position. She rubbed her eyes. "You're late."

Less chance of witnesses.

"You have the items?"

She nodded.

"Get them. We're in a hurry."

She got to her feet and headed for the bedroom.

He followed.

To his surprise, she climbed up on the dresser and reached for the heating vent.

Huh. She was smarter than he'd expected, yet not bright enough to know what was coming.

Pulling the dingy grate back, she retrieved a black velvet pouch and a bundle of letters held in place by a thick rubber band.

"Hand them over," he said.

She hopped down and hesitated. "I get my cut, right?" She clutched the items to her pale chest.

"You'll get your cut," he said, wrapping his hands around the garrote.

She released her hold. Taking the bag first, he slid it into his upper jacket pocket, then slipped the letters into his pant pocket. "Good job."

She brushed a strand of hair behind her ear, revealing her creamy neck. "Thanks."

Restless energy pulsed through him.

"Are we done here?" she asked, shifting her stance, her arms wrapped around her slender waist.

"Just about."

"What's left to do?" she asked, her head cocked, and then she stilled. She took a step back. So she'd finally figured it out.

"No." She shook her head, backing into the paneled wall. In one movement, left hand to right shoulder, he spun her around and slipped the garrote over her head.

He'd intended to give her the option—the easy way with a gunshot to the head or the hard way with the garrote. But the hard way was far more pleasurable, giving him the best elated high.

It really was a shame. She was a pretty thing.

Five minutes later, he was back in the van, leaving the body behind.

"You got everything?" Casey asked as they pulled onto the street, their headlights off.

Cyrus smiled and handed both items to him. They were a go. The appetite for what was to come gnawed at Cyrus's gut, but in a good way. It was time to feed the anticipation that had been growing in him for nigh on a year. It was time to scratch that itch.

LYNETTE EASON is the *USA Today* bestselling author of *Double Take*, *Target Acquired*, and *Serial Burn*, as well as the Extreme Measures, Danger Never Sleeps, Blue Justice, Women of Justice, Deadly Reunions, Hidden Identity, and Elite Guardians series. She is the winner of three ACFW Carol Awards, the Selah Award, and the Inspirational Reader's Choice Award, among others. She is a graduate of the University of South Carolina and has a master's degree in education from Converse College. Eason lives in South Carolina with her husband. They have two adult children. Learn more at LynetteEason.com.

DANI PETTREY is the bestselling author of the Jeopardy Falls series, Coastal Guardians series, Chesapeake Valor series, and the Alaskan Courage series. A three-time Christy Award finalist, Dani has won the National Readers' Choice Award, Daphne du Maurier Award, HOLT Medallion, and Christian Retailing's Best Award for Suspense. She plots murder and mayhem from her home with her husband in Florida. She can be found online at DaniPettrey.com.

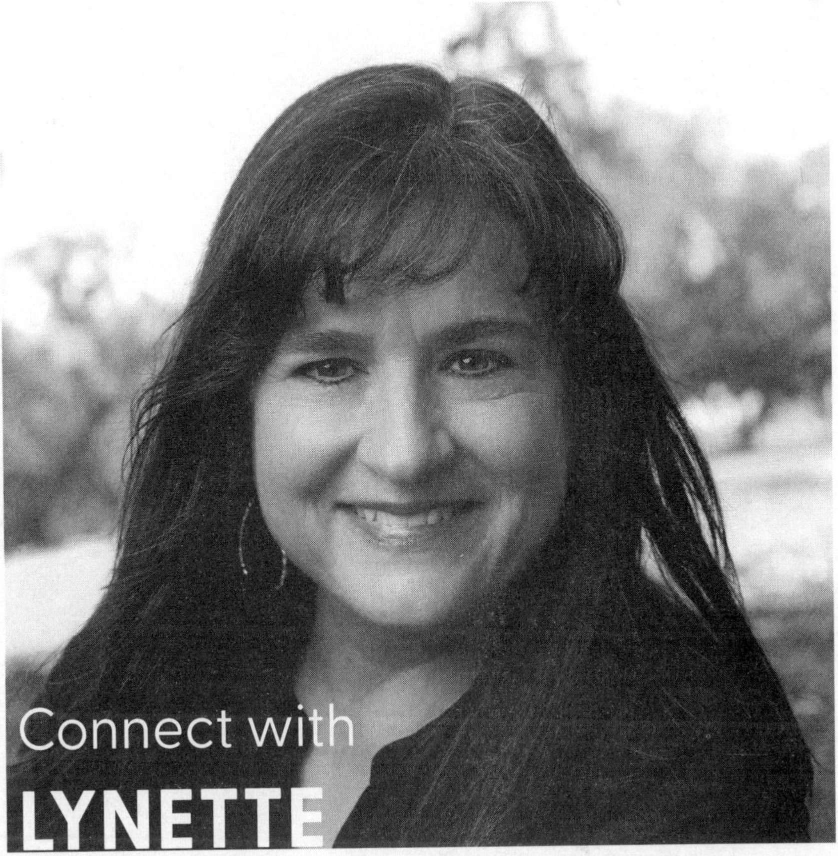

Connect with

LYNETTE

Sign up for Lynette Eason's newsletter to stay in touch on new books, giveaways, and events.

LYNETTEEASON.COM

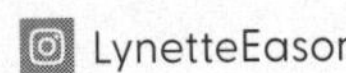

Sign Up for Dani's Newsletter

Keep up to date with Dani's latest news on book releases and events by signing up for her email list at the link below.

DaniPettrey.com

FOLLOW DANI ON SOCIAL MEDIA

Dani Pettrey 

@AuthorDaniPettrey

@DaniPettrey

Be the first to hear about new books from Bethany House!

Stay up to date with our authors and books by signing up for our newsletters at

BethanyHouse.com/SignUp

FOLLOW US ON SOCIAL MEDIA

@BethanyHouseFiction